Like a Buried City

Like a Buried City

Kepar ha Cyta Encledhys

Matthi ab Dewi

evertype
2021

Published by: Evertype, 19A Corso Street, Dundee, DD2 1DR, Scotland. www.evertype.com.

First edition September 2021.

A catalogue record for this book is available from the British Library.

ISBN-10 1-78201-296-6
ISBN-13 978-1-78201-296-2

This is a work of fiction. Names, characters, places, and incidents either are products of the author's imagination or are used fictitiously. Any resemblance to actual events or locales or persons, living or dead, is entirely coincidental.

Set in Minion Pro, New Pelican, 𝒫22 Broadwindsor, and Secret Script Two by Michael Everson.

Cover: Michael Everson.

To the memory of Pamela Westland, 1934–2015
and to that of my father, David Clarke, 1937–2012

Publisher's Note

In this novel Standard Cornish orthography, known in Cornish as Kernowek Standard, is used. Speech and songs by characters from the eighteenth century are spelled in KS according its accommodations for the Late Cornish linguistic register. Some passages representing written text from that time are given in the spelling used at that time, and in fonts which represent handwriting of the period. The font used for the hand of William Bodinar is quite pleasingly similar to the letterforms which he himself used.

Contents

"The ancient Cornish language lies like a buried city under our feet – we pass to and fro above it, but heed it not in the hustle of our everyday life."

John Bellow, 1861
"On the Cornish language"
(A paper for the Royal Cornwall Polytechnic Society)

Prelude

The flash, blast and shower of cement came all at once. It sent Jack Junior flying across the basement to crash into the rear wall. The sound of constant booming and wailing air-raid sirens was terrifying. Layered on top of this cacophony was the ringing of fire-engine bells and the screams of neighbours in the streets. Not even the supposed security of the cellar could mask that.

"If I got my hands on that Hitler," raged Jack Senior, picking himself off the floor and brushing a covering of mortar from his jacket, "I would wring the bastard's neck!"

"Yes—I'm sure you would," cried Loveday above the noise, "but I smell smoke and I think we ought to get out of here."

"I'll get some clothes," Junior shouted as another bomb fell. The house shook above them.

"No time," his father said, "grabbing his son's arm and putting his other around his wife's waist, "we have to get out right now before we end up as ashes."

"We'll lose everything!" she protested while forcing her way out of his grip.

"But we won't lose our lives!" Jack Senior said in an attempt to bring some little comfort amidst the destruction all around.

"What about Granfer's trunk?" demanded Junior.

"Yes," added Loveday, "do you want that up in smoke too?"

Jack Senior's temper was starting to fray.

"Okay—okay—we'll take that—but can we go now?"

The three of them grabbed the wrought ironwork surrounding the locked chest and attempted to heave it up the steps to safety. Just as they reached the top, the most savage explosion of all sent them flying. Jack Junior fell and fell in a cloud of dust. He thought he was plummeting fathoms down a mine shaft. But that was not possible for he was in the lowest level of a townhouse in Plymouth. The falling started to feel like flying among the clouds far above the smoke from the flames of a burning city. Jack Junior was free of the terror as though the hardship and pain of recent years meant nothing anymore.

Then below him, he saw Dartmoor with its towering granite stacks and rugged hillsides. The wind blew across his face as he swooped across the Tamar and soared over ancient landscapes and homesteads. Jack was drawn there for some reason.

"Jack—Jack—can you hear me?" The voice was familiar and loving. He knew the sound but could not place how. All he could tell was there was warmth and love. He shut his eyes to focus on the caressing tones.

"Jack—Jack—open your eyes!"

"That voice again," he told himself as the clouds became thicker around him.

He did as the voice instructed.

When he opened his eyes, he found himself pinned beneath a roof beam which had stopped short of crushing him because of Granfer's oak trunk. It had saved his life.

Light was streaming down from above where he could see open sky and the face of his mother.

"Oh—my darling boy," she wept with joy, "you're alive!"

"Of course, I am," he smiled weakly back.

With that, Loveday was gently led out of the way and a brigade of home-guardsmen moved in with crowbars and props to release the trapped teenager from what had nearly become his grave. They dug and heaved, pushed and tugged—sweating with exertion as the layers of crumbled brick and charred woodwork were peeled away until a stretcher could be lowered down. Once Jack Junior was secured and winched up, he could see how, all around him, Plymouth lay smouldering. It had been rendered to the ground by that storm of Nazi bombs.

It was all he had known. His earliest memories consisted of blissful days playing there in the back yard and out in the road with friends from the street. His father used to take him down for rides on the Sound—even though it was not strictly allowed for him to let a young child on the tugs he piloted. Would any of that be the same again?

"You had a close call there," said his mother, who was now back by his side.

"Where's Dad?" he asked.

His mother turned her face away to hide her tears.

"Where's Dad?" he repeated. Loveday could not hold back the grief any longer and turned to look down at her son.

"Oh—my darling boy," she sobbed, "he's gone to be with Granfer."

At that moment, Junior wished he had just continued flying over the tors. He prayed he could be there amongst the clouds with his Dad and Granfer.

"No—no—no!"

It was all Junior could say for the following few days. It was all he had the will within him to express. The Luftwaffe had robbed him of his world. They might as well have killed him then and there.

"Darling boy," his Mum whispered, "we'll survive. Just you and I."

What was the point of surviving when the stench of smoke and burning flesh lingered in nostrils even when the skies had cleared?

"Oh, my darling boy," Loveday said, "your Dad wanted to move back down to where your Granfer came from."

"Yes—I know," he murmured back, "are we?"

"Yes," she smiled, "we'll move away from here and start again."

I
A Chest of Treasures

The shuffling of feet echoed around the solicitor's office as the light struggled to creep in through the dirt encrusted windows. The Pengilley family were still wearing their black formal clothes following the funeral of Jack Pengilley. He had died the previous month at the grand age of 85 with memories still intact and a list of dreams that he yearned to fulfil.

In life, the old man always enjoyed telling tales about his youth in Plymouth and how times were harder living once he and his mother returned to Cornwall. But no one really listened. Those stories about boyhood on the beach and playing around Newlyn's "bowgie" were all lost now. His voice was silent leaving his meagre possessions to be squabbled over by his relatives.

His children and grandchildren all huddled around a battered and rutted oak table in the centre of the room on which was placed a large wooden chest. It had been sitting in Jack's attic gathering dust for as long as anyone could remember.

Not a word of conversation was exchanged save for occasional apologetic half utterances as more relatives pushed into the restricted space. Even the children's usual excited addiction to playing games or chatting with friends on their phones had been brought to a solemn halt as the entire Pengilley clan gathered around the wooden casket. Long years of wear-and-tear were scratched into every facet but its rusty brackets and hinges still held it firmly together. One could still even make out the scorch marks bestowed on it by the Blitz.

Adventurous children of each generation had played in the attic where it had been stored. They had made up stories of how it contained treasure from a far-distant land and had been recovered by Jack in his earlier days while serving as a heroic merchant seaman. They had all joked that he was actually a terrifying pirate who had plundered the riches of Caribbean islands and had forced captives to their death by making them walk the plank. However, the truth was that no-one in the family knew what was inside.

All they could go on was that it had black writing on its lid instructing them not to open it until 2014. Jack had spent his life wanting to see what was inside. In his younger years, he was able to climb the rickety wooden ladder into the loft and examine it. His wife used to stand at the bottom of the ladder and shout up to him things like; "stop talking your gibberish to that old box." Granny Geraldine had died some years earlier and had been laid to rest in exactly the same graveyard as Jack—under the gnarled oak tree that spread its branches over the church porch.

Geraldine had died from stress, so it was said, at trying to marry off her daughters Elaine and Josie. Others claimed her demise was brought about by Jack's infatuation with talking to inanimate objects—such as this very box. He used to mumble so softly that no one could make out his words. He had hoped to live to see the contents too. Unfortunately, for anyone desperate to dig deeper into family history, he died from a bout of pneumonia over Christmas and thus left the task of making the discovery to those who remained.

All the secrets were preserved by a sturdy padlock which had become parted from its key along time ago. Determined children had tried to release it many times over the years—but it had stubbornly refused to release under the persuasion of everything from hammers to mock spells. The ceremonial job of finally breaking its spell was given to a short bespectacled locksmith who asked the Pengilleys to give him some space as he lifted up an evil-looking bolt-cropper.

He wheezed and puffed for several minutes as he struggled with the antique. For a moment, he stopped and rubbed his forehead as though he was about to give in. His eyes flitted across the room to see how his audience was coping with the suspense. He found them to be breathless with anticipation. Thus, he returned to his task with another bout of battling the mechanism. Then, all of a sudden, there was a dull crack. The obstinate padlock had been successfully severed from the iron rings. Another crack rang around the room as it bounced off the table and onto the floor with a mighty thud—narrowly avoiding Elaine's perfectly pedicured feet. She screamed briefly and backed into a rearguard of uncles.

Elaine, a squat spinster wearing open-toed high-heeled stilettos and a denim skirt, knew how to dress for a night at the pub but had no room in her wardrobe for clothes designed for more sombre occasions. Her brothers Eddie and Joe grimaced at her for, once again, letting the family down by arriving poorly attired. Elaine had no qualms about upsetting them and simply grinned back sarcastically.

The old man's grandchildren were handed the task of opening the heavy lid. They all copied the locksmith with their own interpretations of his heaving and puffing. Slowly, it creaked open and released the smell of almost two centuries of stale dry air. It was a mix of odours from old paper, parchment, a strong hint of ancient tobacco and an earthy smell. The solicitor gestured to them to move back as he took the weight from them and fully opened the lid.

The huddle of twenty-four family members all moved in to geek inside and become the first to see the sparkling coins, rings, and maybe even diamonds. However, there was no such delight to greet their eyes. A torch was produced by their solicitor and shone down into the dark recesses. The expectation of unclaimed family wealth had built up to this moment—now to be lost in a sudden realization that those foreign holidays and new homes were not going to be fulfilled.

"So, what have we come here to see?" huffed Joe, only to be given a look of disdain by his wife, Jenny. Her rebuke was met by a marital scowl which embarrassed her enough to look around the room in a hope no one had noticed—but they had.

"Well?" continued Joe, the eldest of Jack's children, "we have been waiting forever for this moment and all we get is a box of paper."

It was true; all there was within this time-capsule was several bundles of paper in various stages of decay and deterioration. They were accompanied by a solitary tin of what appeared to be tobacco and a delicate example of glazed pottery that was large enough to hold a litre of liquid at the most. It was still in excellent condition with no evidence of breakage or even discolouration in the dark blue glaze.

If the worst came to the worst, the family could attempt to auction it or get it valued on TV.

"I think we had better contact the museum for this," remarked the solicitor, "as I fear that if we handle these papers right away then they may just fall into a pile of dust and be of no use to anyone."

Josie, the youngest of Jack's children had stood remarkably quiet up until now. She decided now was the time to add her thoughts on the matter. She stepped up to the box and turned towards the rest of the family, adjusted her black cardigan, before turning to address her sister, Elaine; "You know what Jack would have said—y'knaw—he taught us?"

"We don't want to put up with anymore disruption by you upsetting the family with Jack's gobbledygook," barked Jenny, standing forward from her husband. He found the old man's mumblings disturbing and didn't want the practice continued any longer. Joe simply stood there nodding in agreement.

"But this is Jack's funeral," erupted Elaine, spinning around on a stiletto heel as though she was performing a drunken dance-move on a Saturday night, "and I think we should remember his mumblings—whatever *you* think."

Elaine was not to be stopped. *"Taranseith na geweith a skelly—"*

"That's quite enough," retorted Joe, letting rip a rarely seen fiery temper, "we must move on from all of this rubbish about this box."

With that, there was more mumbling and the pulling of glum faces from the grandchildren as everyone was herded towards the door. Joe was the first out of the office. He was eager to settle his annoyance with a beer while Jenny didn't wish to get into conversation with Elaine. In her opinion, Elaine was quite plainly mad.

Geoff and Sarah shepherded their two boys, Gary and Eddie out of the building and into the sunlight, giving Elaine a cursory nod. On his way past, Gary looked back at his aunt inquisitively—his curiosity sparked by the earlier outburst.

From this moment onwards, the box became quite forgotten by nearly everyone. It was sent away to be inspected by academics, who in turn decided that more experienced conservators were needed. Most, if not all, of the family had been praying that the documents might contain some deeds to a large house somewhere with a view of the sea spreading out beyond a manicured lawn. Alternatively, it would be nice to discover the details of a bank account which had been accruing interest for two centuries.

So, the family went down to the pub and commandeered a long table in the corner. At one end sat Jenny, Joe, Geoff, and Sarah. At the other was a huddle of children consuming countless packets of crisps and bottles of Coke. Their parents, uncles and aunts drank several rounds of beer to drown their sorrows. The spinsters had been exiled to a small table in the far corner where they sipped on sherry and discussed the day's events and arguments in private.

Geoff sighed to himself with the hope the wake would begin the process of creating new family legends to replace the one about the oak box. Even he had spent more than enough time wondering about it. He smiled with the realization that was all in the past now and the only way to knock it on the head was with a toast.

"Here's to the Pengilleys—one and all," he said as he stumbled to his feet and then crashed back down onto his stool. Clearly, he had not realized how much he had consumed.

"One and all," echoed the family.

"And rest in peace Jacka Pengilley," laughed his wife Sarah—now on her third glass of red wine.

"Rest in peace Jacka!" came the shout.

And that was it. The Pengilleys continued their lives for another year and forgot all about the box, papers, Jack's mumblings and Jacka—the man who had started this all by locking the trunk two-hundred-years earlier. Life returned to normal and no one took any further notice of the eccentric sisters.

It was late on a Thursday evening when Geoff Pengilley opened up his email so that he could clear through a list of spam and bill-payment reminders. Among them was a message waiting in his inbox from James Wilson—the solicitor in charge of his father's estate. It had been sent to him with a message: "you might find this rather interesting." So, Geoff opened it.

Tuesday 6 January 2015

Dear Sir,

I have been contacted by the team of conservators working at the university who have instructed me that the papers left to you are of great historical interest. They contain a daily diary kept by Jacka Pengilley who lived in West Cornwall near the village of Morvah.

They are of interest, not only because they contain large amounts of detail about day-to-day community life but also for the fact that they are written in the Cornish language.

The historians who have examined these diaries say that you have been left the largest amount of traditional written late-Cornish ever found.

The university team would be most happy to show you and explain more.

Yours sincerely,
James Wilson.

He read the email again and rubbed his chin thoughtfully. He was unsure what to make of it. Up until now, his connection with the family history and his Cornish background involved going down to the local pub and singing "Little Lize" while drunk and once making a journey to Twickenham to watch Cornwall beat Yorkshire in the rugby finals. Now he was discovering that his heritage had a deeper and important connection with a way of life and culture that hardly sat alongside his Saturday night love of *X-Factor* and supporting England in the football.

Sarah entered the room still dressed in overalls from her workshop. She was spattered in flecks of paint as though she had been turned into a work of art herself. So, she kept her distance while awkwardly craning her neck over her husband's shoulder in the hope of catching a glimpse of the letter.

"What's that all about?" she said casually—trying not to pry too deeply while letting Geoff know that he could not let anything slip under her radar.

"Oh, it's just from the solicitor," he muttered dismissively, "you know—about that box."

"Oh right," she continued while making her way over to the utility room sink to clean the paint off her hands.

"I'd seen that one earlier—something in it about Cornish."

Sarah was on top of everything indeed and took great delight in seeing her husband come to the realization that he was not telling her anything new at all. Eventually, after reading the contents of the communication, she packed a surprise.

"You know that'll be of interest to Gary then."

Immediately, Sarah wandered out of the kitchen to clean herself up. Geoff looked through the utility room door as she vigorously scrubbed her hands. His inquisitive smirk was lost on her as she continued to ruthlessly attack every hint of dirt under her nails.

"What do you mean 'of interest to Gary'?"

She stopped scouring her flesh for a moment and turned around with disdain on her face.

"Don't you talk to your children about anything?"

"Well, I do—" Geoff started answering, only to be cut off before being able to defend himself any further.

"If—if—you had been talking to them about their school work you would know that Edward has attained an A-star in his biology mock exam—"

"Well, what has that got to do wi—" Geoff angrily retorted, only to be talked down again.

"—and Gary has joined an after-school club where he has been learning Cornish!"

"Oh."

And that was all he could really answer as it dawned on him that he had been to blame for the whole way through his fatherly existence for not paying enough attention to his children and their schoolwork.

Geoff felt a proper fool as he slumped down in his armchair. There, he resolved to make up for his paternal faults by catching up with his kids. He also needed to discover why those dusty diaries might be in some strange language that his son had suddenly taken an interest in.

Plan "A" had to involve a day out with his sons—maybe go down to the park and kick a ball about—do some real father-sons bonding. After all, it was about time.

II

Wheal an Gweal

Jacka Pengilley awoke with the sun streaming through his granite cottage window. It framed the beauty of the hills outside as though they were in a painting scratched onto an old piece of wood. He peered through the panes to examine what sort of day beckoned. The sun was rising up over Watch Croft and Carn Galva, picking out the craggy rocks which formed a crest along the top of the hill. He took a few seconds watching the spectacle. However bright it was, he knew he faced another day below ground and would not get the chance to enjoy much daylight later on.

For a moment more he cherished the far distant glint of light reflecting off the sea. As he looked down into his yard, he spotted his cat, Gwydn, gingerly pacing across the roof of his *crowjy*—a shambolic structure which he himself had built against the stones laid by his ancestors as an ancient hedge. The shed contained a mixture of joys for himself, his children and his wife. He had his small selection of tools such as his pal—a sort of Cornish shovel. There was also some craft equipment handed down through both sides of the family. They included chisels, a potter's wheel, and some very basic brushes.

Jacka scuttled down stairs to find Mary, his wife, already making bread. "*Nanj yw hanter oja pymp*, Jacka," she rebuked, telling her husband that it was already half past five in the morning.

"*Eâ, eâ, yn certan—th'eroma mos dha'n bal oja croust, abar' Duw!*" Jacka grumbled back at Mary. He was explaining how he had to go to the mine after elevenses and so this gave him plenty of time to walk over the downs.

Mary grinned knowing this simple exchange was the essence of her family. It was the kind of utterings expected of them when some wandering antiquarians passed by hoping for a taste of their customs and language. It was just how she was though. It was how her parents were—and their parents too. Indeed, she could remember the time, not so long ago when everyone in Morvah spoke like it. The memory made her face drop. The sweetness became a bitterness. Things weren't now as they once were back along twenty years. Times had become even tougher and family life in this dull grey cottage, perched on the north coast of Penwith, had taken on the frugality alien to so many from further up country. She felt like she had become an exhibit to be mocked and poked by learned people in posh clothes just because the lifestyle was rudimentary and the speech was deemed to be an outcast of Babel.

"Jacka and Mary Pengilley are among the last of a breed", was the remark from one neighbour on being interrogated by some wandering man with a quill and a large notebook. They knew it though and Mary could even hear her own father boasting to anyone who would listen; "Our parents, forefathers and foremothers all worked the land above and below the soil for generations. Our birthright is our language. Our birthright is *Kernowek*."

Just like the smile on Mary's face, the distinctive sounds of Cornish which she heard as a child, up and down the coast, were fading fast. She could barely even remember the old stories and songs her aunts and uncles used to drag out when there was a need for a party. But, Jacka was lucky in that a handful of men down the mine and one or two bal maidens on the surface still chatted in *Kernowek*. Mary, however, felt isolated with both cottages either side having neighbours who spoke mainly English—or as they termed it *Sowsnek*.

This worried Jacka severely for he knew how Mary found it difficult to socialize in the village anymore—and she barely understood a word the vicar was preaching. Jacka's fears were enhanced by more *Sowsnek* creeping into the bal. He had to be able to say in this imposter tongue "please" and "thank you" to the mine-captain—especially when it came to collecting his pay. Sometimes, he was simply too tired to try and think in the language after a long day in the dark straining to see a lode of tin or copper under the flickering light from a single tallow candle.

His two sons, Wella, Davy and his daughter Jane were all finding it difficult when they attended Bible classes held by the vicar's wife. They all begged not to have to go. "Your father and I are too busy winning the bread," she told them, "and for just one day a week we need you learning something and getting you out of our hair."

Mary counted her blessings knowing the village indeed was a rarity in offering such lessons. The down side, though, was that the teacher, Charlotte Prendergast, was conducting everything through *Sowsnek* and all her children were punished regularly to encourage more proficient English.

The eldest, Wella, was now twelve years old and had come home crying the previous day after being slapped for not understanding a Bible reading. Wella, however, was *not* keen to learn. He preferred to spend his time trying to shape models out of wood and random pieces of off-cut metal from the mine's workshops or the nearest smithy.

Davy was a precocious eight-year old who was more like his father in that he would keenly listen to old stories of Cornwall's past. He loved to try and repeat them back to anyone who would listen. Davy was particularly thrilled to find out about Cornish giants such as Cormoran and Bolster. When he came to performing these ageless tales himself, he would re-enact his father's exact emphasis and body-language. He particularly loved the drolls which revealed the hidden worlds of piskies, spriggian, knockers, and buccas. They had a songlike rhythm too. In this way, Davy was like any other child who was smitten with fairy tales and fables.

Davy and Jacka would spend many an hour sitting together by the flickering fire while sharing in these legends. Wella would prefer to continue fiddling with his seemingly bizarre contraptions. They were all based on the machines he had observed working at the mine. He was especially fascinated by the rocking movement of the large wooden beam as the magical power of steam heaved it up and down; seemingly in defiance of every natural law. It had a musical rhythmic quality to it with clanks and clunks—punctuated by a regular thud which shook the floor around it.

Meanwhile, Mary would be sitting in her shed with her pottery, ably assisted by six-year-old Jane—possibly the most naturally musical in the family. She was blessed with the sweetest voice. She formed every note as though it was being sung by an angel high in the eaves

13

of the church. Her perfect pitch made her an acknowledged asset at mass; even though she struggled to understand the real meaning of most of the words.

One of her favourite pastimes was to fit her songs to the clicks and scrapes made by the pottery wheel as it spun around before her:

"Ha me ow mos, ha me ow mos, ha me ow mos i'n ûn las,
Me a glôwas, a glôwas, a glôwas son an pùscas munys.
Bùs me a drouvyas udn pysk brôas naw y lostyow,
Oll an bobel i'n Porth Ia ha Marhas Jowan, nevra na wor dha y
  gessenjy."[1]

However, when it came to singing nursery rhymes with Mrs Prendergast, even though her pure tones cut through the more mundane chorus of the rest of the children, she tended to turn the English language into gibberish:

"Rei der cock oss dû Babm bry crows,
Dû sia vabm maidn podna whei toss."[2]

Her renditions were legendary, but they won her little praise from the vicar's wife. She would stand at the front dressed in a long skirt and pinafore, almost touching the floor, and cry out at the top of her voice for Jane to stop the singing with a despairing; "No, no, no Jane! Not the ungodly babble you speak at home now." Everyone else would be bent over in stitches of laughter.

Wella would usually sit quietly and try not to receive any more beatings. Davy, though, was more likely to spend the rest of the day standing in the corner with a sore backside after shouting back in Cornish something like: *"Nag yw flows vëth!"* which translates as "it is not a babble at all".

Life was changing fast in their granite-hedged, gull-swooped, enchanted little corner of Cornwall under the forbiddingly beauti-

---

1   *"As I was going, going, going in the green moor,*
     I heard, heard, heard, heard the sound of little fish,
     But I found one large fish nine its tails,
     All the people in Marazion, never knew how to hold it."
2   *"Ride a cock horse to Banbury Cross*
     To see a fine maiden upon a white horse."

ful shadow of Watch Croft. For a start, Jacka lived in fear of what lay around the corner. Mining, as he could see it, was going through hard times. He still muttered about what happened only two years earlier when a large amount of copper was found near the surface in North Wales.

"The abundance of cheap ore is flooding the market," he'd moan to Mary in Cornish while doing his best to make himself sound Welsh. "It will make many of our deep Cornish mines a waste of effort," he would continue with the approximation of a sing-song cadence to his lament.

"Moreover," he would say after thinking about the predicament further, "the depth of our tin and copper workings means our pumps are reaching their limits."

"What about that nice Mr Newcomen's pump?" Mary would ask.

"Mr Newcomen—pah!" Jacka would spit in disdain. "His engines just eat up vast amounts of coal from The Valleys—"

"They furreners come down here," he would continue, "puttin sugar in their tay an all!"

Mary for once was in agreement with his complaint as she completely agreed with refraining from the use of something paid for with people's misery in a far-flung lands.

Jacka could go on forever; lurching from one pitiful situation to another until he saw Mary's eyes narrow in annoyance. That is where Jacka would tail off his preaching, far preferring to stank about the cottage and internalize the rant. Mary could easily predict what he was planning to say anyway after hearing it all so many times before.

"And the deeper they go the more apparent it is our engines lack the power."

She was more concerned about the challenges nearer to her hearthside—such as having people to talk to. Yes, there were still some families up and down the coast who maintained the old ways—but they were fewer and further between as the years rolled by. There were the Manns, Quicks, and Davys for certain. Each and every member of those families would give a cheery "*Dëdh dâ da why*" (good day to you) or a warm "*Fatl'yw genough why?*" (how are you?). Sadly, these days were fast nearing their end leaving the Pengilleys feeling like strangers in their own land.

It was for such a reason that on this very morning Jacka sat down at the kitchen table for the first time with a large pile of paper. He had bought it in the market, or *an varhaz*, only a couple of days before with the express desire to record a little of his humble existence in a way which would endure long after he had gone to meet his maker. With quill in hand and a fresh bottle of ink, he began to laboriously scratch onto the paper his very first diary entry.

The intent with which he formed every letter, word and sentence was to remind himself of who he was and to pass that knowledge down to Wella, Davy and Jane. This was going to be his legacy.

The cause for recounting his days may have also been influenced by him recently reaching his fortieth year and Mary about to celebrate her two-score years' birthday in just a couple of months'. When he first went down the mines at the age of fifteen, he was full of unbridled energy and enthusiasm. He was devoted to the concept of using his earlier years to save some money and find some exciting adventure in his life. However, he was nearly completely bald now and had rough hands like the chiselled face of a block of granite. He had seen fellow miners' health fail at similar ages and realized that, if he was going to do something memorable with the existence that God had granted him, he had better start doing something towards it fairly soon.

Jacka Pengilley oma. Den bal boolgack gen gureg a try floh—[3]

Jacka squinted at the page through the flickering half-light of the tallow candle flame. His first few lines were still wet ink on a page but he felt he was making a vital contact with the future. This was the only way to preserve a little of his ancient knowledge. Mary lent over his shoulder to examine what he was up to.

"*Dr'yw hedna, Jacka?*" she asked her husband—nosily finding out what he was writing.

"*Th'eroma screfa neppëth dro dha'm bôwnas,*" he answered—telling her how he was writing something about his life.

---

3   *Jacka Pengilley oma. Den bal bohojak gèn gwreg a try flogh—*
    I, Jacka Pengilley, a poor miner, with a wife and three children—

"*Nag eus nagonen a wrella y redya,*" Mary said. She thought no-one would want to read it.

With solemn determination, Jacka continued scratching away until his eyes were tired and he realized he ought to be packing his *croust*-bag with his pasty and making the short stank down to Wheal an Gweal Mine. So, he gave his wife a big *abm* on the cheek and sped off down the track as fast as his feet could carry him.

Mary stood at the door watching him disappear around a far hedge brimming with sea-pinks and wild mustard. She then continued to take the air as a cool breeze arose from the surface of the sea and over Trevowhan Cliff. Her daydreaming was interrupted by her neighbour.

"What are ee doin standin there like tha, Mary Pengilley? Still ken't mind how t'say the Lord's Prayer?" laughed Mrs Tredinnick who was proudly fluent in English and looked with disdain at anyone continuing to chatter in a dying language.

Mary darted back inside and slammed the door without even understanding what had been said. She knew it wasn't nice and she thought it might be about the debacle at church last Sunday when the rest of the congregation began sniggering at her trying to say the Lord's Prayer in English: "Our Father, whose cart is in Devon—hello be thine aim."

She turned around from the door to see the children sitting at the table. They were picking at a loaf of bread which was still warm from the oven. Wella, Davy and Jane were all dressed and ready to head off to the vicarage for more lessons from Mrs Prendergast.

"*Mabm, na vanam mos da scol hedhyw,*" wailed Davy. He was desperate to stay home rather than going back to that stuffy room. The vicar's wife made him stand in the corner with a dunce hat on his head most times because all he could really speak was *Kernowek*. The day before, he had been hit across the hand because he refused to count in English. So-called "friends" would corner him on the way home shouting hurtful things about him and his family.

"You're the bastard son of a knocker," was one foul-mouthed slant. A separate incident saw Davy picked up by his feet and hung with his head half in the stone trough in the next field. It was full of muck and flies, leaving him stinking for the rest of the day. When he returned to class minutes later, he was severely told off for getting so dirty.

Mary knew all these things, but had limited powers to change the world. What she could do was offer her children comfort during their troubles. So, she came around the table and picked Davy up off the kitchen chair and gave him a big hug and an *abm* on his cheek.

"*Metessen gwell via dha ny dha saya desky nebes Sowsnek, Davy.*"

Her words of comfort were intended to encourage her children to attempt to learn some English—but she was faced with the fact that she found it difficult enough herself and was not really wanting to break a habit of a lifetime by speaking the foreign language which made her feel so isolated.

"*Me a vedn pobas tesen spladn hedhyw,*" she continued while explaining she would bake a splendid cake and that when all of them returned home again, they could eat a big dinner.

"*Ha pa wrellough why oll dos tre arta, ny a ell debry kynyow brâs.*"

So, Mary packed off her three children out of the house and settled into her routine tasks of cleaning, washing, baking and tending the animals in the back field. Her life was filled with sheer, nail-tearing, back-breaking hard work. However, she wouldn't want for anything else than to be sure her children were properly cared for, fed and healthy. In the few brief moments that she had to herself, she retreated to that small outbuilding where she kept her father's pottery-wheel. Jacka had also built her a small kiln out of stone and bricks—begged for, borrowed, and even stolen.

Her skill in throwing clay was not exactly at the master craftsman level, but she had the full belief in herself that, if she practiced, she could maintain the skills her family had shown across the generations. There was also an extra motive in her persistence. Mary had decided that an extra source of money could be necessary in the future if times became tough.

"Breadwinner," her father would snort at her, "you; a breadwinner. You can't do that." He would cruelly mock her dreams of doing something other than baking and cleaning. It didn't mean she had to wave her wishes goodbye though.

Today was one of those days when she retreated to what she called her "*crowjy creft*". It was her craft shed where she could transform her maternal body into the creative spirit that she believed herself to be. She hacked a ball of clay from the block which sat on the shelf.

She then proceeded to work it to the state where it was ready to be dumped onto the middle of the wheel.

It was in these times of working out her anxieties on the prehistoric layers of sediment that she allowed her brain to come up with solutions. Mary must have passed at least three hours moulding the clay into a jug. Her hands gently caressed the clay upwards and downwards creating tiny ripples resembling waves on the shore at Porthmeor. The final two things she needed to do with her masterwork were to attach a delicate handle and then leave it ready for Jacka to give it a first firing.

The time had sped by mulling over the multitude of problems her family faced. Indeed, things had certainly become worse since the new vicar and his wife had arrived from Exeter. These foreigners displayed no conception of *Kernowek* and were not even willing to accept that the children should be allowed to play using it. Mrs Prendergast's sole campaign seemed to be to instil good spoken English throughout the parish—even if it had to be beaten into some.

Occasionally, when he could find time, Jacka would take Wella and Davy on the back of a mule for an adventure to the other side of Penwith. It was a chance to meet some of the people down on the south coast with whom they could converse without fear of rebuke. They would go down to Porthenys and drop in on a family friend— one Mister William Bodinar. He would take the three of them out in his lugger for a day's fishing. The journey there and back would take a fair portion of the day and so the family would make the most of the beauty around them while traversing the windy downs.

Jacka took great pleasure in telling stories along the rutted road to Madron. As the father and two boys ventured past Trehyllys, Kerrowe, and Bosullow, he would recount legends of giants and feared little folk who inhabited this world and other mystical places not so far away. The most important giant for the people who lived in the shadow of Watch Croft and Carn Galva was the Kind Giant— though they knew him as "An Cawr Keef". This nameless towering man was the most considerate creature that anyone had ever heard tales about. He would protect communities along the north coast between Morvah and Zennor by throwing boulders at other giants.

It was, of course, totally true. The proof was in the evidence left by the rocks strewn along the slopes of nearby hills. Even though some might say the booming heard down by the cliffs at Portheras was that of the waves crashing in wild seas, others would maintain to their final breath that it was the noise made by rocks landing hard on the tails of aggressive beings. Another *droll* that Jacka told every time he took his children along this moorland route was about how An Cawr Keef built Zennor Quoit in the space of one night in order that he would have something to tire him out and send him fast to sleep.

Jacka never claimed to be a droll-teller, or story-teller, but he was good enough at it to make sure the journey never seemed as long or tiring as it might otherwise have been. Once the track left Carn Galva and Lanyon Quoit far behind, he would begin singing songs about characters such as Gogmagog and Cormoran.

> "I'n termyn eus passys warlergh drolla gwir,
> Th'era mytern, y hanow o Lir,
> Ha trigys wàr Garrek Loos i'n Coos,
> Ha ladha cowr Gogmagog—cowr pòr boos,
> Ev a wrug tôwla an cowr pell i'n mor,
> Oja y jassya dres treth ha dor,
> Nena veu scrifys an drolla mar deg,
> Ha can dha'm flehes—flehes pòr wheg."[4]

As soon as one song was over, Davy would instantly thrust a fist into the air and shout for more and more. Eventually, Jacka's voice would become hoarse with drolling, singing and laughing. Sometimes, he never even got to tell the stories about Cormoran because of the joyful strain on his throat.

Out of the three Pengilley children, Davy was the most likely to be able to recite all of the stories back to his father while Jane was the best at remembering the songs. Wella, meanwhile, would give the impression that he was listening while having half of his mind con-

---

4   "In the time that is past according to a true tale,
There was a king, his name was Lear,'
And he lived on St Michael's Mount,
And killed the giant Gogmagog—a very heavy giant,
He threw the giant far out to sea,
After chasing him across beaches and land,
Then the very fine tale was written,
And sung to my children—very sweet children."

templating more technical objectives. It was probable that, despite Jacka's showmanship, the eldest son spent most of the journey trying to work out ways to make the track smoother or boat-hoists to be less of an exertion for the operator.

It is not to say, however, that Wella did not appreciate music and poetry but that he inhabited a slightly different realm from that of his family. As far as Jacka and Mary were concerned, this was nothing but positive as engineering was fashionable and could earn good money. They had been quick to note how the children from as far away as Laneast or Camborne were inspired when any famous engineer visited the local mine to examine its operation. This was becoming a frequent event now that ore prices had plummeted so low that talk went around the parish about plans to close the bal. Whoever was able to improve the efficiency of the pumps would surely make themselves wealthy.

Whether the two boys fully appreciated their father's talents or not, it was a source of solace for Jacka to be out walking with his sons for he could spend the entire day without having to utter a single word of *Sowsnek*. The three of them would, on a Friday, head out on their *stank* as the sun rose and then return late on the following evening laden with pilchards to be salted and kept in the spence. The days immediately after fishing trips with William Bodinar were usually filled with some of the most flavoursome fish pasties that anyone in the area could bake. Even the local ladies, who refrained from lowering themselves enough to speak Cornish, would poke their heads around the front door of the cottage to sniff the sweet aromas wafting from Mary's oven. Sometimes, they would be so desperate to try some of the *oggies* that they would even revert to their childhood language and ask in Cornish for a taste.

"*Ellam' tastya dyjyn, mar pleg?*" they would politely enquire—asking for a small corner of a pasty. Mary would never refuse and politely break off a piece and hand it, with a kindly smile, to any neighbour who requested it in the correct manner.

However, Mary and Jane rarely had the opportunity of joining the family adventures outside of the parish as they only had one mule—unless Jacka managed to borrow a cart. But who amongst their immediate neighbours would lend them such an expensive vehicle? For this reason, Jane would get a full briefing from Davy about every detail of the excursion and he would use the experience for the eager audience of one little girl to practice his own version of the myths and legends.

Davy was particularly thrilled to go to Porthenys and enjoy time with Bodinar for he was much older than himself and had spent his days accumulating more drolls to tell than anyone else he knew. Even his father, who had passed down countless ancient songs and poems at a very early age, did not match the wealth of culture that could be gleaned from this fisherman. There were some trips that he would always remember and discuss afterwards with his mother and sister where they had been becalmed by the sea in Mounts Bay. His hands would mime the action of the boats on the water as he described sitting on the deck with the sun beating down and waves gently lapping against the barnacle-encrusted sides of the boat.

Bodinar would tell tales old and new. Some of them had only been heard once or twice in the tavern in Porthenys. Davy treasured the names of every character which appeared in them and spoke each consonant and vowel within them as they were poems in their own right. These were his true friends—even though he had never chanced upon any of them in real life. What he *did* know was that this old man was passing on treasures from Doll Pentreath, John Nancarrow and Arthur Boase.

So, that is what amused the Pengilley "tackers" in those dark days of few pleasures. Though, what entertained the men of the district was a wholly different affair. Mary would castigate Jacka for partaking in any excess at all and would scowl in horror as miners grabbed any opportunity they could to drink mead, beer, wine or cider. Many a time she would be walking down the road to Zennor and smelt some sweet odour drifting in the breeze. Her nose was that good. It only had to be a slight tinge hiding in the air escaping from a back shed. There were many such as these which haphazardly leant on the ancient granite hedges. Word would fly around the outlying communities about who was making the best tipple at that particular moment. Jacka loved such unofficial dens, or "kiddleywinks", where he could attempt, with a mixture of broken English and song-like Cornish, to enjoy a heady mix of conversation, politics, religion and even debauchery.

The nearest example to Jacka's house was conveniently on his daily stank home from "Wheal an Gweal" and was just too irresistible for him not to sneak in. Though he managed to maintain a modicum of self-restraint in the amount he consumed, there were others who would frequently become so piskie-laden that they had to be physically dragged out like a sack of tatties and thrown from the building. This only ever happened when the owner had clearly had a gutful himself and wished to catch his night's sleep.

Despite Mary's opinion that the wink was a haven for liquid-fuelled sin, she would give a half-smile at any mention of the place for she recognized it played an essential part in the community's soul.

"There's nothing wrong with venting a little steam," she would tell herself on spotting a staggering fool collapsing in the lane from a night of merriment. Occasionally, men of all ages, along with their womenfolk too, would bare the pain of their lives to one another within the dark front-room set aside for consumption of whatever the vicar declared in his sermons as "the devil's water". Whereas, on a Sunday, they would ask the Lord for forgiveness for their sinful ways, every other was spent in this establishment where tobacco leeched from the stones. It was where they counselled one another about dark hours passed underground.

The last ten years had seen many miners take their own lives by throwing themselves off the cliffs at Bosigran. It was a sad ceremony that Jacka had often taken a role in where a group of locals had to suddenly leave the drinking house to go and pull a body from the sea. On the odd and fortuitous episode, they would arrive in time to stop someone making the leap. On those occasions, no-one needed to ask why they had been driven to such desperation. Nearly all of them knew or had considered the option for themselves at one time or another.

Jacka knew it was down to a combined pressure of a hard existence and the stress created by their way of life dying out around them. He wept for those innocent days of childhood when he played without any worries about watching what he said. Indeed, why should he have taken care of his words—for they were simply the words his mother used—as did her mother before her? The truth of the matter was everyone who still had any *Kernowek* left in them felt keenly aware of this deep sadness.

Jacka had lost track of the number of funerals he had attended in Morvah church where, as each spade of earth hit the coffin lid, the family would flinch in the agony of losing another friend. Each of these poor souls had made up an intrinsic part of that heritage. Each one of them might have ended their days as a name and date engraved into stone in English, but they also left a hole in lives. Each took with them another droll or song—never to be spoken or sung again. Thus, when entertainment was mentioned, the raucous melodies that mixed with the cider, beer and mead were not solely a means of laughing, but also their way of bidding farewell to a way of life.

Mary and Jane had to make their fun as best as possible along the rugged landscape of West Penwith. A rare adventure consisted of a day out to Laneast or Poria. For the greater part of their lives though, most days were very much the same and dreams of travelling to far distant lands were just that—dreams. Every now and again, Jacka would come in and talk about the adventures enjoyed by friends and relatives such as "Billy Bod"—as they all called William Bodinar. Billy Bod often took his son (Billy Bod Bian) in a boat over to Breten Vian. It was a place spoken about in a reverent way by many of the older people. For this land, often also known as Armorica or Brittany, had a history that ran alongside Cornwall's like a silk thread added to a garment. Billy Bod's other son was not so keen at risking his life on the water and preferred to spend his days working in the local smithy. Both of them rarely uttered any Cornish for the simple reason that they only had a basic smattering of the language.

The two Bods frequently went on fishing trips on a lugger across to Brest, hauling in all sorts of fish; among them species known locally as *briel, hern, morgy, bothak* and a good number of *legest*. The fishermen, who now sailed these same waters without their traditional knowledge, referred to them as mackerel, pilchard, dogfish, pout, and lobster. On one occasion, they had been gone for two whole weeks before sailing back. They were loaded with all sorts of goods that no-one would mention, apart from in a secret code of winks and smirks, because of the fear the customs and excise men might find out. The venture paid well and the crew had luckily avoided all run-ins with the law. If they had been caught, they would surely have been dealt with harshly—maybe even deported.

One of Billy Bod's earliest memories of mixing fishing and free-trade was in his younger days when he had sailed in a smuggling cutter across to Morlaix/Montroulez. It was his first time in this fabled land across the sea that he had heard so much talk about. The ship's master ordered him ashore to buy provisions and vegetables for the rest of the voyage. It was on this adventure when he discovered his lack of French was no setback. To his amazement, he was readily able to converse with all the locals in the Cornish he had picked up as a young boy.

Jacka and Mary, however, were more likely to avoid risk and preferred to stay within the law as much as possible by attending church on Sundays and saying their prayers—albeit in *Kernowek*. So, when any of the family got into trouble, it felt like the skies were falling in on them and that the Lord himself was wreaking havoc with their lives. With this thought that they may be bringing their pitiful state of affairs upon themselves, Mary fell to her knees and started mouthing the Lord's Prayer—"*Pader Duw*" or "*Pader agan Arlùth*".

"*Gàn Tas eus in nev, benegys bo da hanow—gwra da gwlasketh dos—ha bodh bo gwrës i'n nor pecar ha'n nev—*" and then her solitary time with Jesus was brought to an abrupt conclusion by a rattling on the door and the sorrowful cry of a voice which sounded like George Angove.

"Mary, Mary come us quick," he wailed through a crack in the door as he shook the handle furiously, "somethun fearful ave appened up to bal."

"*Cows Kernowek*, George," begged Mary, "*na orama ger veth ath lavarow!*"

She demanded for George to speak in *Kernowek* as she could barely understand a single word.

"*Dro Jacka yw—stagys yw i'n bal oja meur a veyn da godha warnodho.*"

George sobbed as he explained that Jacka had become trapped in the mine after a tunnel had collapsed on him. Just the thought of that poor man buried under a pile of broken granite and wooden props. Mary grabbed her gowk, tied it haphazardly over her head, and then hurried out of the door trailing behind George as he ran back to the mine. When she arrived, she found panic on the surface as a body was dragged out of the shaft. It was limp and lifeless. She couldn't make neither head nor tail of what anyone was saying as there was some dreadful *hùbbadùllya* going on in what was a most ugly mix of English and *Kernowek*.

George hugged her tightly as she screamed in distress.

"*Pyle ma gour vy?*" she wailed as if anyone was going to answer her with the exact location and condition of her husband.

"Stay stout, Mary. I knaw the Cap'n ave got un in hand."

It was about fifty fathoms down where the rock fall had occurred. Jacka and his team had spent the previous day boring holes into the face to set charges. They were well-practiced at the process, taking turns to hold the drill-bit steady while two others rhythmically hammered the top. This was, in itself, a dangerous operation for anyone who had little bodily co-ordination, for it needed one bold individual to bravely wedge the bit in place on the rock surface while two large hammers slammed it in. When Jacka did this in the claustrophobic darkness of a mine, he would come up with Cornish rhymes to keep the timing spot on.

With each slug of the hammer, the bit had to be rotated; "*Onen, dew, try, sqwat!*"

A series of holes had been bored in the rock-face which had all been packed with explosive and fuses. The team was about to evacuate the area for blasting when one of the wooden supports which held up the ceiling cracked and gave way. Down rolled an avalanche of rocks with a roar that could be heard throughout the mine. A cloud of dust was thrown up. It left anyone who had not been knocked to the ground in a state of panic as they desperately attempted to gasp in uncontaminated air. Once the thunder died away along the manmade passageways, it became clear that the gallery had been blocked.

Jacka had narrowly avoided being struck by the falling rubble. He sat up and shook his head to ascertain as to whether or not he was still taking part in the joy of human existence. A minute of being dazed passed and he soon felt himself being heaved and hauled to his feet by a couple of fellow miners.

"*Owgh why brôwys?*" asked one of them to check that Jacka had not been injured.

"*Eâ—dâ lowr ov vy—bùs ma parra vy in dadn an carygy-na,*" he replied explaining that he was okay but his team was under the pile of rock.

Before long there were ten miners who had joined in the rescue operation. They needed to heave away the rubble without causing any further falls. So, while five of them desperately set about trying to remove the rock, another team organized itself into bringing in more props in order to secure the roof.

Every now and again they would stop to listen for movement or cries for help—only to be greeted with silence. The situation did not seem good. Jacka had started to try and help in the rescue operation. However, after only moving a couple of pieces of debris, he had to sit back down as the sheer shock of what had just happened hit him more forcefully than the pile of rock. The noise of the panic drifted in and out along with his consciousness.

The shouts of desperate miners attempting to save their workmates suddenly stopped. The silence alone was enough to bring Jacka out of his shock-induced state.

"*Rag fra yw stoppys geno'why?*" he asked to find out why they had stopped. No answer was needed as he looked down the gallery to where the accident had occurred. He saw the men standing around in a mournful silence looking at two lifeless bodies in the flickering candlelight. Then they solemnly started reciting the Lord's prayer:

"*Gàn Tas eus in nev—*"

As they continued, Jacka could see the way the tallowy light picked out tears running down the cheeks of every miner. For a moment Jacka wished he had been under the rubble instead of them as he had been in charge. His pair was his team and his team was his band of brothers.

It was a good two hours before Wella, Davy and Jane were out of the care of Mrs Prendergast and heading back home. They had been told about the disaster as they left. Another group of children, who had been helping out the bal-maidens as they broke up the ore into smaller pieces, had gathered on one side of a hedge to watch the rescue. They were swiftly joined by Mrs Prendergast. She urged them to stay out of the way. It was another half-an-hour before a shout came from the shaft and another person was hauled out coughing and spluttering—it was Jacka.

Mary pulled herself out of George's grasp and ran over to where he was being sat down outside the count-house. His face was heavily bruised and slightly cut, his shirt had become ripped in several places, and he had an ashen glaze in his eyes—but he was alive. The three children had also broken away from their charge and had hurdled over the granite hedge towards the reunion. The tears flowed and the fears turned into relief.

Davy hugged his father tightly while Jane, smiling through her tears, placed a gentle kiss on Jacka's forehead. Wella was more restrained, not because of any lack of love or for holding any enmity, but for the mere difficulty he experienced in showing such raw emotions.

For a matter of hours, Mary believed she was about to become a widow in the same way that she had seen so many women lose their husbands. In the past five years, she knew of twenty men who had died in accidents down this one hole in the ground. It was not unusual to lose younger children down the mine either. Most of the older boys in the village were involved in winning tin and copper. Many had been at it from their early teens while younger boys would help out in the surface workings by shifting wagons loaded to the top with ore. Even though they were not in danger of being killed in a rock-fall, they were still at peril from being crushed by heavy carts and machinery.

Mary could barely begin to think how she would have coped with life if Jacka had not been around to support her. As she looked at him, she saw the man who had once winked at her as she carried home a basket of eggs to her own mother. The surprise had nearly made her drop the whole lot. Such memories made her smile and forget the harshness of mining life.

One of her friends down the road in Pendeen had lost her father, husband and one son in a series of accidents over the years. Alice Trengweath was now permanently covered in a black shawl and gowk. She was always the first into church to pray and the last to leave too. But what good was praying? In her case, it had achieved nothing.

However, in Mary's case her tear-drowned prayers had brought her husband back—and that was one encounter with death too many.

"Jacka, Jacka—*fatla gene'che, cuv colon vy?*" she cried as she begged Jacka to tell her how he was.

"*Mary wheg oll vy—th'erom obba whath ha bêw,*" Jacka softly whispered that he was here and alive. Though, there was something different in his eyes now. For so many years, he had been the brave hero in the family's life who went out daily to do battle with the landscape and the elements, "keeping the wolf from the door". Now, his stare told Mary that he had lost some of that fight down "Wheal

an Gweal" that day. When those rocks had come crashing down—
so had his confidence.

For several months, Jacka went to work at the mine but did not go
below grass. He had been given the job of stoking the boiler in the
pump house. He had to create enough steam to keep the forty-foot
cylinder operating. Without his consistent dedication, the mine
would flood and it could be fatal for the whole village. Even a slight
let-up in his work would have led to a drop in efficiency—and that
was all important.

"We've got to beat the Welsh at this now," the captain would roar
with a hearty grin.

"You know their copper is fifty pounds per ton," he would lecture
with an attitude like a Roman barge coxswain coercing the crew to
row faster. "We're nowhere near that—we must do better!"

Jacka could do little but curse under his breath as he was already
struggling to keep up: "*Duw! Pajer ugans dha hanter-cans!*" If the
vicar had heard him call on God in such a way, he would have been
rebuked there and then—even if he was right.

As he loaded in the shovels of coal, there emerged in his mind a
plan. He desired a real change to his family's fortunes without having to consign his sons to the dark depths of tin and copper mines
or his daughter slugging a large hammer alongside the rest of the
bal-maidens. Her life was not to be one where her days were valued
in the amount of ore she demolished into smaller pieces. He had a
plan, sure enough—but how would he actually find the money to
get it underway?

III

Lifting the Lid

If there was one thing which irritated Gary Pengilley—it was Thursday afternoon classes. He had to cope with double maths and then single chemistry. He wasn't a natural at the sciences, even though he tried his utmost to be at least marginally good with at least one of them. In truth, he was a complete disaster at both. The mathematical equations looked quite interesting on his notepad once he had added some colours and doodles around them. His teacher had tried to offer encouragement by telling him to think about them as beautiful insights into the rhythms of nature.

The maths master presumed that trying some basic re-framing techniques would make all the difference to Gary. However, the obstinate teenager was already resigned to the fact that this realm of study was beyond him and more for the likes of his brother. Eddie delighted in scientific pursuits! He grabbed every opportunity he could to pull apart a flower and examine it. He also had more of a clue about advanced algebra—despite being the younger of the two.

If there was one thing that Gary loved about Thursdays, it was Cornish language club after school. He was one of five boys who had been inspired by Miss James's diversions into "*Kernowek*" during French, English and Spanish. Undoubtedly, she was deviating grossly from the accepted syllabus as the study of Cornish did not fit anywhere within those three topics. However, she had always found a way.

Eventually, she announced at the end of one French lesson that she would be setting up a club where pupils could learn as much or as little of the language as they wished. Gary was the first to thrust his hand up. He was so bad at maths that he supposed the timing of the club would allow him to avoid half of the chemistry lesson. He was wrong about that—but went along anyway.

There was another element which sparked Gary's fascination; those bizarre mumblings that he had heard for the first time when the oak box was opened. Aunt Elaine's insistence on repeating Granfer Jack's "gibberish" was not lost on the teenager. The jumble of strange-sounding words had actually transported him back to the days when he was even younger and sat on Jack Pengilley's knee. He could almost hear the old man burbling. Maybe it had not been nonsense after all?

What few realized at the time, including Miss James, was the amount of tension that would develop from something as harmless as learning a minority language. When the first notice went up on the school notice-board in the entrance hall it was covered almost instantly in graffiti. Someone (who was never caught) had scrawled across it in heavy black pen "fuckin pasty-gobbling twats". Miss James had not long taken it down and put up a fresh one when another was ruined with the phrase "learn to talk like a fuckin inbred".

By now Miss James had decided it was safer just to identify the pupils who were most likely to be interested and tell them directly. However, the word had got about and a small, but antagonistic element of the school, had begun to make life decidedly uncomfortable. Eventually, the first club meeting came around and, despite the threats and general nastiness, Gary was hooked on the language from the outset. He realized he could start revealing a wonderful new layer to the landscape around him by understanding some of the place names.

Before he knew it, his mind was trying to translate every village and town name that he saw on his travels. He began noting them down and then checking an online dictionary to see what they meant. Soon, he realized that *everywhere* had a meaning and a fascinating story to tell. This is what he loved as he started to imagine the happenings hundreds of years ago when the names first appeared. Why was it that the place was called "Pencalennick" and what was happening in the lives of the people who lived there?

And so, when Great Grandad Jack died and the family peered into that dusty casket, he was the only one who really saw the possibilities. He had remained in email contact with the museum curator who was examining the pile of papers left by Jacka Pengilley two hundred years earlier. He had even been sent a number of diary pages with some basic annotations added by a certain researcher called Dr Julian Casement.

It was not at all easy to read the manuscripts as they were all written in a very unfamiliar, but beautiful, style of writing. There were copious flowing tails to letters such as *g, f, s,* and *y.* They appeared to resemble his own doodling perfected during innumerable science lessons. Each flick of a feather quill waved incantations down the ages to him. They danced in his eyes and he became entranced.

The next hurdle in understanding what Jacka had written was that it was written in late Cornish. It was as though the language had just leapt from the map and the multitudinous *pedns, zawns,* and *veors* had all arranged themselves before him. They were begging him to unveil their meanings.

Gary began to hear these ancient sounds take flight around his head and thought that he could even identify the music and tones of an age passed. He would laboriously try to mimic what he thought they should sound like as tunes on his violin. Maybe his scrapes and screeches were realistic. He liked to think so.

He also represented the landscape of the time through paintings and devised a plan to release his emotions about what he was sensing through clay as well; for he believed this earthy and tactile form had deep relevance to his journey. He could still smell the odours which wafted out of that box when it was first opened. One was from the bundle of paper with its sepia curled edges. Another was from the pungent tobacco tin. However, the most intriguing was the earthy smell emanating from the clay jug.

Gary opened up a dictionary app on his phone to find the word for clay. It was simply *pry*—a short combination of letters which somehow resonated with him. It was pronounced as though it was *pree* in English. There were certainly many poetic possibilities there.

"Gary Pengilley," roared the chemistry teacher, "stop daydreaming!"

A snigger went around the lab,

"The inbred twat's knackered from gobbling so many pasties," came a shout from the back. Another added; "he can't stay awake because he's been shagging his auntie."

"Enough!" shouted Dr Matthews.

Gary awoke from his thoughts with a jolt and no idea how long he had been blissfully drifting in his other enchanted existence.

"Daydreaming?" he questioned. Another giggle flew around the room faster than a Mexican wave.

"Yes—daydreaming Mister Pengilley—and don't try and deny it as I've been watching you not paying attention during your practical."

Gary's body-language slipped into a submissive apologetic hunch as he realized that he had been caught out fair and square. The compound for testing with a litmus paper had all boiled off leaving a collection of anti-bumping granules in the bottom of the beaker.

"Start again Mister Pengilley—and no flying with the fearies this time," suggested the master as he stanked off to check over some other pupils' attempts. Gary looked at his watch to see whether he still had twenty minutes more of the lesson and could not escape setting the experiment up again. Indeed, twenty more minutes until Cornish Club and an end to a day of scientific torture.

The time dragged and the seconds seemed to take more than twice as long as usual to pass. He kept looking back at his watch to see that only thirty seconds had passed when he thought that a minute or more should have elapsed. His brother would have found fascination in this experience too. Eddie would have been thrilled with the Bunsen burners and test tubes as well as the experience in observing the passage of time. He would have probably started explaining the ins and outs of relativity and how our perception was controlled by heart-rate; thereby allowing us to deal with primeval dangerous situations. Gary smirked—ridiculing the bizarre concept of him being pursued down Fore Street by a famished leopard.

The end of chemistry did eventually come and Gary left the lab under a disapproving glare from his teacher. He had almost made it through the doorway when he was summoned back.

"Mister Pengilley," Dr Matthews called out in a voice which echoed around the empty room.

"I realize that you have no interest whatsoever in the study of science. However, I will consider myself an abject failure if I do not, somehow, succeed in some small way in revealing its mystical beauty to you."

Gary maintained his grim silence while wincing against the sarcastic rebuke.

"And to that end, you are in detention next Thursday when you will carry out that experiment properly—and successfully! Do you understand?"

Gary did comprehend but really could not care less for Dr Matthews' motives—however honourable they may be. As far as the teacher was concerned, he was helping a struggling pupil achieve great things in life. He saw every boy in his lab as a future Nobel Prize winner. He believed that every one of them was capable.

That may have been over-optimistic and considered by many as a false assumption. For, indeed, Gary Pengilley's mind was not wired to be able to cope with the complex nature of matter. Dr Matthews would have argued that he was de-coding reality where this troubled teenager would reply with a painting, sculpture, poem or song that represented his own view of what reality looked and felt like.

Dr Matthews handed Gary a detention-slip to be shown to his form tutor and parents, finally adding, "I do have your best interests at heart Mister Pengilley!"

He was wasting his breath. All that mattered to Gary, for now, was Cornish Club next week. Unless he could find some way to escape detention, that would be it—one week without his new-found means of self-expression.

IV

Free Trading

Jacka knew his days as an effective member of the local working community were over. He still looked like the old Jacka. He still spoke like the old Jacka. He even walked and joked like the old one. Despite all outward appearances—there was something missing.

"A pile of rocks cannot tumble upon you and leave you completely unblemished," had been the mine captain's words—but Jacka felt the scars deep within.

He lay awake long hours at night as his family slept soundly around him. All that went through his mind was how he could avoid total destitution. He looked across to Mary, curled up next to him under the eiderdown, and imagined how she would cope if the poor house became their home.

"*A via hedda gwell ès bôwnans i'n bal?*" he asked himself. Who indeed would dispute that a life underground was the perfect way to earn a crust? Jacka certainly did not think so.

He would miss it though: the strong companionship that soldiers must feel on a battlefield. For him, there was nothing better than the comradery with his fellow-workers—his "pair". He would have done anything for them—and they for him.

Now, unfortunately, that support was gone and all he had was his family at home and the piskie-laden party in the wink. Indeed, he couldn't ask for a more supportive and close-knit bubble. Mary worked hard alongside him with the animals, cooking and washing—even the children rarely needed to be asked to help out. It was in their very nature to want to collect some eggs or muck out the chickens. Though, no one, apart from Jacka, ever wanted to go anywhere near the goat. It was the most severe beast with the fieriest of tempers. However, looking at it without afore-knowledge would leave you wondering how on earth that could ever be, for it had been blessed with the cutest face.

It had now come to a time when a sober decision on the family's future was needed. Luckily, Jacka had avoided the wink for two whole days, mainly because funds were running low and he could not buy anymore drink. He needed the remaining pennies for his wife and children. So, he sat down one evening, with the flames roaring in the hearth and the solemn faces of the ones he loved staring back, and began to discuss the future.

Jane pretended to be involved with very adult-looking nods and noises of agreement, but she was too young really to understand what the nature of the impending discussion was about. Wella was once more taken up in his own piston-driven thoughts. However, Mary and Davy were fully cognisant of the relevance. Davy, for one, was looking for answers: would his old "*sîra*" find his way back and revert to the one that used to tell him drolls of spriggian and sea beasts?

"*Res ew dhebm mos ker' rag dendyl mona,*" Jacka said as softly as he could without letting his own voice break through the emotion. He was telling the family that he had to go away to earn money to keep a roof over their heads and plenty of food on the table. Mary instantly grabbed Davy and Jane to her breast to comfort them. She, herself, let slip a single tear—wiping it away quickly with her sleeve. Once rectified, she elevated her head once more to show how brave she was.

"*Fatell yllyn ny bêwa obba ha che in telhar pell?*" she asked with her own voice still faintly trembling to make up for the sturdiness displayed in the rest of her body. Her words were full of the fear for life without Jacka and worries about how the rest of the family would endure their day-to-day lives.

"*Heb me dha wil hebma, na vëdh mona vëth oll dha nei,*" replied Jacka, attempting his best to remain calm. He told Mary that he had to go away in search of a living as, without taking this extreme action, there wouldn't be any money for them anyway.

Luckily, they had always lived frugally and made sure there were some other skills to fall back on. Mary could throw some pots and maybe sell some too. While, if push came to shove, the children could also earn some pennies working at the surface of "Wheal an

Gweal" as many of their friends already did. It would be hard, but not as dangerous as going underground. Maybe, they would end up better-off anyway.

This was not the outcome that Wella, Davy, Jane, or Mary had expected or wanted. Somehow, they had always hoped that their lives would avoid this bleakness—particularly in the case of Wella. He might have been an aloof child, but was cultured in other ways that Mrs Prendergast continually failed to contemplate. Wella believed he would become an engineer and devise amazing machines to make lives better. Maybe, he could work out a way of turning those great mining engines into something to move wagons along tracks by means of steam. Maybe, even, his ingenuity could find a method of increasing the power of those great pistons. If only that were possible then the whole community could benefit.

The disappointment was plainly evident on Wella's face that he would turn out just like all the other children in the district—condemned to poverty and at the beck and call of the local mine captain. The thought even passed through his mind that maybe he was condemning himself to this future by not trying to learn the language of progress. Yes, maybe that was his problem.

Whatever separate conclusions they each arrived at, they were unified in knowing that something had to be done.

So, the following day was the one that Jacka had decided to pay a call to his pard, Billy Bod, down at Porthenys. He spent all day walking across the high moors of Penwith and down to the tiny fishing port. He arrived late in the evening to find William Bodinar helping some friends with the boat, the *Gwicker Frank*.

They all joked in the bar every evening about their friend called "Frank" because they enjoyed some humour from time to time in *Kernowek*—especially if it was against the taxman. "*Gwicker Frank* is a smuggler, me ansome," they'd jest under hushed beery voices at the end of the night.

That is an honest description of the life that Jacka was now getting himself into. If he had the choice, yes—he would have stuck to living by the rules and staying out of trouble. The desperate truth of the matter was that he did *not* have a choice. Thus, in order to find the money to provide his family with the means to secure their future and ensure that he didn't die a hundred fathoms down a hole in the ground, then he had to harden up and take a leaf out of Billy Bod's book.

The memory of too many men and youngsters who had worked themselves into an early grave populated his mind with their ghosts. These lost souls all spoke to Jacka in his dreams telling him to make this difficult, yet important, change.

Jacka stood alongside Billy Bod on the quayside as he puffed considerately on a long slender clay pipe. The highly perfumed clouds of smoke wafted over his face as he took a few more long drags on the sweet tobacco. It was quite obvious that he was thinking deeply. And so Jacka saw fit to just stand there and watch him in mid deliberation.

Time seemed to stop as this contemplative mood hung in the salty, fishy air. Soon, however, time resumed its normal course and Billy removed the pipe from his mouth and simply stated: "*Nag yw pysketsha dhana!*"

William Bodinar had been a hundred percent correct in summing up Jacka's reasons for suddenly arriving in Porthenys and realized that it wasn't about fishing. Indeed, the only thing in common between fishing and what Jacka had in mind was the need of a boat—and maybe the sideshow of actually doing some catching to distract attention.

"*Nag yw, dha wir,*" agreed Jacka—stating that it indeed wasn't about fishing.

"*Me a vedn mos tramor rag gwerra taclow—che a or,*" Jacka clarified that he wanted to go abroad to sell stuff. The truth of it was, though, that he was also suggesting doing a return run.

"*Pandra vedno'whei dry tre y'n scath dhana?*" Billy Bod asked what he wanted to bring home in the boat.

"*Backa dâ rag megy,*" answered Jacka pointing at the tobacco in his pipe.

Billy Bod laughed and strode off across the quay with a plume of smoke following behind him and shouting: "*Gwell via dhis bos obba myttyn abrës!*" So, William Bodinar had more or less agreed to take Jacka in his boat so long as he turned up at daybreak the next morning.

That night, Jacka found a space on the floor at his aunt Jane's cottage far up in the narrow back streets. It was an old shambolic granite building, snuggled in a small gap between a chapel and a dilapidated cluster of sheds, but with a portion of a view across to the island. Jane placed a big bowl of steaming soup on the table in front of him and scowled.

"Are you an Mary still pretendin t'knaw naw English?"

Jacka returned the scowl and looked back at his soup again to take the first few gentle sips.

"I knaw both of ee knaw a liddle English an I just ken't see, for the life o me, why you are so set against your childern learnin ob'm."

There was an answer, but he was not in the mood to start on how he felt deeply linked to his history—and so he retained his silent composure.

"I feel some sorry for they poor liddle cheelds, sufferin every day an believin you knaw awnly Cornish."

Aunt Jane brought a bowl of soup for herself over to the table where Jacka held his counsel despite the inquisition over his Cornish-only policy at home.

"Ess, fay! I knaw some English," Jacka retorted, "an nuff ob'm t'do your understand quite well."

It was quite probably the first words of English he had uttered all year. They had been forced out of him by circumstance. Playing games was not going to win him favour with board and lodging for the night at his aunt's house—particularly as she spoke about as much Cornish as he spoke English.

Jane looked across her soup at Jacka with her maternal emotions in full flow. She smiled supportively and leant over to tap his hand reassuringly.

"I believe that when you must, the pair of ee, you will enter modern times an suffer they childern to speak the awnly way that will leave them go forth in the world an earn their fit livin."

It was indeed a reality of life that Jacka and Mary had been all too aware of; the fact that ways were changing very fast and the Pengilley family was struggling to keep up. The encroachment of the next century was all too apparent with everyone talking the foreign tongue from way across the Tamar and all the new-fangled steam engines around driving the mines. It confused the hell out of Jacka and left Mary stone cold. She could see these marvels were certainly bringing new opportunities. She could remember how long it used to take to get a letter to the other end of Cornwall. Now everything was getting faster and faster. Too fast for her to contemplate.

Jacka had come to take steam for granted in the granite engine-houses with their smoothly pivoted beams and tuneful clanking. But even he had gasped when the suggestion came up in the wink about some engineers postulating how it could drive some sort of horse-less carriage all the way up to London. As far as Jacka knew—that was a long way in the future and nothing that he would see in his lifetime. His only reply to someone's claim it was happening sooner than he thought was: *"metessen!"*—perhaps.

The question for him was more to do with whether his family should embrace change by abandoning Cornish and embrace English—just as most others around them were doing. Jacka was stubborn and quite adamant that he would rather curl up and die than give in to this element of "progress".

He grimaced as Jane gave him a patronizing tap on his hand—then he began to sing:

> *"Pà'th'era pobel 'clappya Kernowek coth,*
> *Pà'th'era tus heb otham mos gen toth,*
> *Pà'th'en vy lowen dres jorna howlyek hir,*
> *Nag era dhymm whans a dhybarth vëth a'n tir."*[5]

Jane looked confused by the song as she could only make out one or two words. Jacka leaned back in his chair and smiled at her.

"Meur ras dha whei a'n cowl," Jacka continued as he got up from the table and thanked Jane for the soup. It was bedtime and he had a very long week ahead of him.

"Dùrnostadha," Jacka whispered as he found a space on a big wooden settle next to the dresser.

"Dùrnostadha," Jane replied, "good night, Jacka."

Morning came and the sun was casting its first rays; skimming them across the calm sea around Porthenys. Jacka gently pulled Jane's front gate shut. He scuttled down the hill and around the corner to the quayside. Billy Bod and Billy Bod Bian were waiting along

---

5   *"When there were people chatting in old Cornish,*
    When there were men without a need to move with speed,
    When I was happy through a long sunny day,
    There was not to me a desire to leave this land at all."

with three other deck hands ready for the voyage across to Brittany. It was as though Billy Bod had never moved from his spot as he stood there once more puffing on his pipe in a way that intimated to the world that he was fully in command. Billy Bod Bian grinned at his father's nonchalance; recognizing a little of himself in the old man's ways. He, however, hated the taste of tobacco and had broken with generations of Bodinar tradition to abstain from it. Even a slight whiff of the sweet smoke carried towards him in the wind would make him break out in a fit of disgusted coughing.

"*Pandr'yw an towl?*" asked Bill Bod between puffs as he searched out his pard's plan for this "free trade" trip.

"*Wèl—me a vedn gwerra hebma!*" Jacka exclaimed as he pulled something heavy wrapped in a cloth from his sack. He set the weighty lump down on the ground and peeled back the cloth.

"*Dr'yw hedna?*" asked Billy Bod Bian—wanting to know what it was. His Cornish was very stilted even on a short sentence. Both Jacka and the young man's father always fell silent when he attempted to use the old language as they did not want to hinder such a rare occasion.

Jacka took a step back and smiled as he revealed how he had come to an agreement with the mine captain when he left "Wheal an Gweal". He had always longed to take ownership of a lump of silver ore kept on the Captain's desk. The rock had been handed to him following the accident as a small measure of compensation and farewell gift.

"*Pes pens 'alja nei cawas gen hedna?*" asked Billy Bod—wanting to know how much they could get for the specimen.

"*Na ora vy—bùs hèn yw an towl p'o gwerrys neppëth, nag yw indelha?*" Jacka replied while scratching his head and saying that he didn't know, but that was the point of commerce. In fact, he was plainly excited by the prospect of trying his hand at the open market. He was hoping his galena was going to raise a fair fortune—but to buy what?

"*Alja nei cawas meur a vacka gen hedna?*"

Billy Bod received a series of frowns from the crew and his son in wondering whether they could get anything (tobacco for example) in trade for it. At that, Jacka hurriedly wrapped up the rock once more and put it back in his sack for fear anyone, who could have suspicions aroused, were to pass by. Indeed, that was the key con-

cern now; not so much about how to barter, but how they were
going to get out and back without being spotted by the taxmen.

Billy Bod and his crew had certainly completed such a sprint
across the water several times before and knew the various ways and
means of avoiding the excise officers. They had often sailed to Brittany and back in the pretence of fishing while bringing back tobacco,
salt and wine. Though the quayside auction of fish on the continent
was very changeable in the amount of funds raised, there were only
a couple of occasions when the crew would find little profit in the
venture. Still, it had to be said, it was not unheard of that rogues
would return to Porthenys with the shame of barely breaking even.

With a decent haul of fish, they could easily land plenty of tea,
wine and tobacco to sell in the market. If this was achieved without
paying any tax, then they could ensure a profitable voyage. All Billy
Bod needed to have with him, in order to make sure his plan went
well, was a length of hemp rope and some sacking. These had been
carefully stowed on the lugger along with the fishing gear and provisions for the journey.

The crew were tasked with preparing the means of returning
home without raising even a hair on the brow of a customs-and-
excise man. The three of them casually sloped off from the
impromptu pre-mission meeting and disappeared into a shabby
wooden shed behind an assortment of boats which had been hauled
out of the sea for repair.

Josiah was the burliest of the three deck-hands with muscles that
looked as though they were the cranes that dragged fishing boats
ashore into that very same yard. He had a short black beard and a
mouth stretched into a continuous grin—if it could be spotted at all
beneath his oversized fisherman's hat. He was only twenty-five years
old but appeared as though he had been at sea for all of his life. He
spoke in a mumble and ran all of his words together as though they
were one single syllable.

His younger brother, Tobmas, was also in the crew and shared
many of the same angular bodily features—apart from the muscles.
His lean body might indicate that he shirked any heavy lifting—but
that would be a false assumption. Tommy Tobm, as he was known,
was an industrious worker and a clever one at that. Where Josiah
might grunt and heave for all his worth to make something move,
Tommy had a mind which worked out the most energy efficient

means of using levers, rollers and props to achieve the same result. His name was more ironic than anything because, while his fellow workers were sweating buckets to shift a boat down the hard, he would be as cool as anything—and, as he frequently reminded anyone who would listen, the word "*tobm*" in Cornish meant "warm".

The third deckhand was Jacka Pascoe. He professed to be the most knowledgeable seaman in the whole of Cornwall only because he had indeed sailed across the North Atlantic and back once in his life. At the age of forty-two, Jacka Lacka had accumulated more nicknames than anyone else in Porthenys. His current one referred to the time he had represented the village in the "wrasslin" against St Columb Major. It had been a disastrous competition—notching up the worst score ever for his town team. Hence, he was rewarded with the name "An Lacka"—"the worst" in Cornish.

Billy Bod watched the three of them furtively disappear into the *crow* to prepare ropes, hooks and sacking that they would utilize to smuggle goods back to Cornwall. On previous endeavours, they had worked out a method of using tar to waterproof the sacking and then hiding their contraband under the surface of the water. It was a risky operation for, if the goods were spotted, then they would be hauled before the law. On the other hand, if the waterproofing measures failed then they lost their money. Thus, it was a serious operation which needed to be performed carefully and precisely. Despite the need for attention to detail, the crew set about their work, laughing and joking about cunning ways to hide loot and daring means employed to evade the navy. But they knew that any slip-ups could cost them dearly—maybe even their lives.

The sun was fully up now and was starting to shorten the morning shadows. The warmth gently burned off the remaining *mizzick* that hung above the water, drifting like a silk blanket. Jacka and Billy Bod silently pushed the boat away from the quayside while the other deck hands raised the foresail. It lightly billowed in the morning breeze just enough to help them creep out of port and into the bay, leaving Cornwall's towering cliffs, hidden beaches and sheltered fishing coves behind.

As far as Jacka was concerned, they should treat this stage of the journey as a fishing trip and catch as much *hern* and *bre'all* as they could so that, if a passing ship contained the offices of His Majesty's excise men, they could proudly show off their catch and avoid being searched for illegal contraband. This, he thought, would also be a good way of making some extra money once ashore in Brittany. An ulterior motive was that these spare coins could also pay for a few days keep and drinking.

Meanwhile, Billy Bod had serious misgivings about Jacka's plan for trading his lump of galena. Yes, it looked pretty and had some traces of silver in it, but as far as he could tell, it was next to useless for bartering. He hadn't quite decided whether he should approach the issue directly or just leave Jacka with the hope that it would make a few pounds. At the very least, the piece of rock gave his mate a sense of purpose on the trip.

Billy's previous crossings had usually involved catching as much fish on the way over as possible, selling it on the quayside, and then returning home laden with as plentiful tobacco, tea, spirits or salt as he could safely stow. He was just one of many people running such an operation and was hoping to be as successful as a woman he knew called Martha Blewett. Billy had noted how she had made a sizable fortune out of smuggling untaxed salt into Cornwall right beneath the eyes of HM Customs & Excise officers. It was the talk along the whole coast how one of the sure routes to bring contraband onto the mainland was through the Isles of Scilly.

Billy was the envious sort. It was a healthy form of greed though as he took careful notice of other people's successes and failures— and learnt from them. He was particularly intrigued by Sidney, the First Earl of Godolphin. He had managed to make some much-needed money decades earlier as Governor of Scilly by operating a free-trading racket from his own little island empire. Even though Billy would never admit it openly, he was positively inspired by the way the aristocrat had turned his back on crime after hitting upon more legal means of earning his crust; namely flowers. His name was almost a jibe on the lips of hardened smugglers. "Like Godolphin are ee?" they would tease anyone who may be getting the jitters before setting off on an adventure. While Billy sneered down his nose publicly—there was a sneaking admiration for the man's memory. Many went as far as to hold the earl in high esteem for converting his smuggling prowess into a lucrative business trading in blossoms. However, for Billy and Jacka, straightforward rogueing was their plan.

Their mission started well with a favourable light wind giving some help on the oars when the current flowed against them. The lugger creaked and groaned with the forces of nature exerting pressure on its aged joints. Despite the vessel's audible reluctance, by the end of the morning, it was far from land leaving Jacka out of his true comfort zone. He preferred to be in the inky dark below ground rather than in an unstable boat bobbing about many miles *from* land. Billy was brought up on the waves though and took pride in recounting how, from his earliest days as a young boy, he would go fishing with four of five men all in their eighties.

These days it was not quite the same. Yes, the fish were caught just as ever but the discussion often moved into English. Thus, Billy Bod was pleased to have Jacka aboard for company. It wasn't because of skills in mending nets or experience in sea-craft, fishing or even smuggling—because it wasn't. The pleasure was down to how he maintained eloquent and amusing conversation in his beloved *Kernowek*.

It was about midday and the sun was high in the sky when Jacka and the crew started the preparation for catching some pilchards.

"*Towl an roos!*" yelled Billy Bod with a hoarse crackle in his throat as he, and the deck hands, hurled the net as far as they could into the swirling currents of the sea. The water sparkled, shining bright blue and green, as they watched the net sink.

"*Gûn las yw dha wir hedhyw!*" laughed Jacka as he cheerfully commented on the beautiful colours being reflected back.

Billy Bod cast a glance at Jacka, who was now sitting with his spine against the main mast and examining his lump of galena again. As Jacka shot a look back, he got a wink that was interpreted as "Aren't you clever to fund this whole trip with an ultra-precious piece of silver ore!" However, that was not what the real meaning was. William Bodinar was more astute than that. He really meant to say "You idiot for thinking that worthless lump of rock is going to buy anything!" Of course, he wouldn't be so rude.

It was a few hours later when the nets were hauled back into the boat laden with a healthy catch of pilchards. The important job now was to keep them as fresh as possible. All hands were summoned to the task and Jacka got a fast lesson on how to pack them into a wooden balyer and how to cover each layer with salt. By the time the light was fading, four barrels on the deck had been filled to the brim and sealed. This left the crew feeling exhausted, hungry and thirsty. The evening meal was not exactly a feast fit for a Godolphin—more a lump of bread washed down with a cruskyn of mead.

Everyone slept well that night despite the uncomfortable nature of a hard wooden-boat as a bed and the constant rocking from the rhythm of the waves lapping below. First light came with the sound of Billy Bod Bian forcefully shaking his father's shoulder.

"Wake up—wake up—er—*dyfun yn scon*," he whispered directly into his ear.

A navy ship was moored about a quarter of a mile off their stern and a smaller rowing boat had been decanted with four men on board—the excise officers had already found them.

The British Navy located Billy Bod's tiny boat approximately mid-channel. As far as Jacka knew, they knew nothing and that this was just a routine inspection. However, Billy had run into these four officers before. As soon as he realized what was about to happen, he grabbed Jacka's carefully wrapped lump of galena, unwrapped it, and with an almighty splash, hurled it over the side.

"*Pandr'era whei o qwil?*" yelped Jacka, wanting to know why his precious silver ore had been slung into the briney.

"*I'n kensa—na dal tra vëth—i'n secùnd le—ny vanama ry dhe'n dus toll fraga vëth gofen dro dha dollow.*"

Billy explained to Jacka in an authoritative whisper that the rock had no value and that he did not want to give the tax men any reason to ask about taxes. Just as soon as he had done this, the four officer's boat pulled alongside. They were armed with swords and side-arms and had a hunger flaring in their eyes for a prize to drag ashore. Reluctantly, Billy Bod Bian held out his hand so that the commander could clamber aboard the lugger. He followed with the polite gesture to all the other three who were dressed in smart dark tunics with gold braiding.

"I am Commander Emmanuel Carter and am charged by His Majesty to examine all boats that cross the Channel, least they have goods that evade custom—and to seek any man who might spy for the French," said the tallest in a very haughty accent. He stood nose to nose with an unflinching Billy Bod.

"And I mind to have met thee before on several occasions—each time you pretend to be fishing."

Carter paced around the deck and looked each crew member closely in the eyes until he got to Jacka.

"But I have not seen you aboard before. Name yourself, man."

Billy Bod shot Jacka a "no-messing" look with a slight shake to his head. This was not the time to pretend he knew no *Sowsnek* at all.

"Jacka Pengilley *oma*—er—is my name, *syra*—er—sir," he stammered in half Cornish, half English.

Carter wryly smiled and stood back.

"Taking country dolts aboard now, are you, Bodinar?"

Billy Bod nodded with a short "yes, sir" and caught the look of horror on Jacka's face at how one of his closest pards could agree with a statement like that. Then again, it was better to keep the tax men calm and send them on their way.

"We shall search this vessel from prow to stern and I pray for all your sakes that she is clean of all contraband, for I hate to see any man cast into prison—or worse—for roguing."

With that, the other three officers took great pleasure in overturning the barrels of pilchards onto the deck and searching among the freshly salted fish for any hints of criminal behaviour. They then examined every other corner with careful attention to looking in crates, stowage holes and under anything that could hide tea or tobacco. Billy Bod and Billy Bod Bian stood alongside the other deck hands as confidently as ever they had done before, knowing that this was quite simply a fishing trip. Jacka, however, had never experienced anything quite like this in his life and was visibly quaking.

The search only lasted for about a quarter of an hour before it was apparent to Commander Carter and his men that their mission was futile. This vessel and crew were completely clean! As the three subordinate officers climbed back into their small pilot boat, Carter paced back up to William Bodinar and stared him out eyeball to eyeball. He searched his face for what seemed like a minute for any sign of breaking. It was a matter of seconds, in reality, after which he grinned broadly.

"William Bodinar. You know I *will* catch you one day."

By now he was climbing back into the pilot boat. However, just before pushing away, he shot Billy another glance.

"You know I shall hang thee."

Then they were gone, rowing furiously against the current back over to their tall ship lying gracefully at anchor. Jacka, Billy and the crew stood there silent and unmoving as they watched the boat get smaller and smaller—until it reached its destination. Only then did any of them take leave to relax.

"*Dâ lowr*—leave us load this fish in the oskets again".

V
Bonding and Discovery

Geoff Pengilley's life was a continuous circle of cooking, dropping his sons to Glasney Secondary School and then starting a day sitting at a trade counter answering, what seemed to him, a constant stream of daft questions about drill-bit sizes, plastic guttering and types of wallpaper paste. When he arrived home each evening, his wife Sarah had already picked up the children from school and had started cooking tea. Sarah spent most of the day slaving over a hot laptop trying to sell fuel supplements as part of a "network selling" scheme. She was seriously beginning to doubt the claims she was going to get rich quick. The only person likely to be sunning themselves in the Virgin Islands was the salesperson right at the top of the pyramid. But, with these mundane jobs, the couple managed to hold their lives together and pay the mortgage, run a car and afford some of the standard kit that two teenage boys demand.

The youngest was ten-year-old Edward. He was fascinated by anything from spaceships to what made the slimy stuff come out of a slug. He was a pure scientist at heart—living and breathing chemical formulae and complex mathematics. He was certainly heading for a life in a laboratory. Meanwhile, his elder brother, Gary, was a sixteen-year-old into music, art and high-culture. He had started learning the violin not long after his first week at school. The instrument found him rather than Gary choosing to play it. It was mainly down to his teacher having a spare instrument which just about fitted him.

It was fair enough for Geoff Pengilley to excuse himself from knowing what they were up to all the time, because both boys were fairly solitary. Neither of them charged around shouting much or bringing strange girls home like a cat hunting birds. Edward spent most of his spare time examining bits of plant material under a microscope while Gary practised music and painted. However, he had been caught out fair and square; it was his duty to know what his children were up to.

So, another Saturday arrived and Geoff decided the weather was just too good to have his boys spending the weekend in the confines of their rooms—whether they enjoyed being there or not.

"Right—Gary, Eddie!" he called upstairs. "Do you want to come out for a blast of air on the beach?"

There was no answer apart from the front room door opening and Sarah poking her head around the frame.

"What are you doing?"

"Well," he grinned broadly, "I'm doing exactly what I should have done years ago—and before it is too late."

"Today," he announced, "I will mostly be spending quality time with the boys."

Sarah nodded approvingly and called upstairs too, "come on you two—here's a rare chance that doesn't come around often."

Gary's face emerged at the top of the stairs.

"What sort of chance?"

"You're going to spend some quality father-sons time together—so get Eddie."

"What?" moaned Gary with obvious reluctance, "we never go out with you—so why now?"

"Oh, come on Gary," Geoff pleaded, realizing that making this case for bonding so late in their relationship seemed slightly strange. "I want to find out about some of the great things you're up to that I'm obviously not getting told about."

Gary had come to the bottom of the stairs by now, leaving space for Eddie to follow—which he did.

"But why now?"

That was indeed a good question from the eldest and one that deserved a good answer. All that Geoff could find to say was; "because the sun is out and I feel it's time I bought both of you an ice cream."

It didn't need to be any more refined than that as before he knew it, Gary and Eddie had their trainers on and were waiting eagerly at the front of the house. It took a matter of ten minutes to walk to the nearest beach, though that time felt like an awkward ten hours. Sarah had stayed home for some precious "me time" in her art studio, thus leaving Geoff, Gary and Edward to make conversation. She could only imagine how that would go!

None of them was very good at small-talk and so the three walked down the road in an awkward silence. Geoff assumed that Gary's mind was deep in some artistic pursuit while Eddie was trying to deal with some mind-blowingly complex formulae. How wrong could he have been?

The three arrived at Gyllyngvase Beach where Geoff sidled over to the ice cream kiosk at the back of the sands.

"What do you want to have boys?" he asked chirpily.

Edward selected a whippy with a flake while Gary went for a mint-choc-chip in a cone. Geoff bought a triple chocolate for himself and handed the ices over. It was the perfect father-son bonding activity for him because little real conversation was expected while summer treats were being devoured. It was an all-encompassing and a convenient diversion—but it could not last forever.

"So, how's biology going Eddie?" eventually came the question which should have been asked months ago. By now, the three were sitting on a bench at the back of the beach watching a surf school. A row of raw recruits who had never touched a board before were practicing the routine of standing up. It was clearly an easy thing to master on terra-firma. It was likely to be a little more entertaining once they entered the waves.

"Not bad—I love it though," smiled Eddie as he kicked his feet under the bench in a way that children always do on a seat that is just a little too high for them. It was a good starter as Eddie just wanted to talk science and now had an excuse. The conversation flowed for several minutes until Geoff realized that he had been so engrossed in talking to his youngest that he had totally forgotten to allot a similar amount of time to Gary.

On turning to his left, he saw Gary deep in thought. He was scrolling through pages on his mobile.

"And you?" asked Geoff.

"You know that Gyllyngvase comes from the Cornish that means 'the shallow nook'?"

Gary had barely looked up from his phone as he made the statement. It was performed as a "matter of fact" which hid the true sensitive artist that he really was. Just then, Geoff realized he had brought up reclusive sons who buried their heads in studies of one sort or another. Was it his fault they were failures in being sociable? Should he even be considering that any blame was necessary? Maybe, the best way of looking at this was as a reason for celebration. Both of his sons had found hobbies which fully engaged them.

Eventually, Gary put his phone back in his pocket and looked around at his father. He was still gazing at the horizon as though awaiting the arrival of an armada of ships.

"Thanks for the time out Dad—but you've never really done this before—so why now?"

"Well—it is all after me not having a clue about either your, or Eddie's, latest news," he confessed. "So, I thought it was time I made sure I wasn't missing out on anything."

"I suppose," he continued, "that I was also a little fascinated by the revelations from Jacka Pengilley's box and how it appears to link to what you were up to."

"Yeh," agreed Gary, "it is sort of spooky. I joined the Cornish Club at school—and then it turns out that this long-dead relative left an entire diary to us in the very same language."

The chat continued as the threesome got up from the bench and continued to stroll back through the gardens behind the beach and up Spernen Wyn Road, Eddie continually stopping to intricately inspect the tropical plants on the way. He was fascinated by the large collection of Gunnera with their giant leaves and spikey stems. They looked like something from a mythical world or a far distant civilization—almost alien. Meanwhile, Gary and Geoff wound their way along the paths at a pace which allowed Eddie to carry out his observations. Conversation flitted between diverse topics until another far-removed civilization drew their attention—but this one could hardly be considered alien.

"It is strange," said Geoff, "how we are all buzzing around in our daily lives in a world which would seem completely foreign to our own relatives just a handful of generations ago." Gary was listening intently to his father's titbit of wisdom like a young apprentice might study the teachings of his guru.

"I mean," continued Geoff, "Jacka would have no chance of understanding us or how we live—it would be just like us trying to communicate with people living in Outer Mongolia."

"But I *would* understand some of what he said," insisted Gary, "I mean, for example, look at this road we're walking up."

"What about it?" Geoff replied in utter surprise, "it's a road with houses on it and tennis courts and a beach at the bottom—what more should I be noticing?"

Gary laughed at his father as though he had made a very basic schoolboy error and he was being derided by his mates. His guru clearly wasn't the fount of all wisdom.

"We're walking up Spernen Wyn Road—Jacka would have understood that was a type of tree called 'whitethorn'—and ever since I started learning Cornish, it means exactly the same to me."

The jaunt may have been just a pleasant afternoon out for a father and two sons as far as any onlooker could tell. However, in reality, it was deeper than that. It was the day that a dad truly started bonding with his children—albeit ten years late.

The following weekend, the new policy of parent-offspring bonding became an event for the whole family. Sarah, Geoff, Eddie and Gary all piled into their ageing Ford Sierra, with its rusty orange hub caps and faded red paintwork, and set off for a long day out. The plan was to fulfil the whole family's wishes in one super excursion in the westerly wilds of Penwith.

Sarah had chosen to take a look at a pottery in Newlyn to start the adventure. The family spent almost an hour looking around the kilns and potters' wheels while a number of workers gently caressed the spinning clay.

"It's just like Ghost," laughed Geoff. Sarah went red in the face while the boys sniggered at the embarrassing remark.

Eddie was fascinated by the way that the mechanism on the treadle was totally manual and maintained a steady rotation with very little effort from the operator's foot. Gary was watching the same mechanism but, rather than making mental notes about the gearing, he was soothed by the gentle rhythm of the treadle. Dum de de de dum de de de dum de de de.

Eventually, he snapped out of the trance and blurted out: "*Pry!*"

"There's no Grand Prix on today so don't worry about missing something like that on our trip out," remarked Sarah. She was a bit of a motorsport fan herself.

"No—the clay," Gary tutted. He became exasperated when the rest of the world failed to understand his thoughts.

"What are you talking about?" asked Eddie with the rest of the confused family looking on.

"*Pry* is the Cornish word for clay and I'm sure I saw it mentioned in Jacka's diary."

Such sudden utterances were becoming more and more common where Gary would be deep in thought for a long period. This would build up more and more pressure on his consciousness until it was like a dam bursting and spewing out water in a tsunami-like torrent. Once the thoughts had been released, Gary was free again to return to his trance-like state.

This continued throughout Eddie's pick. He had chosen to spend the next part of the day at Porthcurno Wartime Telegraphy Museum; an adventure deep into a hillside where ancient machines rattled and tapped in a flurry of coded communications delayed by more than seventy years. Sarah was also fascinated as her Granfer had worked there during the war. Apparently, he was involved in making sure secret messages were received from faraway extremities of the British Empire.

Once again Gary was away with the fearies—maybe, this time brought on by the rhythmic tapping of the teleprinters and the rattling of punched-tape-readers. Even though this was more Eddie's domain, he was clearly fascinated by the ancient technology and how it used an assortment of coils, springs and beautifully machined keys.

Sarah watched him with amusement and took her own photograph on her phone. Whatever he was thinking, it was clear that another stream of consciousness was building up. If she could guess her eldest son's next action, it would include an explosive gush of unintelligible words. That moment never came for, just as it seemed he was about to let loose his emotions, he simply looked up and smiled. He then calmly moved on to the next display.

It was another hour before the whole family had exhausted their time in the museum. Geoff and Sarah were eager to have something to eat but both boys needed to be levered out from the underground maze of rattling machinery. It had definitely been a revelation that Gary could find aspects of interest in something she had purely expected Eddie to enjoy.

"I suppose it only makes sense," remarked Sarah as Geoff caught Gary by the shoulders and propelled him towards the exit.

"What do you mean: it only makes sense?" chorused a response from the rest of the family.

"Well, I had thought Gary would be bored senseless by a museum full of old tech—and that we would struggle to drag Eddie out instead."

"Of course, Eddie would enjoy all the clicking and rattling technology with solenoids and coils—but it's the story and the music that surrounds them—isn't it Gary?"

Gary gave a teasing half smile to acknowledge now that he had let slip some of his own innermost workings. He felt just like one of those teleprinters with their covers off—displaying whirring gear wheels and taught springs.

Lunch was enjoyed out of a hamper on the beach. They rarely went into cafes or restaurants as it was expensive for a family of four. The plan was to conclude the day with a meal in the Tinner's Arms at Zennor. That was going to be the part that Geoff was looking forward to particularly as Sarah had offered to drive back and thereby allowing him the opportunity for a couple of beers with his meal. Before that though, was the fulfilment of Gary's request—to see a few ancient stones and a small collection of cottages a short walk away from "Wheal an Gweal Mine".

His mini Penwithian tour was opened with a short stop at Lanyon Quoit.

"This is from the Neolithic era, rebuilt in 1824 by Captain Giddy," he announced with his head buried in a book cataloguing every stone worth its salt in the area.

"Captain Giddy?" laughed Eddie, barely believing such a name existed.

"Yes, that's right," his brother confirmed, pointing to the page showing the very same monument.

"That's what Craig Weatherhill says," he confidently stated. "Craig is the expert!"

Before long, the family were moving on to the final place of interest; the cottages. Gary claimed he had read about them and knew exactly what to expect. "Just a little spooky," laughed his mum. She had only just been watching a documentary a few weeks earlier about such a case where a young boy had begun to recount memories of an existence in the highlands and islands of Scotland.

In a similar way, Gary was becoming increasingly taken up with
the diaries of Jacka Pengilley. He had only briefly been offered a
chance to study them when visiting the museum's archives. Was it
bizarre that a teenage boy should become obsessed with the life of a
family 200 years earlier? Eddie gave his brother a side-on wink to
say, "You are an absolute nutter!" He added a disarming smirk to
avoid any misunderstanding. He could not comprehend why he was
besotted with people who spoke little English and lived a hand-to-
mouth existence.

Gary didn't consider any of it weird whatsoever and certainly
never claimed to have experienced any past life memories. He saw
this as simply "practical research" and desired to recreate Jacka and
Mary Pengilley's lives in his mind. To do so, he needed small
glimpses of their lives. Thus, the four day-trippers parked up on the
bracken-bordered verge of the coast road which wound its way
through Morvah and Rosemergy, ready to engage in a little more
family bonding. Though, Sarah refused point blank to do any ama-
teur historical detective work until she had payed a fleeting visit to
the tiny teashop and art gallery nearby.

"So, Gary," she gently whispered between sips of Earl Grey, "what
are we about to discover?"

Her son stared back at her blankly. He didn't mean to be rude or
spiteful. He just could not deal with the possibilities of imagination
and speaking in the real world at the same time. He was either trying to work out what he was going to look for in this windblown
treeless part of Cornwall or he was daydreaming about a piece of
music he was working on—or both. Eventually, the real world fil-
tered through to him and he smiled broadly.

"We are going to touch the stones and hear the music of the land
which our family lived on two centuries ago."

It was one of those moments in comedy where all the cast exclaim
"okay" while looking at one another nervously. If this were a western film then there would have been tumbleweed blowing across the
set. However, this was Cornwall in the early part of the twenty-first
century and Eddie just started to giggle, followed by Geoff—and
finally Sarah. Her maternal instincts kicked in when a flicker of disappointment in the family's attitude showed through. She grabbed
him around the shoulders and gave him a supportive hug.

"Now, come on—there must be something else you want to do," she half-asked *and half*-told him. Sarah shone a smile which used to be reserved for school home-time when her sons bore news of a tough exam or an aggressive bully.

"Really mum," Gary insisted, pulling himself away in disdain from her limpet-like grip.

"I do want to learn more about our family. I mean, aren't you the slightest bit intrigued by Jacka Pengilley's diary?"

Sarah looked at Geoff. Geoff looked at Eddie. Eddie looked back at Gary. Then a dull spark ignited in her mind as she recreated the moment in that dark oak-panelled room when the trunk was cracked open before their eyes.

"Well, yes—I suppose I am—particularly thinking about that pottery in there," she replied.

"And I suppose I'm fascinated that I'm a direct descendent of Jacka," followed Geoff.

Eddie just looked back at them all and laughed, "I think I'd rather just go and look around some shops somewhere or head down to the beach."

There was no pleasing everyone all the time. The result was that there were now three members of the family setting out on the quest with one member not the slightest bit bothered about hunting down Pengilley heritage. However, Eddie had enjoyed part of the day at Porthcurnow and so was not violently resisting.

It had started to rain when they vacated the teashop. The music of Penwith seemed to consist of drops crashing onto the car roof. It was only a short drive before Gary shouted for them to pull off the road and follow a metalled track further down towards the cliffs with the hills of Carn Galva and Watchcroft towering timelessly over them.

"So how do you know where to hunt?" asked Sarah, turning around to look at Gary behind her. He was staring through the window in deep thought. It was as though he had become psychically linked to the landscape. That of course was just hokery-pokery and did not really exist as far as Sarah knew. Gary eventually allowed her question to break through to his conscious mind.

"I don't know for sure—just that I get a feeling it is somewhere around here—at least I guess so from what I read in those few pages."

Geoff stopped the car on a grassy roadside bank next to a lichen-covered hedge topped with golden gorse. Gary spotted a row of cottages a few hundred metres along the track and started to stride purposefully towards them with the determination of a Victorian sleuth. When he reached the first, he stood stock-still in the lane in front of it and surveyed its tiny windows, simple porch and slate roof. It had been lovingly decorated with a collection of tubs of immaculate petunias and pansies. This was set off with a slate sign declaring it to be "Dunroamin".

Gary snorted and took a couple of paces towards the middle cottage. This one was laid out in a similar fashion without having the same dainty fineries as next-door. The windows certainly needed a good spot of paint. But, in contrast to the posh nameplate next door, this one had a rough piece of wood with the name "Boswicker". Gary's knowledge of Cornish was enough to understand that "*bos*" meant "a dwelling". However, he was uncertain of meaning of the second element.

He paced another couple of steps along to the end cottage. This one was simply named "The Cottage". The interesting feature here was that there was a public footpath following alongside the granite walls which allowed him to continue his quest around to the back gardens. Eddie, Sarah and Geoff dutifully followed. Eddie was now engrossed in the exotic plants growing in this last cottage's back garden—maybe some foreign escapes brought back by a Victorian plant-hunter from Mexico or the Mediterranean.

Gary nosily peeked over the walls to see what else was behind the cottages. All he could see were some washing lines, a few greenhouses and a rather tumble-down outhouse. Sarah tapped him on the shoulder.

"Don't be so nosy—these are people's private gardens."

At that moment up popped a head from behind a clump of dahlias. The head's owner pulled a broad grin radiating peace with the planet. She didn't seem the least bit worried by someone looking into her garden.

"Ansome day!" she stated with a broad smile. "Do you want to come see?"

"Yes, please," replied Eddie and Sarah almost in unison. Geoff was the last to follow through the garden's back gate as the lady creaked the rusty iron antique shut behind him.

"I'm Maureen," she announced cheerfully, beckoning them to come on her guided tour. She must have been in her late seventies and was proudly dressed in as much jewellery as could possibly hang around her neck and off her ears. She had only started recounting the Latin names for the first bed of specimens when a bald-headed man poked his head through the back door and enquired whether they were all "desirous" of a cup of tea.

The couple's hospitality was certainly welcome—if not a little unusual. It was as though the Pengilleys had been immediately accepted into their closest family. It was only a matter of another five minutes before Maureen's husband, David, emerged from the cottage carrying a tray of tea cups, a teapot, a milk jug and a plate of homemade biscuits. Eddie and Gary leapt forward to grab the jammy dodgers as though they were the last-ever specimens on Earth.

Sarah, meanwhile, was taken by the hand-made milk jug.

"This is really lovely," she mused, rotating it carefully and attempting not to spill any of the contents.

"Where did you find such a lovely item?"

"See that small stone shed there?" Maureen gestured across the wall to the next garden, "well Jim next door was turning out the shed about ten years ago as it had never been touched in as long as he knew." Her jewellery rattled excitedly as she continued to gesticulate in the general direction of the discovery.

"Well, there were piles of rotted wood and earth in there which had weeds and bramble growing on them. The roof must have fallen in at some point a long time ago and no-one had bothered to fix it— as you can see." By now, the rest of the family were listening intently as their hostess continued to explain the story behind the antique on the tray in front of them. "Jim managed to clear out all the rubble to find a large stone recess in the back of the shed. We were thrilled to find it contained pottery. It turns out that the recess was actually the remains of a kiln. It had been abandoned without the contents being removed."

A sudden realization hit Geoff and Sarah at the same time as they looked at each other.

"You're not thinking about that jug in the chest, are you?" Sarah mused.

"It can't be!" replied Geoff.

VI

Brittany

The wind had picked up overnight and, as Mary Pengilley awoke with the sunrise, all she could think about was how Jacka was in that tiny boat with Billy Bod and crew. Her imagination was running wild with all kinds of things that could go wrong with a vulnerable wooden craft buffeted by monstrous waves far from the sight of land. All she could see in her mind's eye was Jacka precariously holding onto a rope or the tiller for his dear life.

The thought passed her mind concerning the terrible irony if Jacka were to lose his life crossing to Brittany in an attempt at escaping a dangerous life in Cornwall. She had laughed many times at tragic folk songs telling of this sort of scenario but she doubted there would be anything save tears if Jacka perished. Mary felt the tension in her fingers follow its way right up her arms and reside at the back of her neck where a headache began to pound with the dull sonorous thud she heard at the stamps. There was little that could be achieved by worrying about her husband's safety apart from becoming ill. That would do no good at all when she still had a house to keep and three constantly demanding children to nurture.

Like most mornings, it was an effort to get the chores done at the same time as cajoling her children into going to the vicarage to get any semblance of education. The headache shortened her temper as all three displayed a complete lack of purpose in getting dressed. Jane only had one foot out from under her blankets. Davy was fully covered and pretending to be asleep. Wella was old enough to be acting as the head of the household but was making a better play out of acting-up instead.

Mary had tried everything over the years to encourage them to find joy in learning by using both "carrot and stick" tactics. This time, though, she seemed to be at her wit's end and the arguments failed to flow. Thus, she barked out the only reason left to go.

"Drefen bos otham dhe why a whel dâ i'n termyn vedn dos!"

Indeed, the three of them could not disagree with the logic in that there was a definite need to them of getting good jobs in the future. The evidence of this well-made point was very real. If their father had got more learning behind him as a child, then he would not have to be putting his life in peril down mines or on the high seas. This thought was enough to encourage them to get up. Davy was sitting up now with two feet gingerly touching the wooden planks that made up the upstairs flooring. Once he felt secure that his feet were not going to feel cold, he stood up and stretched.

"Dwee haff-ta lurn good sum Engerlish thanna?" he asked in his best English.

"Ess," replied Mary with her own attempt.

"Bùs, pandra lever Tas p'o va devedhes tre arta?" whined Jane to find out what their father would say when he returned home again. Mary looked back at all of them without speaking a single word. She looked from the youngest up to her oldest in turn to see them staring back miserably awaiting some sort of affirmation. Nothing was said. Nothing needed to be—as they all understood perfectly well that Jacka would not be best pleased if *Sowsnek* was spoken inside the four walls of the cottage.

Eventually, Wella, Davy and Jane reluctantly progressed their morning ritual to the stage of eating a meagre breakfast; a rather dry-looking piece of bread and a boiled egg. Davy resorted to prodding his food while Mary could not find the words to continue the conversation any further. She knew that Jacka was determined not to resign himself to the onward march of what was being called "civilization".

"It's an alien concept," was her own father's insistence, "and it is flourishing everywhere with new words and ideas." Of course—he would never had said such a thing in English! Mary knew he was right even though it was not only about language; it was also about religion and the profusion of billowing chimneys. Mary would not have minded so much about it if it meant more work and better pay. However, her experience was that the clever new machinery every-

61

where usually caused less work. She was also angered that if you spoke only Cornish then there were few opportunities for you.

She could remember listening to the miners and bal-maidens walking home from work past the front door of her childhood home and hearing them discussing everything in words and phrases that she could understand. If she concentrated enough, she could even hear their songs sung at the end of a long stem. Now those ending their shift would walk through the village and chatter away in the ugly tones of *Sowsnek*.

Her focus was drawn back to Wella starting to grumble in a bid to stay home.

"*Na rewgh whei argya genam—ha kewgh scon i'n hens,*" she berated them all. Mary was no longer in the mood for arguing and gave Wella a clip around the ear to hurry him up.

So, the three left the tiny cottage on the Penwith coast and headed off along the track to the vicarage, boldly built to weather the blasts of Atlantic winds. It stood resolutely against all conditions that this western part of Cornwall could throw at it in order that each child would maintain total concentration on their self-improvement as a God-fearing believer. The howling gales could whistle around the granite corners and slate shingles for all they wanted without dissuading the youngsters from chanting passages from scripture.

Mary felt deeply for them as they walked in a stone-kicking meander up the lane, knowing their pain would continue under Mrs Prendergast. The vicar's wife had an up-country accent, was young and was exceedingly well-dressed in a starched white apron and a stern-looking bonnet. Her slender lips thinned as she smiled at the children. Each grimaced back and politely shook her hand as they passed her; with a courteous, "good morning Mrs Prendergast." On receiving the approved greeting, she would nod her head and bade them a good day in return. This was continued correctly and pleasingly until the line reached Wella.

"*Mettyn dâ, Mêstres Prendergast.*"

He had not delivered the incorrect greeting purposely to elicit a flaming stare from her. His words merely cascaded from his tongue by habit; as they had done for the previous vicar's wife. She had been less aggressive in her methods of dissuasion.

Mrs Prendergast was certainly making a terrifying name for herself by running a stricter Bible class than ever before. Word-perfect renditions of "The Lord is my Shepherd" could be heard chanted from that dusty room along with clipped by-heart performances of the Creed and the Lord's Prayer. No child dared miss a word or pronounce anything incorrectly. Every meaningful punctuation mark was to be acknowledged and fully understood. Indeed, her cup did run over with fulfilment at seeing stray souls gathered in. The rumour was that she, along with the reverend, had been placed there by the diocese for the sole reason of swiftly advancing all the children's abilities to read and write "properly".

Mary stood gazing out of her porch for a few seconds more, attempting to let her few blessings seep into her heart, until she heard the rusty scrape of Mrs Tredinnick's door latch grind open. So, in order that a stream of mockery could be avoided, she hastily darted back indoors and closed the lock gently—mindful not to let even the slightest clank be heard. It had come to the point where she was even avoiding her neighbours. It was not only her pitiful offspring who faced the jibes, but her and Jacka too. As many in the community became more comfortable with English through each successive year, those who failed to embrace its strange ways were treated as though they were village idiots. This abuse happened on Mary and Jacka's own doorstep, in the street outside, at work and now there were even sniggers for making errors in reading prayers in church.

Mary found the words tricky to pronounce and was so ashamed at not being able to remember simple phrases when she needed them. The speaking was one thing—the writing was another. She failed to understand how "tough" could rhyme with "cuff". It would have helped if she had someone in the house to practice this all with. There was no use trying with Jacka. The children came home tired from being bombarded with English and were reluctant to help either.

It was no use! Mary desperately needed some solace and thinking space. Thus, she retreated out through her back door, crossing the yard, sending panicked chickens scurrying like ants fleeing a torrent of scolding water from a kettle. She escaped into her world of clay in the *crowjy*. It was her comfort. It was her safety net. Other women of the parish might have considered their "Sunday best" clothes as their favourite attire of the week; but this was not Mary's opinion. A faint smile of self-reassurance flickered across her lips as she put on her apron. It bore many stains and marks from the pursuit of her craft. It didn't matter that the linen was blotchy and smeared with dried clay—Mary loved it just so. She felt protected for that short moment as she smoothed the garment down against her body. This was, undoubtedly, her favourite thing to wear.

Mary was now shielded from the onslaught. Her granite shed was a personal fortress and her beautiful retreat from civilization. In this hallowed space, she could link to a hazily-remembered past stretching back more than two-hundred years. The earthy aromas instantly fired up memories of her own father in his dark and damp workshop in the back streets of Newlyn. Her mind cleared as she visualized him standing there patiently on the quayside with his handcart, waiting for a trader to arrive from up St Agnes—from where he sourced his supply of clay. He would proudly boast in a long rambling droll how the material he used was dug out of the ground from under the nose of Bolster-the-Giant himself—as it had been since pre-Roman times. His voice was as clear as if he had been standing right there with Mary as he excitedly preached that even the Phoenicians had traversed the globe in search of Cornwall's rich minerals. She looked at her pots lined up next to the kiln and wondered if they shared the same substance as that of the fine vessels used in the palaces of Egyptian pharaohs and houses of Greek philosophers. Maybe Roman emperors had sipped wine from Cornish cups as they planned their bloody battles as far away as the Black Sea or the parched sands of Africa.

It was a captivating concept that her humble life in this windswept corner of civilization was linked to the mighty and powerful names of history; names associated with the most heralded victories and bloody battles. The warriors who fought for Rome and, yes, wrought terrifying destruction on her own forefathers too in the savage conquest of the Britons. Could it be that her father's stories and songs were connected too? Was her language, that spoke of fish, tin, copper and clay, the same which rejoiced in iron-clad combat on the plains of Gaul?

She recaptured beautiful times tangibly with her father. It was as though she could reach out and touch them. Her fingers flexed to feel the silky clay and her toes twitched to touch the treadle. Now, her whole body began to pulse with the motor memories developed in her early years. This was when Mary would help *Tas* as he powered his potter's wheel faster and faster. It would spin with such vigour that she was sure it would make the whole frame fly apart it a catastrophic explosion of wood, metal and clay. She would be standing by his side as he attempted to regulate the speed.

Then, something else flitted into her mind that had lain dormant all this time; there was another language he used to speak to her at moments of delight—and it was not *Kernowek*.

"*Pandr'era Tas ow lawl dhebm?*" Mary asked herself in an attempt to remember what her father used to say to her. She could recall the verse's sweet rhythm and its foreign sound but she was struggling with the actual words.

She flung a lump of clay onto her father's wheel and wetted it so that it stuck firmly and was malleable enough to start working. As she got the wheel up to optimum speed, it generated a clunking rhythm which ignited more buried memories. They were of the verses Tas used to recite all those years ago.

> "*Bezet du, bezet ruz,*
> *Ar vran a gar he labous;*
> *Bezet du, bezet gwenn,*
> *Pep gavr a gar he menn.*"

The words returned to Mary and she began chanting them to herself as she moulded the clay into a small pot. When she finished the verse, she would begin again. She continued this over and over each time with increased volume and sonority until she ended up joyfully singing the words in the continental accent that her father had.

Yes, she remembered now; her father once told her when she was very young how he had been born and bred in a small village in the west of *Breten Vian* and that *Kernowek* was her father's second language. His mother tongue was actually *Brezhoneg*—Breton. With that thought she stopped the treadle for a moment as she allowed the images and sounds to gush back faster than the stream hurtled down the Rose Valley to Portheras. She could now hear him as though he was actually standing next to her in the *crowjy*.

This reawakening of hidden memory made sense as that verse was so close to the *Kernowek*. She could easily make out the words and so she tried to chant it slowly in Cornish:

> "*Bedhes du, bedhes rudh,*
> *An vran a gar hy ydhnyk;*

Bedhes du, bedhes gwydn
Pùb gavar a gar hy myn."[6]

At least, that was her best translation of the verse.

Mary continued chanting as she pedalled once more. There, in her hands, as though taking on its own life, emerged the pot between her hands. Its curves formed between her slender fingers as though she was playing a mystical instrument. Grooves of clay spread around the ochre rim as she touched her fingernails to the edge. It was as though this pot had become a sentient vessel drawing its vitality from her soul. This was the piece of cloam which had reunited her with her past family, her father and heritage. She rekindled the awareness within that, though she now lived in Cornwall and was brought up here speaking its beautiful tongue, her father had been raised in a totally different place. He had weathered his boyhood through a similar set of sounds—yet so so different.

This reassuring reconnection was a godsend for it explained the circumstances buffeting her, how her family had always surfed the turbulent waves of changing cultures and why her heart ached. So, she resolved that this special pot would always be hers and so carefully engraved a Breton word from that verse on its base—*"gavr"*.

With all of her deep thoughts in a whirlpool of emotion and her voice hoarse after heartily singing verses from afar, she had quite put out of her mind all her troubles. The real danger was that they would all flood back. So, she took a large breath of air as she opened the door and stood out in the yard amongst a throng of industriously pecking chickens. She waited there for a minute, listening for neighbourly activity in nearby cottages. Then, when she was sure she had the vicinity to herself, Mary let forth her proclamation of purpose that, save for the year, place and her being a Cornishwoman, could have held the majestic importance of an imperial decree:

"Êsy oma vy ha parys rag kenyver tra," she smiled as she announced to the world (and the chickens) that she was comfortable with herself and ready for everything. The decree echoed off the cottage walls, so great was the power with which Mary delivered it. She

---

6   *"Be it black, be it red,*
      The raven loves her chick;
      Be it black, be it white,
      Every goat loves her kid."

listened a while until every last remnant of sound had been absorbed into the granite and landscape. Then she smoothed down her clay-encrusted apron once more and returned to the cottage; empowered at last.

Once Wella, Davy and Jane's problems had been solved, then she could start concerning herself with whatever her husband was up to on his way across to her father's homeland. As a matter of fact, Wella was doing exceedingly well in the care of the vicar's wife and had not suffered a single rebuke. This was surely as a direct result of him impressing her with a near perfect rendition of the Lord's Prayer in English. He had also stunned the other children for the first time with his counting up to thirty. For today, at least, there would be no cause for castigation.

Indeed, Mrs Prendergast was so pleased with his progress that she handed him a small book of hymns to practice.

"*Dhybma vy*—er—sorry—for me?" he asked in surprise at being proffered such a precious thing. He hadn't thought it possible that he would elicit such a proud smile from her.

"Yes, Wella," Charlotte Prendergast replied in the clearest enunciation expected from an educated lady. "You are learning to speak well now and you deserve a reward for making great steps in disposing of that gobbledygook."

Wella understood the "yes" and the word "speak" but was unsure of the rest of what had just been said. However, he was an astute interpreter of body language and realized that this was a gift to celebrate an important moment in his life. He had never owned a book of his own. So, he was not about to spoil the praise.

"Th–th–th–thank you," he stammered. It was not a difficult phrase as it was one of the most often heard in lessons. A "yes, miss", "thank you, miss" and "please, miss" were all highly regarded phrases which earned a boy merit at the end of the day for being something that was called "poll-light". To Wella, however, it sounded like a coastal place with a deep pool frequented by an obscure fisherman called Mr Light. That was just his Cornish brain interpreting instead of the brand-new English consciousness that was fighting its way to the forefront of his thoughts.

Wella ran out of the vicarage laughing at his own personal jokes with his little book clasped tightly in his hand. He found himself a quiet nook in the hedge further along the lane with the high hills of

Carn Galva, Watch Croft and Chun Downs all forlornly gazing upon him. He settled back to attempt to read the lines of the first few hymns. First, he hummed the tunes to the words as though he was in church. Then he had a go at the actual lyrics.

"As pants the hart for flowing streams," he sang softly to himself. These foreign sounds slipped onto his tongue and hung there as though he was tasting a new blend of honey from bees collecting heather pollen on Boswens Common. He then proceeded to mouth just the vowels and let them ring across the inside of his mouth; just as though they were echoing between the granite pillars in the nave.

"A—a—uh—are—or—oh—ee."

"*Pecar ha Sows ancoth osta, me a hevel*," laughed a voice telling him he seemed to be just like an English foreigner. It was his brother Davy looking down at him. He continued to snigger as Wella slammed shut the book and tucked it under his jacket. He jumped up to stand at his full height towering above his black-haired sibling.

"*Nag yw drog cana hympnys!*" Wella raged. Davy was told in no uncertain terms that there was nothing wrong at all in singing hymns as they were, after all, a good Christian family which lived decently and honourably.

"*Me a vydn lawl dhe Das che dha gows Sowsnek lebbyn*," Davy teased as he ran off up the lane out of Wella's reach. Indeed, he would not be in his father's best books if it turned out that he was taking an interest in English and if Davy revealed this new found interest. However, his father was away and his mother had encouraged him. After all, Davy was the one still enduring Mrs Prendergast's castigation—whereas Wella was improving his standing. Certainly, Wella faced a difficult choice; should he honour Pengilley history or should he become at least semi-fluent? This was pondered as he plodded home at the slowest pace possible while booting any sizeable stone or rock along the rutted track.

That night he lit a candle next to his bed as darkness fell. His brother and sister were playing noisily in the corner of the room and his mother was trying to mend some clothes in the other corner under the glow of a dancing tallow flame. He pulled out the little book again and opened the pages at the place where he had been interrupted by his brother.

This time he continued to sing in his head without making any sound whatsoever.

> *"As pants the hart for flowing streams,*
> *When heated in the chase,*
> *So longs my soul, O God, for thee,*
> *And thy refreshing grace."*

Eventually, Wella fell asleep and his mother blew out the candles for bedtime. In his dreams, he became an eloquent trader travelling to faraway places such as London and Rome. He dreamt of the glittering wealth he would earn with these new tones and consonants flowing from his tongue. Mrs Prendergast was indeed right when she told him in very stilted Cornish that *"Kernowek yw marow"*— that Cornish was dead. For him; it was. These dreams were now replacing his old night-time adventures that were driven by wavetossed journeys to sea with father, some stinking fishing nets and a handful of salt-matted old men. This would become his future life opening up a fortune and esteem in places where the clothes were made of fine cloth, the journeys conducted by swift carriages and where the murky darkness of mines and the sea's cold waves frightened him no-more.

Those roaring foamy peaks of freezing water were no dream for Jacka Pengilley though, for at the same time as his son lay subconsciously contemplating a well-paid life of riches, his father was heaving at sodden ropes on the fishing boat in an ugly storm. The crew of the *Gwicker Frank* were labouring to wrestle control of the lugger as it lurched into a small Breton harbour under the cover of darkness. Although, as Cornish traders and fishermen, they always received a friendly welcome from the locals, every one of them battled to hide his fear of being spotted by officials. If *they* became aware of their entry into the country then they could expect many years eating grubs in a dank cell.

Jacka's own dreams now consisted of fighting hand-to-hand in bloody battles in the indeterminably long war with the French. He could smell the terror and saw the flags of armies mutilating each other over a faraway land called "the New World". His dreams would haphazardly flit between that and being dragged up before a court and charged with treason.

These turbulent nightmares were fuelled by the barside tales at the wink telling of the challenging state of relations hitting the old trade between Cornwall and Brittany.

"But—Brittany has lost its independence to the French Crown," one drunk voice laughed in his head.

"But us Cornish will always stay close to them—after all—we are family!" countered another.

"*Breten Vian* means nothing to London," slurred an opinionated regular in an attempt to show alcohol had no impact on his debating skills.

Jacka's dream could easily become a brawl at any point. If only he could wake up or force his dreaming into something nicer—like being back at home.

Suddenly, he was on a calmer sea enjoying a smoke and pleasant discourse with Billy Bod and some other Bretons as they plied their trade from Newlyn to Roscoff. This was indeed the sort of entertainment his subconscious should be laying on for him! He was now enjoying the sun-kissed open sea and the mingling of sweet voices from both coasts. This was when he realized that he was waking once more to the stormy weather and the reality of coming ashore under uncertain circumstances.

The politics did not really bother Billy Bod or Jacka to any degree. All they wanted to be sure of was that they did not get caught. Thus, they struggled in the dark with sodden ropes as the sails billowed in the moonlight, lighting the way into the small harbour. Each member of the crew was soaked through with successive waves pounding down onto the deck. Anyone who might consider the sea to be a god or the realms of Neptune himself would immediately assume they had committed some misdeed which deserved a harsh and salty punishment. The angry ocean relentlessly persisted in its gratuitous assault on the decking; each time knocking a crew member off his feet like a pin in a game of "keels". They would have all been lost to the depths if it had not been for a piece of rope secured around their waists and tethered to a mast or piece of ironmongery.

By the time morning came in Porzhtudi, the spite of the gale had desisted and the Cornish crew secured the lugger against the quayside; right next to a flight of barnacle-encrusted steps. They formed a chain of hands from the deck to the top of the quay to lift the barrels of fish ashore. By now a group of inquisitive locals had begun to form a circle around the operation to give the goods a closer inspection, anticipating an impromptu auction. Billy Bod proudly levered the first barrel open to show the pilchards.

"*Pùscas nowyth mes a'n mor ha dâ dha dhebry*," he announced, indicating they were good and fresh.

"*Pesked mat*," came the cry from one local as he prodded the specimen with one gaunt finger and took a deep lungful of air from the surface of the fish.

"*Gwerzhet vo?*" he asked to see if the catch was for sale.

"*Eâ, gwerthys rag certan, ha na vëdh ker*," replied Billy Bod as he was joined by his son at the top of the steps. He was offering a fair price, as far as he could tell, in the hope of making a tidy profit for the whole crew. Jacka watched as the father-and-son team skilfully conducted an auction in stilted Breton. He recognized a fair amount of what was being said but had decided to stand back and observe. He assumed that, by leaving it to the "professionals", they would be rich enough to buy a large load of tobacco and carry it back across to Cornwall beneath the watch of the excise men.

The shouts of numbers and gesticulations from the surrounding crowd raised to a fury until he heard Billy Bod yell out, "*Gwerthys!*" to indicate proudly the sale was complete and the entire consignment of pilchards had been sold to the highest bidder. That person was the long-fingered buyer who had been first in the pack to prod and inspect. A broad grin of conquest crossed his lips as he pushed the rest of the crowd away and began to count out a series of coins into Billy's hands. This had barely just occurred when more locals arrived at the summoning-whistle of the successful bidder. They heaved the barrels onto a nearby cart and drove it up the quayside and out of sight.

As soon as the excitement had all died down, Jacka, Billy Bod, Billy Bod Bian, and the other deck hands sat around a remaining empty barrel and doled out the coins into equal piles.

"That all?" moaned one as he assessed his loot. Billy Bod looked around his crew to see their eyes looking up from the paucity of coinage and met their gaze one by one. He then sighed as he viewed his own share. It was indeed meagre.

"*Yw!*" he said.

VII

A Foreign Classroom

A small group of girls gathered threateningly around Jane at the corner of the vicarage garden. They were chanting words which she could not understand in a rhythm which she could. The ten-year old cowered beneath their taunting eyes and lashing tongues.

"*Na—na—na*—stop," she wept pitifully.

"Ha ha—you spoke some English," teased one at the utterance.

"What will your *mabm* say about that?" sniggered another.

Jane pulled her body up to its full height and stubbornly attempted to stand her ground.

"Well you just used a word of Cornish—didn't you?" she retaliated furiously; "you said *mabm* instead of *mother!*"

Realizing that they had been on the end of a counter-attack, the mob of long-haired mother's-angels turned back into an army of aggressors and threw more insults. Jane resorted to cowering again as they all took turns in giving her a slap about the head too. Silently, she took the blows until every last one had run off giggling. Then she dropped down against the wall and continued to sob. She bawled so much that she barely saw the approach of a shadow behind her and a gentle hugging arm reach around her shoulders.

She was caringly guided back to her feet and turned around to face her saviour. At first, Jane was unable to recognize who it was for her eyes were so full with tears. They stung as each dripped down her cheeks. A soft handkerchief was wiped across her eyes to clear them and an even softer voice told her, "There, there."

To her surprise, her rescuer was not one of her brothers, her mother, or even the vicar. She almost choked on her last tears when she saw that the tender hands mopping her face belonged to none other than Mrs Prendergast. How could such an evil witch of a woman, who rebuked her family and forbade the speaking of words that made her so happy, be so loving at the same time?

"You poor, poor thing," she continued on taking Jane's hand and leading her back into the house. She had fetched a kibble of warm water with a clean rag to wash Jane's face. Not a word was uttered during the next few minutes. Jane was unsure what she should say now. Should she try those words which won Wella so much praise; *thank you*? Should she stand her ground and say "*gromassy*"? Maybe she should just say nothing at all.

The silence was maintained up to the point where the washing was complete and Mrs Prendergast looked Jane straight in the face.

"How are you my little one?"

Jane recognized the "how" and "you". A squint of one eye and a smile was enough for her meaning to be received and understood. It was then that Jane was surprised even further.

"*Lowen lebbyn?*"

The fact that Mrs Prendergast had understood more Cornish than she had let slip previously was a revelation. The offering of an olive branch in just two words was enough to explain that she was not completely taken by the devil.

"Happy now!" Jane replied.

"*Metessen*—perhaps," she thought, "not every enemy is actually my enemy."

Behind her prim dresses and regimented array of fine bonnets, there hid a friend with whom Jane could find solace if she so wished. The little girl could now see through this woman's life which had been stowed in a leather case ever since arriving in Cornwall. She was not solely there to enlighten this peripheral parish and bring them good, honest and God-fearing education. She was there to recognize the potential in every one of her wards.

Mrs Prendergast smiled back. There was nothing more inspiring for her than to watch a poor wayward wretch grow up and go off into the savage world beyond. It made her heart glow warm with the belief that their ability to endure and respond to exciting opportunities, even the girls, was down to her disciplined approach. Yes— she could now see her purpose quite clearly.

However—not everything was as plain and straightforward as she had hoped. It was not quite as simple as looking nice in the pews on a Sunday morning or encouraging children to follow the path of piety. Mrs Prendergast had been utterly distraught at the lives before her ever since arriving. She had been shocked by how much everyone drank and confused by some of the children's weak grasp on English. In her mind, this was not a good way to form brave citizens in a fast-developing world—and it was definitely not the way to proceed if these dear little ones were going to receive the good news of Jesus Christ.

Charlotte sat in her make-do classroom at the back of the vicarage on that first misty Monday morning in March 1768—and cried. She wept bitterly for a full hour at the onerous responsibility laid before her by the diocese. It was only just as her final tears were drying on her rouged cheeks that the flam-new class noisily entered like a rabble. In an instant, she let out a scream of revulsion at their untamed manners which echoed around the nearby houses. Since that day, she had worked out which of the children would grow up to make something of their lives and which would spend it working down the mines. That is; all apart from the Pengilleys. Mrs Prendergast had never encountered a family before where English was not their first language; let alone not being able to speak it at all.

It was to be her greatest test; could she honestly fulfil the orders signed off in a musty cathedral back-office? This was particularly doubtful if her chances of one-hundred percent success was being thoroughly hampered by a challenge she had never been prepared for. Through the previous wearing weeks and months, she had feared that she was abjectly failing; all because three ragged pupils were not able to fulfil the most basic requirements of reading Bible verses.

The pressure kept her wide awake at night. Often, she would get out of bed when the stars were still shining and the moon casting its light across the silver-tipped ripples of the Celtic Sea. Charlotte would stare out of her cottage window and solemnly watch the reflections in the distance as the moon touched the horizon. Her prayer would be short and to the point:

"Lord, Thou hast given me Thy loyal servants of this poor parish to nurture. Show me Thy will and give me strength in carrying out Thy work in Thy Name. Amen."

Her heartfelt intention each day was to uphold her reputation from former postings as a loving, patient and wonderful vicar's-wife. Unfortunately, each day would end up weighing heavily upon her shoulders and the continued refusal of Davy, Wella and Jane to speak English led her to lashing out with a fierce volley of rebukes. Shouting like this was certainly most unbecoming.

The other day had seen her first glimmers of a breakthrough with Wella. She had proudly rewarded him with a tiny hymn book. Now, Charlotte saw this opportunity with Jane as a way of winning her over in a display of tenderness; and, to her credit, it was a triumph.

Davy was a different bucket of pilchards altogether though. No amount of pleading, cajoling, or shouting had the slightest impact on his defiant demeanour. He stubbornly refused to let any English at all grace the bitter surface of his tongue—and he delighted in it.

Mrs Prendergast had even had to ask forgiveness for her sins on one occasion when she noticed through the window one morning that Davy was being bullied again by the other local boys. She had watched with an uncomfortable sense of enjoyment as he was pinned against the yard's wall and given a good working over. On enquiring as to why they had been acting such, they simply answered, "Davy deserved it."

Secretly, she agreed that he did indeed deserve punishment if it would knock some sense into him and knock the Cornish out of him. Those boys could be helping her fulfil her mission; if only the beating would make Davy give in and start to engage with everyone else. It never did. He would simply brush himself down and smile at her with a cheery, "*Myttyn dâ—era nei o tesky Kernowek hedhyw dhana?*" This meant: Good morning—are we learning Cornish today then?

At the end of a day such as this, she would slam the door hard behind the last pupil as they ran and skipped their way back home. Her energy would be completely spent as though she had been boxing for seven rounds or rowing a boat through stormy waters. Charlotte would collapse in her chair at the front of the empty chalk-dust room and sob once more. She would cry for herself and what she was becoming. She would then cry again that her failure would mean unfulfilled lives lacking in the joys of learning and the expansive opportunities of the world beyond.

It was after such a disastrous day, that had left her emotionally wrecked like a cutter hitting the Brysons, that Charlotte Prendergast was on the point of picking up her pen and some notepaper. She was writing the first lines of her resignation to the bishop when there came a soft knock on the door. It was Jane.

"*Mêstres Prendergast?*" whispered Jane as she poked her head around the door.

"Come in, Jane," beckoned Charlotte, broadly smiling, in the hope that the little girl wouldn't notice the tears still wet upon her cheeks. Jane heaved open the heavy door wider allowing it to swing to its full extent.

"Close the door please," she requested. Jane screwed up her face as though she was trying to work out what she should do. So, Mrs Prendergast gave a hand sign to indicate a door shutting. Jane smiled on understanding the mime and skipped back to complete her instructions.

"Jane," started Charlotte as if choosing her words carefully; which she was, fearful that anything too difficult would just be sounds left meaninglessly floating in the air.

"Jane—I am so very sorry for everything."

This time, she could not hold back the tears and began to sob inconsolably on her desk. Jane stood there hardly knowing what to make of this strange display before her. Ever since Mrs Prendergast had arrived, she had held herself up tall and been a fearful character—so terrifying that it had nearly meant avoiding the classes altogether. Now a different side was being shown. This was a fragile, self-conscious woman.

Jane had originally returned to say her best "thank you" in English for the saintly attitude shown when she was being teased remorselessly in the yard. It was clearly apparent that the forlorn vicar's wife was just as much in need of support as she. Jane stretched up to pat Charlotte on the shoulder. She had started by saying a soothing "*tety valy*" (which meant "deary me" in Cornish) but then quickly followed on with a phrase she had heard other parents saying when a child fell over: "There, there."

"Thank you—er—*gromassy*, Jane."

When Jane had struggled again to close the door and the final clunk confirmed that Charlotte was alone once more, she picked up her notepaper and screwed it up tightly in her hands. Thence, she stood up from her chair, dropped the ball of paper into a basket and straightened out her dress. Her smile and resilience had returned— thanks to one small girl who had more understanding than most.

VIII
Drinking the Money

Jacka wearily rubbed his eyes as yet another cruskyn-full of cider was deposited with a sturdy clunk on the rough-hewn bench before him. He was too tired to count how many had already been gulped down his *clunk* and he doubted that anyone else was keeping tally. His hazy surmising of the alcoholic quantities left him with an extremely doubtful estimate of six so far—at the very least. The first two measures had been downed in a futile race that had set Billy Bod, Billy Bod Bian and Jacka Lacka against Jacka and the remaining crew. Billy Bod Bian was the youngest and the most able at coping with vast amounts of cloudy golden liquid which frothed and sparkled inside his mouth. The following jars had been drunk at a slower pace and without the competitive chants which accompanied the earlier ones.

This fresh measure of sweet cider, however, had all the hallmarks of a drink which would be consumed as governed by the rhythm of a group of singers in the corner. They had been performing a selection of local songs and were just about to burst out with a hearty rendition of yet another. Billy Bod and Jacka looked at each other and gave a shout of joy when they heard the first line.

As the lyrics were belched out by the lead singer (who was totalling more than eight cruskyns-full himself) a roar went up in the bar and everyone raised their drinks to the ceiling. It was quite plain from the closeness of their Cornish with the Breton that this was a song celebrating drinking. As soon as the second verse began, drinking vessels were being thumped down onto story-stained benches and men linking work-worn arms in a long chain. They leapt up to perform a kind of snake-dance around the tables, chairs, behind the bar and then into the back room. Even Tommy Tobm and Josiah had been hauled like a net of pilchards onto the floor to join the endlessly winding chain of revellers. Josiah, with his short burly legs, comically attempted the steps. He had no chance of surpassing the agile mastery of the native Bretons. On several occasions he almost tripped up his younger brother Tobmas whose lean figure was more able to cope with the five-step rhythm.

"*Cabm pymp yw!*" cried Tommy gleefully as he tripped his way clumsily around the room. The only reason he didn't crash to the stone floor was that he was being carried along in a wave of revellers.

One of the more elderly dancers, who was pushing on into his late seventies, had also got up to attempt the dance. His legs, whether by means of age or inebriation, were unable to perform effortlessly. That soon came to an end though when he stumbled over a stool, which had been left in his path, and fell flat onto a table where the local women were gathered. One gave him a drunken sloppy kiss on his forehead and pushed him back into the throng to a roar of laughter.

The song continued verse after verse and grew louder and louder until the final chorus made it almost impossible for anyone else to converse—not that anyone really was intent on holding any important negotiations. Those had ended hours ago and were being swiftly forgotten in the alcoholic haze. The evening was far from over and the Bretons had a reputation of keeping a good party going well into the following day.

As the bombards began playing a gavotte dance straight off the back of the previous song, Jacka saw Billy Bod on the early wane. He had let his head rest on his arms on the table, where he was now snoring: *Ronk—ronk—ronk—*

The snores were loud enough to be heard amongst the immediate group but had no chance of drowning out any of the surrounding musical mayhem. Thus, Jacka and the remaining Cornish contingent continued their party while the trip's captain soundly slept.

Among the laughter and noise, a wisp of a consideration flew briefly through Jacka's mind. It brought to his attention, albeit a very drunken attention, that their current actions were exceedingly foolhardy as they had made little money from selling the fish and now were engaged in pouring the remaining earnings down their throats.

"*Gocky, gocky, gocky on nei*," Jacka laughed while telling his compatriots that they were foolish. He then put his own head on the table and fell swiftly to sleep. There he snored and gurgled with the warm cosy sound of revellers circling the bar gently drifting in and out of his dreams. Occasionally he would stir, look up, smile, and then fall back into a cider-fuelled slumber.

At some point he must have awoken fully and made his way, with his friends, back to the boat. Maybe he was carried or dragged—there was no way of really telling. All that anyone could say for certain is that the entire crew made it safely back to the *Gwicker Frank* without any mishaps. No one ended up in strangers' beds, no one became lost in the back-lanes and no one tripped over the quayside to plummet into the harbour's murky water.

Jacka, Jacka Lacka, Tommy Tobm, Josiah, Billy Bod and Billy Bod Bian awoke with the first light of the new morning laid across the deck of their boat; currently gently bobbing against the seagull-encircled quayside in the harbour. It was a perfect morning with blue cloudless skies and a very light breeze causing the motion of their vessel to rock on the lapping surface of the water. Jacka screwed his eyes shut as soon as he had opened them—as he realized that something was wrong.

For a start, he had little idea how any of them had returned to the boat after the night in the bar. Secondly, he felt his head throbbing violently as a painful after-effect of the copious cruskyn-loads of cider. Thirdly, he had a feeling that the drink had been fairly expensive. Despite these three salient points, Jacka made a second attempt at opening his eyes. It felt like trying to haul open a cargo-hold door on age-rusted hinges. This time he tried them one at a time—starting with his right eye.

He held it open for a full ten seconds while looking around the boat. Finally, he unscrunched his left eye and let the full power of the morning light hit the back of his sore eyeballs. Once the first was open, Jacka gingerly sat upright and gave a yelp of pain as his head throbbed more violently from the *cùrun a spern*; a hangover which felt as though the sufferer was wearing a crown of thorns. From his, more or less, vertical position he could now see how the rest of the crew were starting to shift about and carry out similar post-drinking rituals.

Not everyone was equally able to hold their alcohol, so it would seem, as he glimpsed Billy Bod Bian suddenly throw his head over the side of the boat and emit a loud "wheee-ja" sound. Jacka laughed to himself at the young man's plight and the fact that the sound he made while wretching was almost exactly the same as *wheja*, the word for "to vomit" in *Kernowek*. If only Billy Bod Bian's new wife, Ellen, could see the state he was in. Surely, she would not be laughing at all and more likely giving him a stern rebuke for his unsaintly conduct, condition and the fact that he had spent all his money on drink.

"*An mona!*" screamed Jacka as he suddenly came to the realization that the money, which they had barely earned in their outward voyage, must have been totally spent in the previous night's debacle.

"*Ma spendyes oll an mona genen,*" Jacka cried with incredulity that they could have all been so stupid. By now, Billy Bod, Josiah, and Tobmas were all awake—though a little dazed. If the turn of poor fortune had not been so serious, Jacka would have taken more pleasure in the spectacle. The re-animation of the crew seemed humorously near to what he had witnessed when a visiting theatre of puppeteers had called into Morvah the previous year. They had performed a play with their string-suspended dolls; each exactly resembling the scene enacted aboard that very morning.

"What's that about the money?" grumbled Tobmas—ignorant of the severity of their predicament.

Jacka repeated his previous exclamation for Tobmas's sole benefit. He then watched the morning haziness quickly burn off from the crew's faces as they realized their mad mistake. All Billy Bod could do was to revere the name of God by whispering "*Duw*" while Josiah sat there and uttered absolutely nothing. His silence was not maintained for long though as his habitual grin slowly turned into a chuckle that, in turn, developed into a roaring laugh. By now, despite the hangovers, all of the crew, apart from Jacka, were giggling uncontrollably.

Jacka stared back at them in stunned amazement as they fell around the deck, continuing to laugh at something he did not find in the least bit funny. By now, his shock had turned to anger. How they could all find such a disastrous state of affairs cause for levity? They, in turn, continued to cackle and wheeze with too much laughter—if there could ever be such a thing.

At this, Jacka totally forgot the tender state of his own head, stood up, stormed off the deck and leapt up the quayside steps. At the top, he turned around and glared back at the ship's company in disgust before taking-off in a rage. He could still hear them far in the distance making light of their drunken party. So, he turned around a street corner and set off in a teasy stank towards an unplanned and unknown destination.

Had he taken two turnings and walked three miles or was it three turnings and four miles? Little did it matter to Jacka as he was still fuming. It could only be cured by getting himself as far away from the "*tus wocky*" as possible. Anyone passing him would have heard him mumbling those words several times and, very likely, would have been able to translate them into Breton; with a meaning of "stupid men".

Eventually, Jacka found a horse-block to rest on after a good half-an-hour of striding at full pace. He had covered nearly every street in the fishing port and was now opposite a workshop where he could hear a familiar rhythmic sound and a very familiar smell; clay!

"*Pryweyth!*" whispered Jacka to himself as his nostrils caught the familiar scent of fresh pottery. It transported him back to the little outhouse in his own back yard where Mary spent rare spare hours fashioning pots in the same way that many generations of her family always had done. He sat there on the step for a good many minutes while listening to the sounds, breathing in the aroma and casting his mind back across the sea to his own home. Eventually he could not resist the pull of his inquisitive mind and so ambled across the road and peered into the workshop.

He could feel the natural warmth of the building envelop him. The heat was being thrown out of the brickwork from a kiln at the back. From its size, it was quite plainly obvious that a serious quantity of pottery was being manufactured here. This was clear from the shelves along one wall which were lined with pre-firing pots. Then, on the floor, there were wooden crates loaded-up with examples that had just been taken out.

"*Demat deoc'h,*" smiled the thin little woman in an apron with a greeting in Breton. Her husband looked up and called across a cheery welcome too.

"*Kernow o vy,*" Jacka replied clearly to indicate he was from Cornwall. The woman, who looked like she was in her eighties but more likely only about fifty years old, took Jacka by the hand over to her husband. As her tiny wrinkled fingers pressed against the palm of his hand, she continued in the clearest Breton he had heard yet.

"Eñ a gomz brezhoneg deus tu all ag ar mor."

As far as Jacka could tell, she was saying; "he speaks Breton from the other side of the sea".

Jacka sat with the old potter for the next two hours chatting as he worked. The two conversed like long lost friends. They discussed everything from pottery, drink, politics, the pressures of life, to how Jacka had just ended up on his doorstep. The potter hummed and nodded as he listened to the plight that had just beset his visitor— yet he maintained a steady rhythm on his treadle throughout. He managed to power the wheel round at a pace that far exceeded his wife's efforts. As time progressed and the dusk light faded, Jacka learnt about his new friend's life too.

It turned out that he had been born in Hayle in Cornwall and moved over to Brittany with his family when he was young. His father had worked down the mines but had decided to escape to the continent when he lost his job for the fifth time in as many years. Jacka also gleaned that his name was Joshua Trengove and his father was Joshua too.

"Yw dâ geno'whei preiweyth?" asked Joshua as he pointed to the shelves of ware around the workshop. Jacka keenly replied that he was indeed very interested in pottery and particularly as his wife was an enthusiastic potter. With that, the connection between the two men was forged. By now, Jacka had totally forgotten his concerns about not making any money from the fishing and then drinking the remaining profits. The conversation had him ensnared.

He was even more fascinated to discover how Joshua was involved with a trading network spanning far and wide to ports he had never heard of and places he could only dream of—and it all earned him a fair living. If he could achieve the same success back in Cornwall by hooking into this ring, then his family's problems could be solved forever. Jacka was now building a clear mental picture of his potential new life working with Mary to create a business across Europe— maybe further.

It was becoming pitch dark when he departed the workshop and left his new friends. As they gave him a traditional two cheek farewell-kiss, Joshua's wife Nolwenn handed him a parting gift of a tiny little milk jug of exquisite design and craftsmanship. Jacka's feet sped over the cobbles with a renewed vigour as he held onto the dream that his life was about to change for the better. His mind was bursting with fresh plans and was eager to discuss them with Billy Bod. However, when he reached the quayside, there was not a sign of the lugger. Maybe it had just been moved to another berth. Maybe it was the poor light that meant he was missing it. After wandering around both sides of the harbour for more than a quarter-of-an-hour it became apparent that the reason he could not locate the boat was because it had left. The optimism which had been burning so brightly within him just minutes earlier had now transformed into a mixture of panic and depression. How could Billy Bod and the crew have abandoned him?

Jacka was desperate. He returned to the tavern where they had partied through the previous night to see if anyone there knew about what had happened. Luckily, Jacka's deduction was correct as, when he approached the bar, he was summoned over by the landlord who pushed into his palm a small piece of paper.

Jacka sos—

Drog ew genam boas othom a ponya ker heb warnyans. Nei a glowas boas soudorian Frenk a toas. Betha whei saw sos kear.

—William Bodinar [7]

Jacka sank back forlornly onto a bench near the tavern door with the note in one hand and the milk jug in the other. What on earth was he going to do about returning home?

---

7   *Jacka sos— Drog yw genam' bos otham a ponya 'ker heb warnyans.*
    Ny a glôwas bos soudoryon Frynk ow tos. Bedhowgh why saw, sos ker.
    —William Bodinar.

    Dear Jacka— Sorry for having to flee without warning. We heard
    there were French soldiers coming. Be safe mate. —William Bodinar.

IX
Campaign

Though the homeward-bound Pengilley family was stuck on a traffic-logged A30, their discussion continued about their many discoveries. Everyone had gained something: Eddie had indulged his scientific fascination in a cavern full of World War Two technology, Sarah had explored her fascination with crafts, Geoff had enjoyed a pub lunch, and Gary had seen the area from where Jacka Pengilley had come.

Gary had answered some of his questions—though many remained: where exactly was Jacka's house and why was the pot left in that wooden box? It was clear that there would only be one way to discover the nature of the link—and the solution would come from reading the entire diary. There was one thing that bothered him about making the next steps—his weak grasp of Cornish. It was simply not of a high enough standard to comprehend what was in the antique documentation.

Another stumbling block was that the diary was still only viewable at the museum during pre-arranged and limited opening hours. On top of all of this, he had everyday life to deal with too. It was a mixture of dull exam revision for subjects for which he cared little and aggravation from a group of boys who had singled him out for being "different". They mocked him and his fellow members of the Cornish Club for being "square". They considered anything that didn't include chasing girls, wittering on about football or cars as being the pursuits of a "bell-end". Their harassment had started out as fairly low-level bullying; a spiteful comment whispered from the back of class or in passing in a corridor. It then grew to taking on a particularly nasty twenty-first-century shape over his mobile phone.

LIKE A BURIED CITY

It had also erupted into vicious physical violence leaving him with purple stinging bruises on regular occasions.

He would often be deep in thought while attempting to get his head around a tricky subject when his phone would vibrate on reception of another taunt. A quick scan of his texts would reveal a stream of threats or expletives from one of the gang. They were certainly adept at making his life a misery through means of savage language and psychological control. There had been some occasions when they would grab him after school and just push him around. Other times, they would jump him and deal a brutal working over.

These boys usually managed to get away with their crimes because they knew how far they could beat Gary without it becoming visible. However, as of late, it was becoming much worse. They also managed to maintain their respectability amongst their teachers by means of acting the part of perfect students. They gave well-reasoned responses to any of Gary's complaints. How could such a group of well-mannered and smartly dressed students be lying?

The most recent attack came when a particularly surly individual noticed Gary with his head buried in a book about Cornish history. He darted back to the gang with the news. They spent the next few minutes huddled in the corner of the playground plotting what they wanted to do as their lunchtime bit of fun.

When Gary returned to the cloakroom at the end of the break, he was caught unaware and jumped by them. Just as he realized what was happening, he heard a door slam, trapping him. The only escape route was being guarded by a grinning thick-set boy with a enough bulk to block any attempt to flee.

Gary could cope with taunts about being a nerd or a swot. He could even deal with a certain amount of being pushed around. But it had just escalated into something a lot more serious, for he was currently pinned into the corner of the cloakroom.

"How do you say 'ouch' in Cornish, then?" laughed the boy bearing down on him with a clenched fist poised to strike.

"*Kyj dhe ves*," said Gary defiantly.

"That didn't sound like 'ouch' to me," he replied with a threatening growl in his voice. "Time for you to learn some manners then."

With that a fist was launched into Gary's stomach, instantly knocking the wind out of him. He choked from the impact, only stopping because another thump was powered into him almost immediately. The onslaught seemed to go on for ever and there wasn't much he could do to avoid the strikes. Gary resorted to distracting himself from the pain with mental diversion tactics. He tried to take notice of how the cloakroom ceiling was poorly decorated and desperately needed fresh paint. He probably was able to count the number of red coats or sports bags hanging up. His mind wandered into noting how one of the gang had a choir badge on his lapel. That raised other interesting questions about how someone who enjoyed cultural activities of such finesse could resort to such savagery for his sport.

He considered the case of many a Roman emperor who had appreciated poetry while planning the slaughter of thousands. He was aware how the most savage battles were fought with swords engraved with the most delectable designs in Celtic history. Why would it concern a hardened warrior that his weapon was adorned with elaborate knotwork and the most precious of gems? He pondered also how the Third Reich had displayed a deep passion for the finest works of art plundered from the nations it had subdued under thousands of jackboots.

This particular attack was designed to leave no visible bruising, which would raise the concern of teachers or parents, while being particularly painful. What good would grassing-up do anyway? It would only lead to something even worse down the line. Luckily, Gary could just about cope with what was levelled against him as he continued to transport himself deep into his imagination.

It did eventually stop once the boys had had their fun. They ran out of the cloakroom laughing leaving Gary feeling sorry for himself and in a great deal of pain. It was at this point that the thought crossed his mind; "was it worth standing out like this?" Clearly, life would be far simpler if he just blended in and didn't give the thugs an easy target. "Perhaps," he told himself while gathering his belongings together again, "just perhaps I should take the route of least resistance!"

Later that afternoon, Gary sat alone in a lab coat. It was half-past-three when nearly everyone else in the school had disappeared off home. Dr Matthews walked into the room with a big mad-professor grin on his face and bellowed at the top of his voice, "Pengilley—we *are* going to have some fun."

Gary stared back blankly in a mixture of disdain and resignation. He knew he was there reluctantly to complete a task. It was an unwilling attendance though—and it certainly was *not* going to be fun.

"Fun sir?" he replied with a hint of sarcasm in his voice. "Fun for me is music. Fun for me is art. Fun for me is history—not Bunsen burners and anti-bumping granules!"

The chemistry tutor stood there shocked at the insolence.

"Pengilley—I can only try and help you pass your exams but you have to help *me* to help *you*."

It was no good. The one hour of detention dragged. Time appeared to be slowing in a way which could have encouraged Einstein to scribble endless formulae on his black board. Gary realized the ironic humour in that Eddie would have taken complete delight in spending an extra hour in a sulphur-stained chemistry lab with Dr Matthews. For him, however, this was tedious—and tedium did nothing for his mood.

"If only every hour of every day could be a tune or a painting," he thought, wandering off into another day-dream, "or the pleasure of a beautiful construction of Cornish grammar."

If only every day did not have to be burdened with exam preparation in subjects which he had zero desire to learn about!

"So, Pengilley," laughed the doctor, swilling a beaker as the liquid developed a purple iodine tint, "we have successfully completed the experiment—even if I did most of the real work for you."

Gary nodded in the hope that playing along, at this point, would speed forward the time when he would be given permission to go home.

"Don't you think science is beautiful at all?"

"Not really considered it like that."

"You love language and art, don't you Pengilley?" Matthews asked, pouring the solution down the sink. "Well, just try and see the beauty in nature and think of the formulae as a kind of grammar that wasn't conceived by man."

Indeed, Gary could see an elegance and grace in all these reactions and benzene rings. However, it would never take precedence over the joy of decoding an ancient language. This was the pre-occupation which burned within him. It was this passion which had left his stomach with a burning sensation too.

Gary impatiently grabbed his bag to leave detention.

"Oh—one more thing," Dr Matthews added. He had started nervously rubbing his beard as though he could not quite form the next series of words.

"I noticed there was some—er—how should I put it —nastiness towards you in class the other day. Is everything all right?"

Gary was taken aback; totally unprepared for someone unexpected to care about him. He was too stubborn though to let his surprise show through. So, he simply gave a sheepish smile before scurrying out of the room. Dr Matthews was left gazing at the empty doorway and no happier now that Gary had given his non-verbal answer.

Gary fled down an empty corridor into the deserted entrance lobby and found a graffiti-covered seat beneath the noticeboard. This place had seen "war of the Cornish Club notices" break-out just a couple of weeks earlier. Dr Matthews' concern had begun to have its effect.

"What sort of person takes fun in causing misery?" he muttered. He sat waiting for calm to descend; it only needed a couple of minutes. Then Gary was ready to head home. On that short journey, decisions were made and resolutions forged. By the time he had slammed the front door and pounded upstairs to his room, he had come to the belief that Cornish was not worth it. He tipped the contents of his bag on the floor, pulled any *Kernowek* book out of the pile, and then unceremoniously slung them into the bin.

"There," he thought, "that's it done and dusted!"

Tea was ready half an hour later and his mum's regular announcement was made. It would have been out of character if he didn't leave showing up until the second call. His father was just making that when Gary sat down at the table.

"How was school?" Sarah asked.

"Okay!" The reply was half muffled with the first forkful of mash being sent mouth-wards.

"Anymore news about Cornish Club?" asked Geoff. Gary put down the second forkful with a grimace.

"Is this an interrogation?"

"No, dear," his mum answered, trying to pick her words carefully, "we are just interested."

"Well," Gary answered, stabbing a sausage with his knife, "I'm not doing it anymore."

There was a full-house of surprised stares. Even his brother lost control of the contents of his fork at the bombshell.

"You loved it! Why for heaven's sake?" Mum was completely confused. Gary had just persuaded the whole family to take up his cause—and then he suddenly loses interest.

"Is everything all right?" she continued.

"I'd really rather not go into it," Gary insisted.

The remainder of mealtime passed with an awkward silence. Once pudding had been dealt with, Gary ran back upstairs calling, "I've got lots of homework to do!"

"There must be something wrong," Geoff said as he collected the plates off the table.

"He's not going to tell us," Sarah said, still sitting at the table with worry stretching her face.

"Leave it a bit," his brother suggested, "he's just in a mood for some reason."

"You sure?" Sarah asked.

The next morning, Gary remained resolutely unwilling to divulge his problem. No matter the amount of questioning was about to nudge him into submission. He slung his backpack over his shoulder and hurried out the door to school, shouting, "Love you Mum," in his wake.

Sarah waited at the door watching her son sprint up the road with his shirt tails untucked and unkempt hair dutifully rearranging itself with the flow of the wind through it. Once she was sure he was not about to return for any forgotten items, she took the chance to investigate further.

She pushed open his bedroom door and surveyed it for any evidence of uncharacteristic behaviour. The violin was perched ready for playing in its opened case on his bed. There was a pile of dirty clothes on the floor as expected in any teenager's room. His desk displayed signs of study; which was positive in itself. Below it was his bin.

Sarah fetched the discarded books from amongst the unwanted pieces of packaging and snotty tissues and lay them back on his desk. Something was definitely awry. For a moment, it crossed her mind that her son might have become entangled in something like drugs.

Then again, she told herself, there had been no other evidence; no previous mood swings or dazed appearance. He didn't have any narcotics paraphernalia which was apparent.

"Hopefully," Sarah prayed, "he will talk about it when the time is right."

The time was definitely not right for admitting anything to anyone now that Gary was back at school. He had been cornered once again.

"So, Mr Pastyhead," jibed Duncan Menzies with his left hand placed tightly around his victim's windpipe, "you're just so feeble—aren't you?" His hand tightened causing Gary to choke. The boy watched with enjoyment as he elicited a sense of panic. Finally, he released his grip after ten seconds to leave Pengilley to drop to the floor, coughing severely.

"You're just pathetic," laughed chief henchman Dan Philp, planting the toe of his left foot sharply in Gary's side. Both ran out of the deserted classroom chuckling at another successful proof of their superiority.

"Am I pathetic?" spluttered Gary as he hauled himself up onto a chair.

That evening, Eddie knocked on his brother's door.

"What do you want?"

"*Fatla genes*?" he asked, pushing his head around to see how he was. It was certainly a surprise for real affection from his younger sibling—let alone for it to be expressed in the language he had just tried distancing himself from.

Eddie found him with his head in his hands staring at the pile of books which had rescued from the bin.

"Did you come in here and get these out the rubbish?"

Eddie shook his head.

"Not me, bro—wanna talk about it?"

"Am I pathetic?"

Eddie laughed.

"You know you are—but that's what I love about you, Bro!"

"No," repeated Gary, "am I really pathetic?"

"Depends what you call pathetic," he replied sitting down on his brother's bed; narrowly missing crushing a much-loved violin in the process.

"If pathetic is you doing what you are passionate about," he smiled, "then you are utterly pathetic."

"Well thanks a bunch!"

"And," Eddie added, "if pathetic is being made to give something up when you love it—then yes you are being pathetic."

"Thanks again!"

"No worries, bro."

Eddie left his brother to his thoughts in peace. That solitude was disturbed within a minute with the regular-as-clockwork call for tea. This time Gary beat his brother to the table. Next to his spoon was another book which he thought he had disposed of the evening before.

"I found this one in the bin too," Sarah smiled as she landed a plate of spag bol down in front of her eldest. "Want to discuss it yet?"

"No thanks, Mum," he said with a fork already twirling the stringy mess, "I have it in hand."

Indeed, Gary had come to a new conclusion; that (for the first time ever) his brother was right. He would, indeed, be pathetic to let some idiots get the better of him. Within twenty minutes, he was back in his room to get his homework done. He didn't have a cure for his bullying problem, but he could re-evaluate himself.

"It's going to have to be fix-it as I go along!" he told himself.

His only short-term solution was to pull his phone out of his inside pocket and start typing another email to Dr Julian Casement.

> Dear Dr Casement,
>
> Thank you for your help with Jacka Pengilley's diaries so far. I would really like to see a full translation at some point. When do you think this might be possible? I am still just beginning to study Cornish with an after-school club and it is all fairly basic stuff.
>
> I was wondering, in particular, if there is any evidence that you have seen in the diary about links to pottery. After all, there was a rather splendid pot in the trunk that contained the diary. I am particularly interested, because the design is similar to a jug we saw when, at the weekend, we visited a house in the area where Jacka Pengilley lived.
>
> I look forward to hearing back from you.
>
> Oll an gwella
> Gary Pengilley.

Gary was still deep in contemplation the next afternoon on his walk home when he was awoken from his thoughts by a voice from behind. For a moment, he was ready to defend himself from Duncan "Dough-head" Menzies and Dan Philp, his little imp.

"*Fatla genes*, Gary?" came a yell across the street. Josh Johns skipped behind a passing cyclist to join him. He was particularly proud of himself that he had mastered how to ask "how are you?" at Cornish Club.

"Why weren't you at Cornish Club the other day then?"

Gary gave a small exasperated shake of the head with his eyes pointing skywards as though he would receive some divine support.

"I had to do a detention with Dr Matthews. What did I miss?"

"Well, there has been a bit of a fight between Miss James and the head."

It turned out that Josh Johns was underplaying the disagreement in reporting that there had been a bit of a set-to. There had, in fact, been a full-on stand-up row which, very nearly, resulted in a resignation. Miss James was determined that her students were going to learn *Kernowek*. Thus, she did not see eye-to-eye with Glasney Secondary School's management. They considered it a "complete waste of time".

Miss James had attempted to storm out of the principal's office while threatening to find a job at another school which had more respect for the humanities. James Turner had to physically block her exit to prevent her from leaving. She then yelled at him to move aside—a request which he stubbornly refused. The shouting continued for five minutes before the deputy principal arrived and calmed down the school's very own edition of a television reality show stand-off. Turner realized that he had made a severe misjudgement. He knew for certain that Miss James achieved consistently high scores with her students and helped maintain a clean run of spotless Ofsted inspections.

Gary smirked at Josh's animated recounting of the disagreement. His hands gave a better idea of what had ensued in the principal's office than the limited expression in his English.

"So, what about Cornish Club next week, then?" asked Gary, fearing that one of the few socially engaging pursuits in his life was about to be brought to a sudden halt—even if he had only just tried to do that himself.

"The head has ordered the club to close—claiming it is taking our focus off of exam work," Josh replied glumly.

"That is bloody outrageous! I'm sure there must be some sort of rule against stopping us!" Gary shouted in exasperation, causing everyone else in the vicinity to turn around. At that moment, Gary Pengilley definitely did *not* feel pathetic. He felt enraged and in a mood to kick-ass.

Indeed, it was outrageous; the headmaster could not deduce from a mere two weeks of the club that it was having any such affect at all. Firstly; the club had suffered two graffiti attacks. Secondly; bullying could be added to the charge sheet. Now there was institutional censorship to top off this teenage dystopian nightmare.

Gary's blood was boiling in a way he did not think was possible. Mostly, he would be described as a mild-mannered artistic student who spent most of his time day-dreaming and partaking in pursuits which could be accomplished without any teamwork. Solitary was the word. Introverted was his nature.

Now Gary felt something different within him. He felt that he was a true outsider who had a campaign burgeoning within him. It was not of his own volition though, as all he truly wanted to do was to be left alone learning a little Cornish. But *this* goal could now only be achieved by having a battle of wills. It was *his* against the bullies and the headmaster. The big question was; why did anyone feel that it was necessary to scupper his interests?

"Thank you Eddie," smiled Gary. Josh looked back in confusion. "What do you mean?"

"If we let this go," Gary explained, "then everything we stand for will be utterly pathetic."

If Gary had had the power of psychic thought or the ability to transform into a fly and wait on the wall of his oppressors, then he would have been able to see their machinations and plots in progress. He could have viewed the headmaster's office where Miss James was now waiting.

She was a slender thirty-year old brunette. Her hair cascaded down over her right shoulder like a waterfall. It swayed every time she used her left hand to re-arrange with a subconscious regularity. In these stressful times, however, she would grab hold of strands and play with them without realizing. The anxiety, on this occasion, was due to her being in her boss's office immediately following a fiery exchange with him over The Cornish Club earlier that same day. James Turner, the head, was a sixty-year old, balding rake of a man. Miss James felt the need to acknowledge him in some way when he swept into his office in his pin-striped suit. So, she mumbled a "good afternoon" as though she was a wayward pupil in detention.

"Miss James," he began as he sat down on the other side of his desk, "I fear I have had to ask you to not continue this Cornish Club because it interferes with vital exams and, also—" He paused to open a folder containing correspondence before continuing. "Also—I have received a few letters from parents who allege that you have been going off topic in French and Spanish lessons into the realms of Cornish."

Turner peered up to see how Miss James was taking the telling-off. He noticed that she was furiously twiddling her long hair with a scrunched-up expression creasing her face.

"We do appreciate your admirable passion for Cornish," he continued looking back down at the notes scrawled in her employee file, "but it is not a real language for school education. Children should be encouraged to spend more time learning something—er—*useful*."

He looked up again to see whether her expression had changed—briefly pausing to allot her an opportunity to reply.

"Firstly, Cornish *is* a real living language as recognized by the government," she began defiantly in her defence.

"Secondly, learning about heritage and roots is an important part of building a rounded education." By now Miss James was getting into the flow. "Thirdly, this is just a club—it is no different from spending time learning a musical instrument outside of curriculum time."

She could have continued her oration for a good many extra points but James Turner silenced her with a dismissive hand. He was not about to allow her to continue her animated case and definitely did not wish it to all get out of control.

"This is not a matter for debate, Miss James. I have made my decision."

The headmaster had brought the debate to an abrupt halt. Whatever was laid on the table in favour of running the club, he was certainly not going to give in.

If Gary Pengilley was indeed such an investigative fly which could spy on situations beyond his physical body, then he could have then been able to transport himself to the house of one of the boys who had been making unpleasant jibes against him. It was a very upmarket abode in beautiful rolling countryside that swept down to the shores of the Carrick Roads. He would have seen inside the finely furnished lounge where the mother was talking politics during mealtime.

"The Left is not interested in *us!*" she expounded while dumping a pile of plates in the middle of the table. "Liberal values are being forced on *our* way of life and all my family fought for in the war is at stake!" When she came to a particularly hot topic which agitated her, she would cut aggressively at a piece of ham on the plate while espousing her opinions.

Catherine had been a councillor when she was younger and was well acquainted with turning every situation into a political comment. Though she was in the dining room with her nearest and dearest around her, she imagined herself to still be in a council chamber fighting for what she thought was right. Each morsel of food was aggressively chewed and swallowed as quickly as possible so that she could continue reasoning her point with only the briefest intervals for chewing.

"What a waste of time," she laughed in derision, "the school will be coming up with such rubbish that Cornwall is not part of England before long in the history lessons."

The father, son, and elder daughter would have all been caught cheering their mother on as the Pengilley-fly landed. However, Gary Pengilley had none of these abilities and was totally unaware of what was unfolding behind the scenes. All he knew was that his passion was being hindered—and he did not like that in the least.

That very night, Gary finished his tea and slipped off to his room, just as he usually did. Sarah looked to Geoff and Eddie as he left the room.

"What do you think?" she said, still concerned about the mental state of her eldest. Eddie knew as much as his parents; very little. However, he did have a feeling his little chat had made a difference.

"I think he's okay Mum."

Once Gary was back in the safe solitude of his room, he switched on his keyboard and started to bash out a tune in the key of A-minor. The heart-rending moody chords hung in the air above him as his fingers flew across the keys. Each time he created a sharp-attack and long sustain. The final notes of each phrase were left to hang angrily in the air.

Gary let the music die off into silence—and then flicked the power-switch as he began to cry.

X

Pardons, Pipes, and Lace

How it is to look above the doorways and to hear every building shout back at you in an unfamiliar voice. How it is to smell the same salty sea in the harbour and hear the same cry of a seagull as you knew from childhood—but then also hear a chorus of muddled voices which tell you, from their subtle tones, that you were no longer home. How it is to feel so lost.

Jacka was feeling in such a way now that he was marooned in a foreign land which still felt distinctly familiar. He was aware of being among friends even though in an occupied territory. He knew he had to be circumspect and go to ground to avoid being caught by the French army. They patrolled the streets, banged on doors, held locals at gunpoint and dragged many off to a silent and anonymous demise. What did he fear most but being declared a spy and condemned to death? He could almost hear the sobs Mary would make on receiving news of his capture and execution. What would become of his beloved family if that were to transpire? Thus, he needed to devise a plan—and quickly.

The only people he had the acquaintance of in the town were Joshua and Nolwenn at the pottery. So, with the streets now only lit by flickering oil-lamps in the lace-bordered windows of each house and shop, Jacka circumspectly made his way back up to the far side of the fishing village. He gave an impatient rat-a-tat-tat of panicked knocks on the stable door at the side of the workshop. After a minute, which dragged on to feel like an eternity, he heard a shuffling of feet—and then a hushed voice:

"*Petra a fell deoc'h?*" whispered Nolwenn through the door to ask what Jacka wanted. His Breton was not good enough fully to understand this much and so he gave the loudest whisper he could, without raising unwanted attention, back through the door.

"*Jacka ywa—ma otham dhybm a socour,*" telling her he needed help. She caught the word *otham* which was near enough to her *ezhomm* for her to get the meaning. The door was swiftly unbolted and once more Jacka was led by the cuff of his jacket into the workshop and up the steps at the rear to the living space above.

Joshua welcomed Jacka back with a big hug as though he was his long-lost brother—even though he had only been gone for an hour. They sat down at the kitchen table while Nolwenn prepared crêpes. The conversation started out with what had just occurred and how he had been left stranded in Brittany by his friends. Eventually, the topic came around to his urgent need for somewhere to lie low until the French troops had left the area.

Trying to make light of Jacka's terrible anguish, Joshua laughed and joked at the predicament for a couple of minutes. Nolwenn looked around and egged him on as she sliced and diced onions. Soon enough, he grabbed Jacka's hand and assured him there was a safe roof and bed for him for as long as he needed it. The Trengoves were fully aware of the danger.

Joshua, being originally from Cornwall, felt a strong sense of compatriotism while also remembering back to how difficult it had been for him when he first settled in *Breten Vian*. He had studied hard to learn both Breton and French in order to appear fully integrated. Now, it was difficult to detect any residual Cornish accent. He had surely accomplished a full transition and could easily fool nearly anyone into believing he had been raised in the land of pardons, pipes and lace. He had even learned how to partake in the traditional village dances to accompany Nolwenn. He knew a five-step just as well as any Breton.

The three dined as though they had always known each other. They ate sweetmeats rolled in crêpes and drank jug-loads of sweet mead. Eventually, the poor lost soul found his way up to the small room at the back of the cottage. There, he dropped to sleep almost as soon as his weary head hit the pillow.

Jacka's dreams were a convoluted mess of recounted recent events. At one moment, he believed himself to be wedged under a pile of rock which had fallen away from the roof in "Wheal an Gweal Mine". He could feel the weight pressing down on his chest so that he could barely breathe. The next moment his dreams set him back on the boat in the middle of the *Mor Bretednek*, or the Channel, as the customs and excise men dragged him off under arrest for a long list of heinous crimes. Without much of a gap in the time-line, Jacka found himself back on the quayside of Porzhtudi as he pleaded Billy Bod not to leave without him. Then he felt that he was tumbling off the quayside and hitting the water.

At the moment, there was a splash of water on his face which suddenly awoke him. It was Joshua throwing a jug of water over his head.

"*Pandra wher*?" shouted Jacka, asking what was going on and still fighting confusion. His host indicated for him to hush. He paused a moment as if to attempt to make out the meaning of the shouting in nearby streets. Once he was sure that their safety was assured for the time being, he explained.

"*Ma soudoryon i'n dre*," he whispered, telling Jacka how soldiers were going from door to door. It seemed, from what he could hear, that they were asking about a group of foreign fishermen. Some of the properties were given rigorous searches if officers had reason to believe they were actively anti-French. Of course, in a place like Porzhtudi, this meant a large proportion of the population.

All Jacka said once the disorientation had left him was a knowing "tut-tut" for he recognized this as a sad parallel to what had happened in Cornwall. His own father had told him how Cornwall had once been proudly independent. Indeed, Jacka himself still told the stories to his own children, recounting the many uprisings. One of his favourites was that of Myhal Josef an Gov and Tobmas Flamank marching against Henry VII's taxes in 1497. The history bit deeply into his soul as he knew his own great-great grandfather had taken part.

However strongly Jacka felt political unity at the plight, he needed to stay out of sight. So, he was moved out through the back door and into a store shed. There he stayed utterly silent while hiding behind stacks of pottery. Five minutes passed—but felt more like half-an-hour. He could hear the knock on the door and orders being barked in French. He also heard Joshua and Nolwenn answering the officer's long list of questions. These turned into shouting and then a crash. It sounded as though a table of pottery had been sent flying.

Jacka was unable to see the peril his hosts were presently in. The officers were doing their best to frighten and intimidate—and it was working. Nolwenn was weeping and had taken refuge in the arms of Joshua. He hugged her tightly as he made his best efforts to answer the soldiers' questions. Each was levelled at him with phlegm carrying droplets of sour hate.

Joshua resisted answering with a hundred-percent truthfulness. There was no need for him or his cowering wife to cross themselves. No forgiveness was required from the Virgin Mary who in her mercy watched over them every minute of the day as, in his strictest interpretation of the way things were, no sin had been committed. The soldiers wanted to know of any *English* fishermen in town. Jacka was absolutely *not* English. As far as Joshua was concerned, he was *Cornish*—he was a fellow Briton.

It was highly probable that this kind of distinction was too subtle for the ignorant French soldiers. This cultural point would have been completely lost on them as all they really cared for was nothing more than a solemn imperial duty. Joshua could feel a wave of relief break over his body on realizing he had successfully convinced them.

Back in his hideout, Jacka heard the ordeal reach its conclusion with the commander shouting a sarcastic *"bonne nuit et au revoir"*. He didn't instantly give up his cover, though, until he could hear the troop's boots clacking on the cobbles in the far distance. It had been a desperately close call and Jacka was relieved that he had made friends with the right people.

The next morning, Jacka pulled a bundle of ragged paper out of his sack and untied the hemp binding. The workshop had a wide assortment of dyes, glazes and chemicals available for the artistic finish on vases and jugs. They all emitted their own unique odours; some sharp which could create a fit of sneezing—others more earthy to transport the mind back to nature. He also discovered a stylus, for writing, amongst the assortment of tools. So, he sat down as the sun streamed through the workshop window and scratched another entry in his notes about his sorrowful life.

An hour elapsed and his arm became weak. By this time, Nolwenn had arrived in the downstairs area and beckoned him up to the kitchen to share breakfast. The topic of discussion was on what had transpired during the night and the questions that were asked at the door. One interesting new piece of information emerged—it seemed as though Billy Bod and the crew had made a clean escape. It was likely, if this were true, that the lugger was making fast progress fleeing back across the Channel (or as Jacka called it, "*an Mor Bretednek*"). Sadly, no free-trading had been possible on this mission and so it would seem logical to assume that they would be attempting more fishing on the return leg.

This, while good news, left Jacka in a predicament—how to get home? The presence of French soldiers overturning homes in Porzhtudi, like a ravenous pack of wolves hunting meagre scraps, highlighted the difficulties being faced. There was a strange atmosphere strongly hinting that a fight would be readily picked so long as the results could be profitable. However, this might also offer him a welcome opportunity. What if there were enough unhappy people in the village for him to arrange a boat with them back to Cornwall?

That evening, Jacka returned to the bar and ordered, in his rudimentary Breton, a pint of beer for himself and a fizzing cruskyn of cider for Joshua.

"*Ur banne bier hag ur banne chistr, marplij ganeoc'h.*"

Then as the two savoured their first few sips, Jacka laid down the first elements of his plan.

"*Me a vedn whelas dhe clappya Sowsnek lebbyn rag ma moy a dus obma a or Frynkek ha Brezonek,*" Jacka whispered to say that he would attempt some English as there were more people who understood French and Breton around than any English.

"I am needing a way to steal home and believe there be many folks here who would cast off the Frenchmen's hold on them."

Joshua gave a light chuckle as he took another gulp of cider.

"But if we went to Cornwall, who is to say it would be any better there?" he replied as he scratched the side of his head. Clearly, the very discussion brought him out with a nervous reaction.

"I'm not saying it would be much better—yet we have no soldiers for ever searching our houses for any who might dislike the rule of Paris."

Jacka was watching to see if he could detect any body language that would give away Joshua's readiness to accept. There was none—and so he continued.

"Find us a boat, *mar costa*? Then we would seem innocent and guileless to the Frenchmen and we might help you and Nolwenn flee."

There was still barely any indication of a favourable reception.

"—and if you were to return home to your native Cornwall," continued Jacka, "then we four could all work together—Mary, Nolwenn, you and I—and make cloamen pots to sell."

Now there was a response. Jacka saw Joshua's eyes sparkle. He had managed to hit the right message at the right time. Joshua carefully settled his tankard on the bar and stared thoughtfully into the bubbles gently flying up through the amber nectar and breaking on the surface. He thought it was like a foaming shoal of mackerel. It almost made him want to shout "*hev-va hev-va!*" to alert everyone.

"*Lebbyn, ot ena tybyans dâ,*" Joshua responded thoughtfully to reveal how he considered it to be a good idea indeed.

"*Bùs pandr'yw an gwelha vordh dha wil hedda?*" he asked—clearly plotting the best way to achieve this all.

Silence descended for a moment as contingencies were anticipated and options investigated. It was difficult to say how much time flowed by the two men as they sat there thinking—but it was certain to say more drink was consumed and a few songs sung too. Eventually Joshua rested a hand on his new friend's shoulder to say "*Ma dhybm towl.*" The truth of the matter was that Joshua had always had a plan to escape back home but he had not, until now, had a real cause to enact it.

Jacka had gained his ticket home. All he wanted now was to know the plan.

"*Lavar dhybm an towl dhana!*"

XI

Anseth Tor

The rain beat down ferociously for the fourth day in a row and the Pengilleys were reluctantly marooned in their little house in Penryn. Rivers of muddy water coursed down the narrow streets as a few brave shoppers scurried from trader to trader in a futile effort at avoiding a soaking. It was a Saturday; and so the usual plan for a wet weekend was panning out again with Mum in her studio working on her latest creation, Eddie curled up on the sofa with another technical journal, Dad was flicking through the sport channels trying to find something worth watching and Gary was staring into a blank space awaiting inspiration.

Eventually, he picked up his violin and secured it beneath his chin. Then, he carefully layered rosin on the bow, dragging the Jurassic block of amber up and down its length a full ten times before throwing the lump of resin back into the case. As he started to tune up, his phone pinged an incoming email alert. It was a message from Dr Julian Casement at the university. There was a sizeable file attached to it.

Without a single note being played, Gary quickly forgot about his practice. He dumped the fiddle on the nearest chair without even slackening-off the bow. Then, he scanned the email's contents in expectation of revelations galore. He was not disappointed.

Dear Gary,

It is with great pleasure that I attach a file with my first attempt at translating Jacka Pengilley's writings into English. As you will see, he had an interesting life which started out in abject poverty, but eventually his family became relatively well off. I will let you read this text to discover for yourself how that happened.

I also think he is trying to tell us something. Unfortunately, as I do not know the circumstances in which the diary was found, I cannot surmise his meaning. All I know is that he mentions a place that I cannot find on any map of Cornwall—or indeed anywhere else.

He mentions an Anseth Tor. I have examined the histories of Dartmoor and Bodmin Moor to no avail. Maybe you might be able to cast some light on this.

Yours
Dr Julian Casement.

The email suddenly transformed Gary's day from being one of window-pane-drenched boredom into one in which he could become a sleuth. There was a mystery hidden in these papers—but how could it be solved?

He decided that the first move should involve the full and careful reading of the translation. So, he went downstairs to the lounge where Eddie was engrossed in a book on the workings of experimental fusion reactors and found a space at the other end of the sofa for his adventure to commence. It was then that he heard Jacka's voice in his head more clearly than ever before:

I am Jacka Pengilley and am aged 35 years old. I live with my wife and three children on the coast of Cornwall near to the tiny village of Morvah. Most of my time is spent working down a nearby mine. On the occasion when I do have a spare moment or two, I like to help Mary firing her pots in the hand-built kiln or tending our chickens, goats and pigs.

Our tiny cottage is called Boswicker and has two rooms above and two at ground level. It is in a terrace of cottages along a lane that leads down to the cliffs at one end and up onto the moors at the other. We do not speak that much with our neighbours as they understand little Cornish where we choose not to converse much in English.

I am a proud Cornishman who cherishes his history and stories told by fathers and grandfathers before me. However, I am severely saddened by how the language, which all my friends spoke around me in my childhood, has declined. My children are severely pressured by friends and the local vicar's wife to stop speaking it. Thus, I fear my attempts to maintain Kernowek with them will fail.

On the other hand, I am fully aware of how they need to be brought up to earn a good standard of living because a life down the mines is unhealthy and dangerous. To that end, I am resigned to the thought that they may end up moving away from this beautiful place and leaving their traditional tongue behind them to wither.

Dear reader, whoever you may be, I intend that this description of my life will show you a little of the lives led by a fast-disappearing community. We are not only battered by the winds and waves that roll off the Atlantic Ocean but are also caught in a storm of cultures. Our ways are old but weak against a society that is beginning to rule the world. The English sail out of nearby Plymouth to land colonizing troops on foreign shores. While they conquer with fanfare and royal pageant, the destruction they wreak on our tiny language goes without consequence.

Maybe, one day, my words will be read and understood by someone. So, let me begin to tell you how my life was first transformed by a terrifying accident way below the sweet green grass of our home pastures—'

Gary was instantly entranced with these opening paragraphs and felt himself magically transported through time. While the words soaked into his soul, much as the rain outside was now soaking into the front garden, something suddenly struck him from his recent past.

"Mum—mum," he bellowed, causing Eddie to look up and scowl at his inconsiderate noise.

"What do you want?" she irritably replied on leaving her studio for the kitchen to wash layers of clay from her hands.

"What was the name of that cottage we saw the other week when we went to Penwith?"

"What—the one where we had tea?"

"No," snapped Gary, impatient at not being instantly understood.

"I mean the one next door where that milk jug had been found."

Gary's mother wandered into the lounge while still drying her hands with a tea-towel.

"Why do you want to know?"

"Just—I'm interested!"

Sarah picked up her tablet and started flicking through images taken on their recent excursion. After a pause, she handed it to Gary, showing a picture of him standing in front of the cottage. He winced to make out the name-plate. Eventually, he was able to decipher the name: Boswicker!

"Oh my god!" exclaimed Gary, almost dropping the tablet to the floor.

"Mum—that cottage was Jacka Pengilley's."

Sarah was now captivated enough for her to forget being called away from her own indulgences with clay. She sat down on a chair next to her son who was fired up in excitement like never before. He passed her his tablet containing the translated paragraph where Jacka revealed where he lived. As she began to echo Gary's "oh my God," she was joined by Eddie peering over her shoulder.

It wasn't long before the whole family was reading the opening paragraphs. Eventually, the excitement had bubbled over so much that it was enough to extract Geoff from his armchair in front of the television—a major feat in itself. There was no chance that he was going to miss out—particularly as there was very little, in the way of any sport on the TV.

"But what does Boswicker mean?" he pitched into the discussion while hitting the television mute button.

It was a salient question but not instantly solvable. With an outstretched hand which was usually reserved for commanding the relinquishment of the remote-control for the box, Geoff gestured to Gary to pass him the tablet.

Geoff stood reading the text for a couple of hushed minutes as the rest of the family returned to their previous occupations. Eventually, he pulled up an online guide to Cornish place names. He began to scan through a long list under the letter B: Bosavern, Boscarn, Boscaswell, Boscawen Rose, Boscawen Un, Bosigran, Boswednack, Boswens—but no Boswicker.

"*Bos* means dwelling and causes second-state mutation," Gary excitedly started to theorize, "which means that the *wicker* part might be found in a dictionary as *gwicker*."

"My God, you have been learning this Cornish language, haven't you!" Geoff said, handing the tablet back.

"Well, yeah," Gary laughed with a tinge of disdain. "It's like being an archaeologist of sorts. In fact, lots of these place names have been researched by the guy who wrote that book on the stones of Penwith."

"What—Craig—er?"

"Craig Weatherhill," Gary said—completing his father's sentence.

"But, what do you mean by a second-state mutation?"

"That's simple," Gary replied with a growing belief that his studiousness had found an application at last.

"It means that the first letter of a word is changed by what comes in front of it. That could be its gender, for example—as it is in this case."

The boy, still wearing his favourite sweater indoors, poked a finger from the overlong sleeves and pointed at another page. This one catalogued the word "*bos*" and how it mutated the word for "wind".

"As you can see," Gary gabbled in an attempt to get to his point as fast as possible. "'*Gwens*' or '*gwyns*' becomes '*wens*' or '*wyns*'."

He was now positively screeching with joy.

"Therefore, Boswens could be translated as 'dwelling of the wind'."

Gary was clearly very chuffed with himself by his detective-work—but was only just getting into his stride.

"So," he grinned at his audience, "if I now look for a word in the dictionary that fits *gwicker*, then we might be able to presume a meaning for Jacka's cottage name."

This part of the logic-trail took Geoff and Gary longer than the earlier fast-flowing revelations. While the teen poked about on the tablet, leaping from one web-article to another, his father had pulled a weighty Cornish dictionary off a shelf in the lounge that had been conquered by an empire of Gary's *Kernowek* research literature.

A good twenty minutes had crept by when Geoff paced over to where Gary was sitting.

"Have a look at this—there is a *gwycor* here. That's the closest I can find."

Gary casually tossed the tablet aside and cradled the dog-eared second-hand dictionary on his lap. Its pages were ripped and dog-eared with random markers peeking out of the ruffled leaves. Some were time-discoloured articles on quoits. Others were old shopping receipts. A few pages were even stained by pressed-flowers. None of these really registered at this moment as the big-reveal was tangible. Gary's eyes scanned the listing for *gwycor*.

"If this is right, then the cottage name means 'dwelling of a trader'."

He paused as he read further.

"But there is also *gwycor frank*—meaning a 'free trader'—or 'smuggler'."

Gary and Geoff exchanged glances and began to laugh.

"Here's to the Cornish detectives solving it as Tony Robinson does on Time Team—"

"—or Indiana Jones," interrupted Gary.

Geoff gave his son a massive bear-hug; something which hadn't been frequent enough in recent years. Now, both were united as some might do as their favourite football team scores a goal.

This scholarly translation of an old family diary from two-hundred-years earlier had now become the must-read text. Sarah was excited to learn bit-by-bit that there was a heritage in pottery—an all-embracing passion of hers. Geoff was simply intrigued to discover that his direct family-line led back to something a little less mundane than his own life. But, for Gary, this was the unfolding of a narrative which he could grasp and claim ownership over. If there had been a moment in the past week where he had fallen out of love with the project, there was no sign of it now.

Even Eddie began to see something of himself in the lives lived by the Pengilleys two-hundred years earlier. He latched onto how Jacka spoke about his son Wella:

"I am so proud of Wella," began one section of Jacka's writings in Cornish. Dr Julian Casement had been as faithful to the language in his translation as possible. However, even Eddie, as a want-to-be engineer, could tell that he was not going to understand the full nature of the commentary without understanding the original language. Despite this obstacle, he continued to read—

> *Wella has turned out to be a fine boy with great intelligence. He spends his life learning by doing. We were not a rich family in the beginning as I was injured down "Wheal an Gweal" and, apart from some good-will from the local parish, I was out on my own. As luck would have it, Mary's*

pottery developed, with my help, into our main income—and what an income that was!

I must make the point to you though, that our survival as a family would not have been possible had it not been for Wella. His ingenuity and ability to speak good English enabled us to achieve things that I had never thought possible—but at what cost?

As you well know, I treasure my family's long lineage in this parish and how it has spoken Cornish before anyone can remember. I have sung the songs that my father sang. My father sang the songs taught to him by his father and I would not be surprised if he was singing the same songs that were sung as Angove and Flamank marched to London in their rebellions. Though, while success in a trade that allowed us to live more comfortably brought much relief after a tragic accident, it meant that, for a while, I was distanced from my values.

With luck and a great number of prayers of apology before the graves of my forefathers, I managed to save my conscience. I will tell you about this later. Of course, I will also tell you more about how Wella's self-taught skills got us to that point in the first place.

You must be wondering what happened to that wealth once we returned to our roots. You will learn about this as you read—though, as I complete this passage of my journal, a key message for you must be to think of Anseth Tor. Nothing more will be said of this.'

Eddie read the passage again, then again, and then once more to convince himself that he was not fooling himself. Yes, he had checked three times, like any engineer would, before committing himself.

"This is a clue to some mystery—how cool—a mystery," he told himself before leaping out of his chair and hurtling into the lounge where the rest of the family were sitting.

"Have you read the clue in this that tells us about Anseth Tor?"

"Uh huh," chorused the family. They had obviously had a good discussion on this point already.

"But where is Anseth Tor?" asked Sarah, pulling out a map of Cornwall from the bookshelf.

"This is getting better and better," smiled Geoff.

And it was.

XII

Graffiti

Gary's zeal had returned. But it was not the kind of zeal which would make a person stride forthrightly with purpose and determination. No; this sort was the one which transported the affected to faraway realms while the ordinary lives of those around continued as ever before.

As he ambled through the school gates, he was once more lost in the long distant world of eighteenth-century West Cornwall with only negligible engagement in day-to-day realities. This manifested itself with him having his head perpetually buried in his tablet. The concrete beneath his feet appeared to him to be the uneven granite track between Morvah and the sea.

While he was absorbed in his reading, at least three teachers had to rebuke him for nearly colliding with them. Of course, he didn't even register being told off. He also managed to, totally and unwittingly, blank out the glares of a nearby group of boys whose own ideas concerning zeal consisted of tormenting the easily tormentable. It was the same ones who had been causing him aggravation a couple of days earlier. His ignorance of them may have appeared to be a brazen gesture of stubborn resolve. The fact they read it as such was neither here nor there.

More importantly, he did not look up to notice what had happened to the school sign. At this point, he was learning how some verbs worked in a hope he would be able to better appreciated Jacka's life:

"*Me a wra mos*—I do go—*te a wra mos*—you do go—*ev*—*hi a wra mos*—he, she or it do go," he muttered while wandering aimlessly into the entrance hall. Suddenly, his dream-world was smashed by an angry voice bellowing his name.

"Pengilley," roared the headmaster, "in my office right now!"

Gary was awakened so suddenly that he crashed into another boy and almost dropped the tablet which was casting the spell over him. He turned around to see Mr Turner striding towards him. He stood stock still—stagged to the spot in terror.

"Why? What on earth have I done?" he retorted in a shaky voice trembling with shock. It was a revelation to many that he was someone deserving the head's fiery temper.

"In my office!" he ordered, bordering on the point where he completely lost self-control.

Gary followed James Turner into his office. Miss James was already sitting there. Her cheeks were reddened and her forehead was perspiring so much that she needed to grab a handkerchief from her bag to mop the beads of worry gathering on her skin. Usually, she was smiley and ready to laugh her way around life—whatever the circumstances. But not this time—not now.

"Did *you* do it, Pengilley?"

"Do what?"

"Come on boy—you cannot tell me you didn't see the school sign on your way in?"

"No," replied Gary honestly.

"Someone has sprayed graffiti across it—*in Cornish!*"

Just then—Gary desperately wanted to laugh and do a little victory-dance. He thought better of it.

"What does it say?"

Turner beckoned him to follow him and then strode out of his study with Miss James and Gary following until they reached the gates.

"There you have it—your handiwork I presume!"

The three stared up at the blue sign—formerly a proud statement of the establishment's upstanding character. Glasney Secondary was now tarnished with three words in a black hazy scrawl: "*Kernow bys vykken*".

"*Kernow bys vycken*! Cornwall forever!" Gary proudly stated.

"So, you *did* do it!" exclaimed Turner angrily. His eyes were almost blazing to a point where Gary thought they would explode from his face.

"No! I certainly didn't—and I think Miss James will be able to confirm that this sign is all the evidence we need to prove that no-one in the Cornish class carried out this act of vandalism."

Miss James and Gary's eyes met. It was clear that, for a brief moment, she was trying to work out how Gary had come to that fast conclusion. She looked back at the sign with puzzlement still evident on her face.

"Ah yes—I get what you mean," she smiled as the realization hit her. By now, Mr Turner was looking confused by the sudden dissipation in fear and embarrassment. Miss James continued by explaining what Gary meant:

"That means 'Cornwall forever'—but it is not as I would spell it. It's written in a spelling we just don't use here."

"Okay, okay—I understand." The headmaster had become sheepishly embarrassed by his incorrect appropriation of blame. For a moment he stood, with his head bowed in deep thought, attempting to break through his regretful mumbling and come out with a new course of action. He turned to Miss James.

"What I now need are names of people who may have done this and reasons why!"

Gary indeed knew who to name—though he did not know whether it was wise, on his part, to do so. He too needed to re-evaluate his tactics. Should he help out in the investigation and set himself up for retaliation? He would joke with his friends that he was "having the Cornish beaten out of him". But it was no joke.

Gary looked up at the principal and nodded calmly.

"Yes, sir," he smiled bravely, "I will tell you when I know myself."

Later that same day his phone vibrated and once more there was a message from an anonymous sender. It had an image-file attached. Gary opened it to see a picture of the sign obliterated with a normally innocuous phrase in *Kernowek*. Below the image was a line of text, which read: "we'll get you and all your pathetic shit-for-brains Kernow mates."

Gary raised his head to look around the classroom while he replaced the phone in his blazer pocket. His gaze was met head on by Carter. He smiled aggressively and then made a fist sign, completed with an index finger pointing towards his intended victim. The mathematics teacher never saw any of this exchange. Her burbling about quadratic equations continued unabated.

Gary was now reconsidering his offer of information made to the headmaster earlier that morning.

XIII
Farwèl Wella

Money was scarce and Mary could wait no longer for Jacka's return from Brittany. The parish helped her all that it could knowing that she and her three children were victims of the harsh business of tin and copper. She was managing to earn just enough to pay for food by selling the occasional pot to anyone passing through the village or visiting "Wheal an Gweal Mine" on business. That was a rare enough event in itself though because of its remote location. Anyone who had their means liberated by wealth to enjoy travelling the length and breadth of Cornwall for simply their own pleasure would seldom stop in this quiet corner. Her most successful trading had been to antiquarians who traversed the wild quarters of Penwith in the hope of finding a curious ancient stone to sketch or a hint of an historic link between this ragged people and those of a long-lost tribe of Israel. The adventurers who had come simply to see the sights were more likely to visit Mount's Bay or travel by tall-ship around the coast.

These meagre opportunities had barely filled her spence. So, now came the time which would wear heavily upon this twenty-three-year-old mother's brow.

"Wella—Davy—Jane—*ker o'whei ha prysyow yw calys. Wos hedna, res yw dha nei gwil neppeth rag cawas bôwnas gwell*," she told her three children with tears cascading down her cheeks. She mournfully explained how times were tough and, because of this, they needed to do something to make life better.

"*Bùs taclow a vëdh dâ oja tas dha dhos tre arta*," wept Davy as she scrunched up his shirt to mop his eyes. He was sure that everything would be fine once his father returned home. But then, he was a vivacious twelve-year-old who was still naïve to the world. He knew little of the cold hard truths which lay beyond his granite-edged existence and callously awaited him to trip and fall.

Mary protectively drew them close with her wide-opened arms. They huddled around her for comfort leaving her apron damp with the liquid memories of their troubles. For a moment, she hugged them to her breast while landing a gentle kiss on each of their foreheads. She saw how each was still unblemished with the furrows dug deep by years of tribulations. Hers creased up as much with laughter as with lament.

"*Wella ha Davy*," she choked through her own streams of pitiful sadness which had now made it down as far as her chin, "*devedhys yw an prÿs rag whelas whel gàs honen.*"

They all knew it. There was no arguing. Money was needed and the time had come for each to bring in some sort of finance.

Davy was just about old enough to help out on the surface workings. So, the next morning, he approached the mine captain and offered his services. He joined a team of boys who marshalled the wagons which dragged ore from the mine to where it was laboriously "dressed". He spent each day heaving the trucks from one side of the mine site to the other. Each and every truck was accompanied with a whistled tune and a memory of sweeter times. Oh, how circumstances can change and one's perspective can find a whole new meaning. Davy would have given anything to charge through the doors of the vicarage and learn some more English.

Every now and again there would be an opportunity to take a brief rest before another wagon laden with rock appeared out of the entrance on creaky rattling rails. He would listen to the sound of the bal-maidens smashing the ore in the near distance. Their hammers made a dull thud on some of the larger pieces as they were split into even smaller bits. This rhythmic composition enhanced by the distant clanging produced by a stamps engine. It was all a heady and hypnotic mix of sounds which mingled with the wash of the incessant sea on the distance cliffs and the biting blast of the wind on his face.

If only he could learn to play a musical instrument, then he would be able to use some of this natural inspiration to write down tunes. Alas, the very reason he was where he was in the first place was because the family had a distinct lack of financial reserves—and those were definitely needed to pay for any type of fiddle or pipe. Maybe, Wella would be clever enough to construct something musical for him out of what he found around (as he so frequently did for other needs).

Then he remembered how Wella would not be around for a while—if ever again. For, that very day, his elder brother was packing the paucity of his belongings into a sack and preparing to set off on foot to Poria. The mine captain had told him that someone of his skills should be searching out a man called John Smeaton. This gentleman, endowed with a fine tall hat in all public appearances, was in the process of building a sturdy quay in the harbour. Wella had a letter of recommendation from the mine captain to Mr Smeaton explaining that he came from a background of mining knowledge and was also very adept at making nearly anything work.

This was only partially true. Wella was surely adept at designing and building simple levers and gears by carving them out of wood with a knife. He had never chanced to work in cast iron though— and had no experience of building piers into the sea. The limit of his stone-working amounted to helping Jacka construct Mary's kiln and repairing a hedge at the side of their yard.

"Ne'er mind the truth," he muttered to himself as he carefully put his school hymn book into the bag, "I must appeal to Mr Smeaton's good nature to take me on as an apprentice."

He stopped a second at his utterance with amazement and a gentle smile as he cast his mind back to that day when he started to really make an effort at learning English properly. It had all started with that little book handed to him by Mrs Prendergast. Now, here he was about to set out on a mighty adventure into an entirely English-speaking environment.

Wella grabbed his sack and pulled the chord to tighten its neck. On flinging it over his shoulder he bent down to kiss his little sister and then his weeping mother. Finally, he stepped out of the front door with a shakily-bid farewell: "*Anowr.*"

Mary stood trembling at the door with her daughter clinging to her waist for a long ten minutes after Wella disappeared out of sight. She seemed to have spent the better part of the past two months since Jacka left for Brittany in a permanent pool of tears. Her thoughts were caught up with prayers wishing both of her son's safety and prosperity while also dealing with a niggling worry at the back of her mind for her husband's well-being too.

"*Py le ma va?*" she forlornly asked herself while wondering where he had got himself to. It was no use crying anymore for he was old enough and certainly ugly enough to make his own way in the world. However, when he managed to return home, she would be demanding that he showed some good profit from his venture.

A smirk crossed her lips momentarily as she jested with herself that he might return with a cake hiding the sum of nine pounds within it. He might even take the old road home with more than three points of wisdom. If only she knew of Jacka's situation at that point.

There he was on a quayside at first light; climbing into a fishing boat and accompanied by a handful of sturdy fisherfolk (who were intent on little more than succeeding in a healthy-day's haul). It was all a ruse to cover up meeting in the middle of the channel with a Cornish boat and exchanging illegal goods. Joining Jacka's flight back home were Joshua and Nolwenn; neither had ever professed to be experienced on the water, but they were ready to give it their best shot.

Jacka already knew from his earlier run-in with British excise officers that this was not a safe venture by any means. Be that as it may, he could not stay in Brittany. So, once again, Jacka was sailing out of port with the first tender rays of sun glinting over the sea. The only ripples were from the oars as the crew rowed in the dead-calm—a hypnotic sound of splash—splash—splash as the oars hit the water.

Indeed, it was the sounds of this voyage that were noticeably different from when he set sail from Porthenys. When the *Gwicker Frank* cast off from the Cornish quayside just two months ago, there was a mix of *Kernowek* spoken by him and Billy Bod—and English by the deckhands. This time he was being serenaded by Breton's half-familiar vowels and consonants. A gruff voice would blast the first two lines of a *kan-ha-diskan* to be impatiently followed by a squeakier vocal copying the first part. This game of musical chasing seemed to be unending.

At times he thought he was in an entirely foreign environment—only to be followed moments later by a stream of words, or even entire sentences, which sounded as though they were from his, not so distant, childhood in West Cornwall. After all, he was only 28-years-old—and those times were not so long past.

Jacka listened carefully as Nolwenn and Joshua engaged in light chat with the other crew members. As he pushed a wodge of tobacco into his pipe, he thought he heard something that sounded like "*nown brâs*"—words he might use himself to say that he was hungry. As he lit the tobacco and took a few draws, he started to think more intently about home.

How would he be received when he returned? Would Mary and the children all be waiting with smiles and laughter? Would *they* be hungry because he had not come home with any profit? The least he could do was to appropriate some fish from the catch on this journey—maybe even some when he boarded the Cornish boat. At the very least, Jacka could justifiably argue to any customs officer that he was not taking part in any underhand activities. He was simply aboard for his passage. All this thinking added to the gentle swaying of the boat and the calming smoke soon sent him to sleep.

Three hours must have passed before Jacka was awoken by sunlight as the mid-morning rays beat down on the deck. There was also frenetic activity with nets were being laid. If he had been with Billy Bod, then he might have felt guilty at not taking his fair share in the work. However, as he was undeniably a passenger, then his eagerness to chip in was blown away in the salty breeze. For once, it was good to be watching from the sidelines and not having to become involved in tirelessly tugging ropes or burdening barrels on his shoulders.

Jacka heaved himself up from the corner in which he had been sleeping and casually wandered over to one of the barrels. His demeanour was as though he was browsing for carrots or swedes in the marketplace. What he saw when he peered over the rim, however, was not fruit or vegetable—but hessian bags. He could see one was slightly torn and there was a clear sign of salt. This was more than what was needed for preparing the catch of fish.

He sidled over to the next barrel as though he was continuing his perusal of goats at a market. This time he looked inside to see more sacks. These ones were labelled "tobacco". Once again, he found himself in the thick of another rogueing mission. If they were so unfortunate to be stopped by the customs officers again, from either side of the Channel, what would he tell them? How would he convince them he was nothing but an innocent passenger with no afore-knowledge of this illegal bartering?

One of the Breton crew looked up from his conversation with Nolwenn and Joshua. Jacka just smiled as though everything was all above-board. The exchange of glances was enough for Joshua to cast him a suspicious look too. Jacka flicked his head to the right to indicate that he wanted to have a word with him away from everyone else. This was not really that much of a necessary security measure though as both of them were fully able to complicate their level of Cornish enough to confuse any prying Breton ears.

"*Eus neppëth i'n côk yw dyfednys?*" Jacka asked in order that he should ascertain whether they were illegally or lawfully loaded with goods.

Joshua gave a nervous cough followed by an even more uneasy laugh without saying a single word.

"*Aaa—nâ—*" moaned Jacka.

"*Drog yw genam,*" apologized Joshua as he patted Jacka on the shoulder and headed back off to join his wife. Nolwenn was in deep conversation with the boat's owner. The body language showed they had no secrets between them in the way one might expect of a twin sister or brother. It was clear that everyone on board the vessel was fully aware of the situation—save for Jacka.

Once more he retreated to the part of the deck which he had found for resting without getting under anyone's feet. He had no time for sleeping now as there was an urgent need for a plan. What would he tell any French customs officials? Then the realization dawned on him that he would not be able to relate any plan at all as his mastery of French, or *Frynkek*, was pitifully deficient. Previously, there had never been any real reason to learn it and no-one had ever even tried to teach him. The only language which had been forced on him was *Sowsnek*.

There he was, bobbing gently up and down in the middle of the Channel feeling vulnerable because he was now, not only fully reliant on the Breton crew for his safe passage, but also, *they* would have to do any campaigning for his freedom should they be boarded. His grave situation was only eased by the chance that Joshua might be the one who begs for mercy on his behalf.

There was one other possibility; the crew might have just enough time to haul the barrels overboard at the first sight of a tall-ship. If that were to be the case, then they could sink the loot to the sea bed and deny all knowledge of any misdemeanours. Was he sure about the science of it though? Would the barrels sink or would they be left bobbing about on the surface awaiting discovery?

There were too many variables of which he was either mildly unsure or had no concept of. All he could do was sit back, charge another pipe, and pray to be delivered safely to whichever Cornish boat they had arranged.

"*Gwell via dhebm cùsca,*" he muttered in self-assurance that the only plan left was to take a nap. So, Jacka crouched down and slid his legs out before him before leaning back on a pile of spare netting. There he began to sing himself a solemn song which his father had taught him as a child to lull himself asleep.

> "*Th'era den gen corf mar grev,*
> *Ha meur y hanow dâ,*
> *An Gov a gerdhas trev dhe drev,*
> *Gen Flamank, an dhew warbarth,*
> *In mesk an bùsh gen colon len,*
> *In mesk Kernowyon lel,*
> *Th'era tus mes balyow sten,*
> *Davy Pengilley Trevail.*"[8]

There was plenty more that Jacka could have sung, having learnt by heart each and every one of the verses at his father's knee. His eyes were starting to become heavy and sore. His attempt at the following verses became a half-murmuring of slurred sounds. Eventually, they withered away to a gentle gurgling snore. Each *ronk* fell between every other rise in the swell of the sea.

By now, he believed himself to be back with his *sîra* in a cottage in Zennor in 1736. There was laughter and five children within its

8 "*There was a man with such a strong body,*
   And great was his good name,
   An Gof walked town to town,
   With Flamank the two together,
   Among the crowd with loyal hearts,
   Among the loyal Cornish,
   There were men out of the tin mines,
   Davy Pengilley Trevail."

confined granite walls. He could faintly hear the tuneful chime of the church bell and a cart passing in the muddy lane outside. Moreover, he heard the words of his youth ringing around within the damp-ridden walls. His dream-world self was far from aware that he was actually aboard a small Breton fishing boat in the middle of a perilous voyage. All his six-year-old self could sense was the jubilation of being a child again at home in the place he loved and amongst those who were dearest to him.

He skipped from his father's lap and over to the arms of his mother. She was in deep conversation at the cottage door with Mrs Trevail from down-along. He heard them conversing in a flurry of Cornish about the vicar's plans for Guldize. He savoured the sound of *Mabm*'s high-pitched vowels as one word effortlessly collided with another to leave a whole sentence sung in a single breath.

Jacka simply loved any celebration in the village as it meant there were plenty of sweet things for the children to cram into their mucky mouths. They would still be munching on a split, smothered with cream, as they coursed up and down the length of Fore Street playing games with anyone who came into contact with them.

Guldize was certainly always special to him. He enjoyed nothing better than harvest-tide where scrumptious food produced by neighbours up and down the coastline was stacked on rickety tables in the church porch. There would always be the traditional sheaf of corn brought from the nearest scythed park. It would have been rushed straight to the church following Crying the Neck. Jacka could almost hear the shout of "*Ma va genam, ma va genam*—I ave un, I ave un," as the sheaf was held proudly aloft by his Dad.

The boat jolted and, very suddenly, Jacka was wide awake again. The sudden movement had occurred with the force of another, much larger, boat crashing into the side of the one he was currently aboard. There were furious shouts and orders barked in French. The uniformed officers were pushing everyone into a line on the side of the boat. One spotted Jacka in his somnolescent state and hauled him up by his jacket and belligerently thrust him towards the rest of the crew. By now, his vision was clearing and his mind was beginning to make out the finer details of what was transpiring.

A tall-masted ship flying a fleur-de-lys had pulled alongside their humble boat. Three officers, armed with muskets, were screaming commands at the bewildered fishermen. Even Nolwenn had been subjected to a certain amount of shoving and manhandling as though she was being herded around a jail. Then Jacka remembered how, just before he had fallen asleep, he had carried out an inspection of the barrels on deck and had seen the contraband waiting to be covered by fish.

He could see that, during the period of his slumbering, the crew had been busy and had filled all the barrels to the brim with pilchards. He knew that this must have meant he had been asleep for a good four hours as he had witnessed this operation already in a Cornish boat on the way to Brittany just a few months earlier.

By now, another man with a more decorative uniform was making his way, hand over hand, down the rope ladder attached to the side of the forbidding vessel which had just weighed anchor beside them. Jacka resigned himself to being caught and languishing in a French prison without any hope of deliverance. Would he ever see Mary and the children again?

The French commander slowly paced along the line of Breton fishermen, giving each a glare to see if they were sweating or showing any signs of fear. His eyes scanned the captives' eyes to elicit a reaction. Every single pair that met his line of sight stared back brazenly. Eventually, he reached Joshua, then Nolwenn and then Jacka himself.

He paced back to Nolwenn and said something in French which she replied to confidently. Another two paces were taken leaving him staring directly at Jacka. He could feel the beads of sweat gathering on his brow.

"*Je ne vous connais pas!*" whispered the commander into Jacka's left ear. Jacka remained quiet as he was completely clueless as to what had just been said. One of the Breton fishermen cleared his throat and uttered something which attracted the interrogator away. There followed an angry exchange after which the commander paced back to Jacka, smiled, and then walked over to his officers.

Another order was barked and the officers began overturning the pilchard barrels and hunting through the boat for anything that could win an easy conviction for illegal activity. Jacka was cringing at this point in the sure knowledge that they were about to be found out.

One barrel was tipped with a crack onto the deck leaving a slippery splash of wet fish oozing out upon the sun-baked timbers. Jacka knew that only two of the barrels had contraband in them and from the early results of the search, they had started with the ones that had been empty when he saw them. Eventually, there were just two left standing. As the officer heaved them over, more silvery fish flowed out like a wave onto the planks before them.

One of the officers crouched down and was desperately searching through the catch with his bare hands in the hope of finding evidence. However, much to Jacka's complete surprise, there were no sacks of salt and there were no sacks of tobacco. Perhaps he had dreamed about the search he had made earlier and there had not been any roguing going on. He searched his memory while the officer and the commander continued to interrogate the Bretons. No, he was sure that he had been awake. Puzzled, Jacka shot a glance across to Joshua and Nolwenn. Joshua replied with a half grin and a wink.

Further inspections led to nothing being found aboard the boat. The commander was clearly very upset this had not resulted in a triumph. He now began shouting at the crew in a stream of French that bore the hallmarks of irritation and defeat. As he climbed back up the rope ladder, one of the two officers left aboard struck the Breton boat owner in the stomach, leaving him to collapse to the deck. No-one else dared to move. The other officer spat on him and gave a hefty kick in the guts. The fisherman choked and coughed with pain.

They had not finished with him. Now, the two officers grabbed him while he was still wheezing and lifted him up by the feet and hands. His coughing now turned into protestation at the heavy-handed action being taken. It was then that Joshua made an attempt to step forward to stop the beating, but he was given a silent order to stay where he was by one of the other Bretons barring his way with an open hand across his chest. Indeed, it was wise that no-one should step in as this would have provoked the officers into being able to take action against the crew and everything would have been lost.

They had no option apart from standing in the same row they had waited in for the past hour in the baking sunshine. They had not moved from the time the French officers had first boarded. Now, they watched as the owner of the boat in full vocal protest was swung from side to side and thrown over the side of the boat into the water.

A loud splash followed and then silence. The officers peered over the side to see just a stream of bubbles surfacing. They laughed at their brutal actions which had left one man severely beaten and now drowned.

No-one moved as they scuttled back up the rope ladder and lifted their anchor. They stayed glued to their positions watching the ship raise its sails. There was stunned silence at what had happened but it was anger that had to be held at bay inside each of them until the customs patrol had put some distance between them.

As soon as they realized they were safe, every one of them broke their line of inspection and rushed over to the side of the boat from which their crewmate had been tossed. There was nothing but the lapping of the waves and the slapping of the rope holding the nets in place on the surface of the water. Not a word was said at their loss. Minutes passed. As they stared out to the same sea that provided their living but now gave them cause to mourn.

One of them struck up a song in Breton with a sad tune that made the singer's tears well-up. Joshua gently grabbed his wife and gave her a tight hug as she sobbed for someone that had been a familiar face around Porzhtudi for as long as she could remember. Was it sadness? Was it anger? Did they bring this on themselves? Jacka had only just started to ask himself such questions when he heard a cry in the distance. There was a rush to the side from where it had been heard. It was difficult to spot anything in the green-blue salty plain which stretched out before them. Suddenly, Nolwenn spotted a hand waving.

It was the boat owner who had surfaced some four hundred yards away and was shouting for help:

"*Daet amañ da skoazell ac'hanon!*"

Joshua was already heaving his boots off and undoing his belt. Nolwenn tried to stop him but there was little time to conduct a rescue. As swiftly as he had removed his excess garments, he was preparing to dive over the edge. The boat rocked and he lost his footing. Joshua tumbled into the sea with a yelp. Nolwenn was horrified at the clumsy start to his bravery but the rest of the crew welcomed a release of tension. They laughed at the "brave" hero being taken down a peg. He shouted back a hardly-audible rebuke as waves washed over his head to even more laughs.

Eventually, the rescue was underway. Joshua swam out to where the stricken fisherman was struggling. In normal situations, being familiar with the inherent dangers of the sea, he would have been able to make it back unaided. However, the brutal pounding he had received earlier from the French officers had reduced his ability because of a stinging pain in his ribs.

Joshua grabbed the weakened man around his chest and dragged him back to the boat. Each stroke took more effort and the grey-haired man clutched to his body moaned in pain with each one. As a younger man, probably, he would have been able to take such a beating. His fifty-five-year old frame had long forgotten the bar-room brawls that were considered a hobby of his youth. Now, even one or two strikes took their toll. Moreover, his bruised body was weakened by the cold permeating from the Atlantic waters.

Joshua was not that much younger than the person he heaved against each wave. Every time the water cascaded over his face he gasped and felt more of his energy dissipate on the frothy surface. When his face re-emerged, he gulped for another lungful of air and drew strength from seeing his crew-mates waving in the near distance. The shouts of encouragement grew steadily louder until he reached the boat.

Arms swung down into the water to grab the two and lift them to safety. Nolwenn took personal charge of her husband; mopping his face, depositing a barrage of kisses on him as though he had been away for years, and wrapping his shivering body in a blanket. It was like a hospital during the recent wars with concerned nursing staff rushing around and shouting in a disorganized panic of life-saving fervour. This continued for a quarter-of-an-hour before the simple remedies, available on board such a boat, had been delivered and the patient had given his due response, showing that he was not going to die.

One of those simple remedies was a common bottle of rum. It was a cure-all medicine which could disinfect wounds, numb pain and be used to celebrate a successful operation. The latter was what Jacka had in mind as he appropriated the opened bottle for a shifty swig. After all, he was using it for the medicinal purpose of numbing his rattled nerves following the run-in with the French Navy. If he were to feel guilty for taking this measure, then the feeling wouldn't

127

endure for long—for he was swiftly followed by each and every person aboard in draining every drop.

Once again, Jacka collapsed into a deep sleep, aided by the worry and alcohol combining into a toxic mix. As his dreams crystallized into solid visions, he saw the officers board the boat once more. This time they were shouting at him in a stream of incomprehensible French which distilled into a cacophony of strange noises. He then saw a fist fly into his face and a rifle butt into his stomach.

His vision became blurred from the attack. He could only partially view who was conducting the onslaught. He saw a face, a sailor's hat, a jacket, and not much else. He found himself gasping and wheezing for air on the deck as a sailor's boot connected with his ribs and another with his head. The punches and kicking continued and the pain felt real.

Then, he clearly saw Mary standing there watching the assault with tears flowing down her cheeks. His body was in a torment of pain while his mind was crying out; "Mary, Mary—*whegoll—drog yw genam*—"—"Mary, Mary—sweety—I am sorry." Jacka then felt the cold splash of water as it hit his face. Shaking his head violently, he gasped for air as he felt himself hit the waves. Had he just been dumped overboard by the soldiers?

Reality suddenly fought back and he awoke, flaying his arms in terror, still in the sure belief that he had suffered a terrible fate at the hands of the French. It was only momentary, but long enough for someone to notice his reaction. Joshua hauled Jacka off the deck and patted him on the shoulders for reassurance.

"*Dâ lowr?*" he asked to find out if Jacka was okay.

Jacka nodded as his heart-rate began to return to normal and the world took on the appearance of one which he could live comfortably with: a calm sea and blue skies. It was almost just as fishing trips had been when he took to sea with Billy Bod and his sons.

There was much activity aboard the boat again—this time nothing to do with violent inspections. He noticed the crew using a long pole with a hook on the end which was usually meant for grabbing ropes in the water. Indeed, the fisherman gingerly prodding the waves was attempting to catch hold of a rope floating on the surface of the water.

Several prods and curses had to be issued before a cheer went up from everyone standing around. The hook had successfully snared the rope. The team, including Joshua, hauled the floats aboard. That is when Jacka realized that these were not just any old bits of sacking discovered on the surface of the water—these contained the contraband wrapped in watertight tarred-hemp-bags.

That would teach him to fall asleep without noticing what had been occurring around him. If he had kept his wits throughout the voyage, Jacka would have spotted the French ship appearing over the horizon. He would have also been aware of the activity involved in removing the salt and tobacco from the barrels. He would have then witnessed how they were ejected into the water long before the ship ever reached them.

The French had not discovered the contraband because it had been disposed of overboard more than five hundred yards away and, thus, could not be seen from their current position. During Jacka's most recent period of slumber, he had also failed to see how long and hard the crew had searched the surface of the waves to reclaim their goods.

Joshua glimpsed the surprise in Jacka's eyes and patted him once more on the back.

"*O'whei ownekhës?*" he laughed—asking if he had been afraid. Indeed, he had been frightened.

"*Ownek dha wir!*" he replied.

XIV
Defiance

The images flicked through on slow-motion showing the school's front gate with a time and date stamp. So far, headmaster James Turner had spent two hours slowly reviewing frames from the camera. The slightly fuzzy video started from the point when he had left the premises on Friday evening. He had seen hundreds of pedestrians walking past the entrance with its innocuous welcome sign.

One of the first stills he glared at was a pupil who left the premises late after attending a cricket-training session. He still had his whites on and hurried out of the gate without stopping in order that he could reach a waiting bus before it departed. It was quite apparent that he missed it, for the vehicle hurtled past just a split second after the boy went out of frame.

Another cause to hit the pause was when a couple of men in their mid-twenties came into shot on the pavement outside of the school. They were making their way home after closing-time at the Morgawr Tavern in a ten-pint stagger. They didn't have the control to spray any graffiti on the sign. However, one of them stopped right on the edge of the frame and stood looking through the school fence.

What was he doing?

It became apparent when he steadied himself with one hand on the railings and then scrabbled to open his flies with the other. He then let a stream of hot yellow urine flow onto the school property. Turner winced with disgust.

After that point, he continued to review the images but no-one looked up at the sign and no one went anywhere near touching it. There had also been at least ten cars and a couple of vans which had used the gateway as a convenient turning space. Not a single one of the occupants got out and the signage remained in constant view throughout.

James Turner paused the images and crossed his office to where he kept his own cabinet of drinks (purely for guests of course) and poured himself a consolatory scotch. He made up his mind, as he tasted the first sip, that he would aim to finish this review within the next hour—fearing that if he took any longer then he would be allowing other duties to be left untended.

He choked as the whisky hit the back of his throat. With a slight gasp of air to cool the tongue from the fiery malt, he placed the tumbler down on his desk and resumed the tedious task.

More images slid before his tired eyes. By now, he had become so weary that he very nearly missed the couple of frames in which two hooded boys appeared from the shadows and began spraying graffiti onto the sign.

Victoriously, Turner hit the pause key. He squinted and then used the mouse to enlarge the image. The two boys in question had their faces hidden to an extent which meant certain identification would be a problem. However, both were wearing hoodies. For a start, it ruled out Gary Pengilley as, to his knowledge, he had never seen him in, or out, of school wearing such a garment.

Gary was more likely to be seen off the premises in a checked shirt, a pair of jeans and a woolie. He definitely was not a member of the "cool brigade" who always had the latest trainers and "gangsta-style" clothing. School attire was also unlikely to include anything resembling a hoodie as he came from a family which ensured the children always attended on time and dressed in proper uniform; breaking none of the rules.

So, who was it?

James Turner rubbed his eyes and jabbed a key to enlarge the image once more. Now he could make out a logo on the back of the hoodie—and it was not pleasing to the headmaster now that he had reached this stage in the investigation. With one more click, the logo was large enough for him to tell that it was a school rugby team top. For certain, this ruled-out Gary and everyone else in the Cornish Club.

The principal chuckled, incredulous at his own presumptions. In a normal class situation, he would carefully warn pupils away from ever assuming anything. However, in the case of this investigation, he felt these were fair assumptions. His self-rebuke lasted a second or two as he diligently noted the time-index and then, with a sigh of despair, closed down the program.

If he was going to be completely fair, then he would need to apologize to Gary as soon as possible for claiming, without any proof, that he had committed the crime. Thus, he instantly launched his email and began typing a letter, copying it to his parents and Miss James. This apologetic posting started James Turner considering his actions surrounding this affair on a wider scale too.

At the back of his mind, he became aware of half-remembered educational articles where learned researchers had come to the conclusion that bilingualism was beneficial. The question for both him and the school, however, was more to do with using that time to learn a useful "living" language—rather than one spoken by a handful of enthusiasts who wore some weird blue druidic costumes every September—as they had done only recently in Penryn.

Gary was finishing his music homework and about to switch off his computer for the evening when the email dropped into his inbox. Turner had simply put in the subject box that the message concerned "Graffiti". This left Gary palpably nervous about opening it because of the fear he could find himself in further trouble—even though he knew whatever was thrown at him was not warranted.

> *Dear Mr Pengilley,*
>
> *I am truly sorry to have assumed you to be guilty of painting graffiti on the school signage. You have my word that I will continue to investigate in order to find out who did this.*
>
> *I have also had time to reconsider my decision to stop the club. I accept that this is a good use of your time in the research of a subject which is both academic and of good value to the school's reputation.*
>
> *I would like you and your club to prepare a presentation on the language and culture in the expectation that we will be able to display your work before the whole school at assembly.*
>
> *Yours sincerely,*
> *James Turner (Principal)*

Gary could scarcely believe his eyes and needed to reread the email once more to fully convince himself this was a result. The boys who had endeavoured to make his life a misery through bullying had actually been a great help in winning back the Cornish Club.

He shot up out of his seat and punched the air like a heroic warrior on the battle-lines after defeating a Roman invasion. He could almost feel imaginary woad on his cheeks and the weight of an iron sword in his hand. He then conducted a silent tour of his bedroom with bare feet dancing on the carpet.

"*Trygh a'm beus*," he mouthed into the mirror. His brain had barely needed to even translate this from "I have victory". It was almost as though it was naturally on his tongue—chanted across the centuries. He was still celebrating with his imagination running wild over the shape and feel of the presentation when a second email, and then a third, dropped into his inbox.

> *Dear Gary,*
>
> *I am sure you have read the email from the principal about the graffiti.*
>
> *While it is fine to consider this good for the club, please keep your celebrations low-key. We do not want to come across with triumphalism on this matter.*
>
> *I look forward to seeing you after school on Thursday for the club—maybe we can start preparing that assembly presentation?*
>
> *Yours sincerely,*
> *Miss James.*

Then Gary clicked onto the second email to arrive from Mr Turner.

> *Dear Mr Pengilley,*
>
> *Please keep everything we have discussed to yourself for now. I do not want whoever carried out the vandalism to know that you haven't been held responsible. It might help us uncover the pupils who are to blame.*
>
> *Yours sincerely,*
> *James Turner (Principal).*

The relief was palpable. Gary crashed back on his bed and stared at the ceiling for a few moments to let the feeling of stress drain out of every sinew. He had felt he was under attack in a classic pincer-movement; his peers lambasting him for being "geeky" from one direction, and the "establishment" from the other. He laughed quietly to himself as he realized that both sides wanted him to conform—but in slightly different ways.

The irony was even more apparent as his mind catapulted him back to the world of Jacka Pengilley and his family two-hundred years ago. He had only just been reading about the pressures *they* had been facing. From one direction came his heritage demanding he preserved Pengilley traditions. He was also torn by the pressure to speak English and give his family a secure future. All of a sudden, Gary felt comforted. He wasn't alone. He was following a well-trodden path.

"If only Jacka could know what I've been going through," thought Gary as he sat up on the side of his bed. He grabbed the diary translation which he had printed out only the day before. One thing was for certain—Gary could learn from his long distant relatives. He decided, then and there, to split his evening into three parts for each day. Part one was for reading more of the translation, part two was to learn some more Cornish, and part three was to get on with the rest of his schoolwork.

So, living by his new regime, he retreated back into the world of 1768—as had been translated for him:

"*It is a fine summer evening as I write this,*" began Jacka's next diary entry.

"*I am spending my time in deep thought over recent events which have seen me leave my family and travel to Brittany. It appears that I will not be returning to Mary with anything of monetary value. The smuggling part of my operation was a complete failure. However, I am returning with two new friends who have vowed to work alongside Mary and myself to help us grow our pottery business. I could not have had better luck than to stumble into the good care of Joshua and Nolwenn. They took me into their home, hid me from soldiers and found me a route back across the Channel. My ink is running dry as I inform you that we had a narrow escape*" *with the French navy. Sailors boarded us and hunted high and low for contraband. None was found as it had been cunningly hidden from view in the water. We are now making our way into the middle of the Channel where we have planned to meet up with a Cornish boat. I will be exchanged along with Joshua, Nolwenn and the contraband for whatever is being sent from Cornwall to Brittany."*

Jacka's pen had obviously run dry as his entry ended. Gary put the page down with the intention of reading it the following day. As he did so, he spotted an upcoming entry with the words: "my tears for Davy'. It was not part of his plan to read that section right away because, in his mind, he would be breaking his own rules. It was an internal mental fight to put the diary back in its folder without reading any further—but he did.

The battle continued with his concentration throughout the rest of the evening. He was attempting to learn how to use the Cornish conditional verbs but was being put-off by the niggling concern for Davy.

"*Pàn vo chauns dhis,*" Gary chanted from his book of Cornish grammar. He followed this with an incantation containing the English translation, "Whenever you may have a chance."

His eyes slid down the page and skipped over "*pypynag a vo*—whatever may be" and "*Re bo lowena dhis*—may there be joy to you" in the pretence that he had completed the task he had set himself for the evening. He was failing and knew it. Could he give himself the ability to concentrate on his homework if he just allowed himself to read the entry about Davy? With resignation taking a secure hold of him, Gary picked up the translation and looked at it to give himself a few more seconds where his internal self-control could re-assert itself. This was not a successful tactic and his hands almost went into automatic operation as they withdrew the bundle of A4 from the folder.

"Am I addicted?" he wondered in the buzzing confines of his mind. "How can I be under the influence of something like this?"

He had heard boys egging each other on at school about who had drunk the most and who had tried illegal substances. They traded worse and worse stories of dangerous substance abuse as a badge of honour. It was doubtful whether any of them had ever really touched anything really risky. They were all too chicken in real life.

Whatever *their* stories had really been, Gary knew that he could barely put this diary down. If that was addiction—then, yes—he was surely addicted.

An hour had swiftly passed and the Pengilley family was doing what all perfect families plan to do; sitting down together for evening tea. Eddie was devoutly adherent to the regime and had actually been in his seat for several minutes ahead of Sarah, Geoff and himself. That was as far as the "good-boy" image went though as he was slumped; paying no attention to anyone else. His thumb twitched while relentlessly scrolling through something on his phone. It was as though he was under hypnosis, such was the depth of his trance. Gary leaned over to try and have a look, but as soon as he moved, his younger brother adjusted the angle of the screen in order that he couldn't view it. Cleverly, his mother managed to catch a glimpse.

"Oh, I see you're hooked on the diary too!" she laughed.

"But it's no laughing matter," Gary interjected glumly, "because I get the feeling that I'm about to read something which was not at all good."

"Davy?" asked Sarah gently as though the person in question was a real living person known to everyone in 2015.

"Well yes. Have you read that section?"

His mother continued serving up some soup without saying anything.

"What do you know about Davy?" he persisted. It was clear Gary was lagging behind everyone else in Jacka's story. This was more than slightly aggravating as it had been *him* who had taken an interest before anyone else. Now it seemed he was the last to know what had happened.

"I don't think I should tell you," his mother smiled as she slopped some fish chowder into his bowl.

Gary's annoyance dissipated suddenly when it occurred to him that he had actually achieved something great in persuading his whole family to become involved in this adventure. As he took his first sip of the soup, he became aware of contentment. It was such that he could never recall before. He had the school behind him— and his family too. Why would they take away from him the pleasure of finding out for himself the reason for Jacka's tears?

The next morning, Gary headed off to school with his head buzzing over recent events. He had made most of his journey on auto-pilot, hardly noticing anything or anyone around him. That included the school sign. It had been thoroughly scrubbed and was shining like a newly polished mirror. Maybe it was the sparkle which came from the panel that finally grabbed Gary's attention. He stopped in his tracks, took a few paces back, and then stared at it for a few seconds. He smiled wryly before continuing his stride through the gates.

The cleansing of the official frontage of this institution was apt as its principal had taken a fresh approach too. A smile lit his face as he marched through the playground—but moments later, he felt a hand shove him from behind.

"Pengilley," sneered the accompanying voice, "you hanging out with your weirdo mates again tonight?"

Gary twisted his body around into a defensive stance with both feet apart as he realized the aggression came from David Carter and two of his friends. Carter was standing there continuing to chuckle in the most irritating whining tone possible. However, Gary showed no intention of backing down or taking a subordinate posture. The face before him quickly switched to a "hard-man" grimace that could only have been learned from a violent action-thriller.

"Whatcha gonna do about it then—you small-dicked pasty-boy?"

Indeed, for a moment, there passed through Gary's mind about the kind of actions he could take. One option was to swing his bag round into Carter's body to give him a headache. This would result in breaking his tablet though. Another consideration was jabbing a punch into his nose with his left hand. That was a non-starter too for he was simply not built for combat.

Gary opted for the final of three options; to turn away and keep walking. This he did. Ostensibly, this should have been the perfect "good-boy" response to the insults and bullying. His error, unfortunately, was to mutter the word "twat" as he strode off. Carter was instantly enraged into a fury of flying fists. He grabbed Gary by the collar, hauling him violently backwards to the ground while delivering a fast jab to his upper arm. His gang of supporters gathered around and stood over, laughing tauntingly as the assailant planted another punch to his stomach and swung a foot into his ribs as though he was going for a goal.

Gary attempted to stand up and defend himself but was prevented from returning to his feet by Carter. He was now sitting on his chest and had begun, less than playfully, slapping him around the cheeks. Each time his bare open palm made contact with his face, a shout of "shaggin yer goat—eh?—pasty-boy!"

Gary was unaware of the passage of time or the number of punches and kicks targeted to his body. The attack was shorter than he perceived it to be and was interrupted, quite fortuitously, by Miss James. She had been walking into the school at exactly the right moment to witness part of the attack but failed to identify the guilty party as he had grabbed his bag and fled. She only managed a glimpse of what happened and it was from too far away to identify individuals. Still, she screamed out at the top of her high-pitched voice: "get back here now!"

These were not the type of ideal students who would utter a polite "yes miss" and follow obediently into the principal's office. All three boys completely ignored her futile order and had disappeared around the corner of the building in a roar of laughter. Miss James hurried over to where Gary was still lying on the ground clutching his bruised ribs, moaning in pain and trying to haul himself into a sitting position.

"Who were they?" she asked while helping Gary to his feet.

"No idea—they had scarves around their faces." It was a straight-forward lie.

"Well we know which house they were in—don't we!"

True enough, Gary could not cover-up for the gang's identity totally for the school had four houses and wore slightly different ties accordingly. Even from a distance and even with poor eyesight it was possible to identify them.

"Yes, I noticed too they were from Godolphin."

Miss James nodded supportively now that some information was forthcoming and no serious injury seemed to be obvious.

"*Osta dâ lowr*?" she asked.

Gary could do nothing but laugh at this—despite the pain. For the first time in his life, he had been asked a genuine question in the language of his ancestors—and had fully understood it. Miss James had asked him in *Kernowek* whether he was okay.

"*Ov!*" replied Gary, completely forgetting the bruising kick which had been landed in his side.

"*Ov! Dâ lowr ov vy!*" he laughed.

XV
The Storm

The boat's owner was still sore and aching many hours after being severely assaulted and could almost see the boot marks left in his ribs. He rubbed his side fearing that he had suffered an injury more serious than apparent from the red and purple blotches emerging on his skin. However painful it might be, he still had a job to do—deliver his cargo to the Cornish. The problem for him was that the wind had whipped up the waves to become furious monsters clawing incessantly at the tiny wooden craft. It was being tossed about like a toy boat. All hands were set to the task of hauling ropes or tending the rudder. Each time another mountain of water washed over them, it sent everyone helplessly rolling across the deck.

Joshua, Jack, and Nolwenn were not used to being out this far in such horrendous conditions and found keeping balance to be nigh on impossible. On one occasion, Joshua had slipped across the deck and almost gone overboard. His life had been saved by a deckhand grabbing his arm and hanging on until the vessel had levelled itself. The deafening crashing of the water made logical thought a challenge too. The cacophony of shouts and orders were all lost in the white noise from the pounding sea.

Jacka was acquainted with being in life-threatening situations underground. His experience prepared him better for climbing down a sheer rock-face in the pitch dark. There had been several times when his safety had relied on a member of his "pair"; entrusted with holding a piece of rope at the top of a shaft. One misplaced step or a poorly grasped handle was enough to end in a dive into oblivion. He lived in perpetual fear of having to descend into the Earth in such a way. The only light would come from a tallow candle on his cap and he was prevented from falling by a single knot tied around his waist.

That was it! That was what he should do—tie himself, Nolwenn and Joshua onto the boat with some spare rope. It was a plan more easily considered than executed as the powerful swell thrust the boat up into the sky and left a moment of time when the crew seemed to float weightlessly before crashing back down to the deck. Tying a knot when everything was saturated was a task he had never faced in "Wheal an Gweal". His hands were cold and his muscles refused to react as they did in his youth. Jacka had spent too many years of his life gripping a cold iron drill bit while a hammer struck continuously down to create explosive bore holes in a lode of tin or copper. The vibration and the occasional mis-strike had left his grip severely depleted.

Nolwenn came to the rescue. She had very fine and dexterous fingers that were more able to navigate the end around itself and into a knot. Joshua gave his rope, Nolwenn's and Jacka's a tight yank to ensure they were not going to work themselves loose at the wrong moment. Almost as soon as they had been secured, another wall of greeny-blueness thundered over the boat. It sent one of the deck-hands flying across the deck and over the side in a split second—too fast for anyone to grab the poor lad. The boat owner screamed as he saw his employee disappear into the waves knowing there would be no rescue. His horror stood still in time as the world around the battered vessel slowed with his shouts of agony.

Jacka had seen death down a mine but never out at sea. There had been many instances when a fellow miner had taken a tumble. Most of these had resulted in a rescue operation where the injured person was lifted out in the nick of time. Even in a rock fall, there was hope that lengthy digging would find someone alive—even if they were suffering from cuts and broken bones. This was different though: one momentary loss of concentration and a wave at the wrong time had obliterated a life with no chance of redemption. Nolwenn's tears were instant. Jacka and Joshua were not far behind.

The storm seemed to last for hours. Indeed, there was nothing to guide them as to the exact time—apart from glimpses of the sun in the day and momentary gaps in the clouds revealing the tranquil stars far above. Eventually, the ferocity began to subside; leaving the entire complement of the crew completely spent. Moreover, with the force of the storm, it was difficult to estimate how far they had been blown off course.

Night fell and the sea once more returned to a calm rocking motion. The captain issued an order in Breton and Joshua leant over to Jacka to translate it.

"*Prës yw cùsca tereba myttyn.*"

It was time for the crew to sleep until the morning. Even if the order had not been given, Jacka was sure that every single person aboard would have involuntarily gone into a deep slumber after being severely fatigued by the tempest.

"*Wor'tyweth!*" exclaimed Jacka, expressing his delight at being able to sleep once more. As he fell back into the realms of a dreamland, he once more saw his family welcoming him at the door of his cottage under the slopes of the Penwith hills. Wella was there looking even more handsome than ever before. Jane was running towards him with her arms open. Mary just stood there weeping.

"*Rag fra an dagrow?*" he heard himself asking. Why the tears indeed? What was the meaning of this vision of his family? Then he realized that someone was missing. It was Davy that had not greeted him at the door. His voice cried out: "*Ple ma Davy?*" His call, asking where his younger son was, failed to receive an answer for he awoke suddenly in a sweat.

There was a misty morning light bathing Jacka as he levered his body off the netting. It had been a passable bed for the night—considering all the circumstances. A shiver shot through him as he stretched his aching limbs. The pain was either because of the previous evening's exertion or because of a chill from the wet and cold conditions over the last couple of days. He shivered again and instantly grabbed his jacket tightly to his body.

The captain was leaning on the starboard side and using a rudimentary telescope to hunt for far-off vessels. He had scanned across the misty horizon for a number of minutes before stowing the instrument into a leather pouch. His tutting was easy to understand—even though the following discussion in Breton only revealed a handful of words which Jacka could decipher. It seemed the stormy weather had blown them off course and, thus, they could not locate the Cornish boat.

The order was given to raise the sails and even Jacka was handed a rope to grab hold of. What followed was a series of manoeuvres to tack against the south-westerly wind and progress back towards the west in the hope of spotting the vessel. The arduous work of a deck-hand was every bit as tiring as that of a miner. Instead of hauling wagons and slugging hammers, he was now expected to let a hawser chew into the flesh on his palms. After three of four changes in direction, Jacka started to predict when he was needed. After an hour of fighting the wind, which was howling up the Channel, the order was given to rest.

"*Ma an côk 'hans!*" shouted Joshua, excitedly pointing into the near distance to show Jacka the Cornish fishing boat had been spotted.

Jacka leapt up and pushed his head between the throng of crew mates.

"*Pylê? Pylê?*"—"Where? Where?" demanded Jacka as the telescope was passed from one to another, like a tribal pipe, so that each could take a look.

Indeed, it appeared to be a Cornish lugger under sail and progressing steadily towards them. Eventually, Jacka could make out its billowing sails without any visual aids. It took a full hour of sailing, watching and waiting before the two boats pulled up against each other. When they had been lashed together, the crews met with exuberant hugs and shouts of joy. Jacka joined in the celebrations and went, in turn, from hand to hand. Then, as he grabbed the last outstretched welcome, he recognized the face and voice:

"*Fatla geno'whei?*" laughed Billy Bod as he warmly greeted Jacka. The two broke the hand-grasp and hugged heartily as though they had not seen each other for a lifetime.

The following hours turned quickly into a party as a fresh cask of cider was cracked open and cruskyns were handed around. Jacka introduced Nolwenn and Joshua to Billy Bod and then proceeded to eagerly give his detailed account of how he had returned to the quayside in Porzhtudi to find that the *Gwicker Frank* had left in a hurry.

Billy Bod gave Jacka a tight apologetic pat on the back. He explained how his crew had been warned of French soldiers looking for them and how they had only just managed to cast off and clear the harbour when the force appeared. Musket shots were fired at them leaving Jacka an Lacka with a pellet wound in his thigh. More tales of heroism followed and the laughter continued through the day. Both crews almost forgot they needed to transfer cargoes. By the time evening descended, they were completely drunk. The last two sailors able to stand secured the sails for the night and went to sleep on a pile of sacks.

When Jacka next awoke, there was activity all around him. Barrels were being rolled, heaved and exchanged between the boats. Billy Bod had taken possession of the tobacco and the salt. Meanwhile four barrels were hauled across onto the Breton vessel in exchange. Once all the precious cargo had been stowed safely, Billy Bod beckoned with a hand for Jacka, Nolwenn and Joshua to join him on the *Gwicker Frank*. The hand steadied the three passengers as they gingerly stepped across into the Cornish boat.

As his feet landed on the decking, Jacka felt as though he was already home. No time was wasted in casting off and bidding the Breton crew "*kenavo*". The Breton's responded to "goodbye" in their own language with the Cornish equivalent: "*Tereba nessa! Anowr!*"

Just as Jacka had watched the *Gwicker Frank* turn from a tiny dot on the horizon into a full-sized Cornish lugger, he now watched the boat which had carried him thus far as it became smaller and smaller. Eventually, no end of straining his eyes could make it out.

The feeling of being home felt good although the truth of the matter was that they still had to make it across the other half of the Channel without being spotted. The nerves were starting to fray after two run-ins already. Rattled was not Jacka's favoured state-of-being despite a lifetime down a deep hole. His eyes started to flick incessantly around both sides of the boat in the belief that there was a tall-ship about to loom over the horizon. It would not surprise him if his luck amounted to third-time unlucky. He knew how determined customs officers were at catching anyone they could. He had heard of so many people who thought they could raise some easy finance by smuggling goods abroad only to find themselves languishing in a cell awaiting trial.

He imagined what it would be like for his family if they were to witness him swinging from the gallows. He could see how distraught Mary would be with tear-wet cheeks and children left to feed.

Children! He had not even asked Billy Bod if he knew how his family was.

"Billy Bod—*lavar dhybm fatell yw flehes ha gwreg vy.*"

William Bodinar could see the worry in his friend's eyes as he asked how his children and wife were. It was the kind of fear he had seen on the face of women as they waited for news of loved ones who had gone away to fight in wars. There was a particular searching look in the eyes which attempted to dig out the information without a single spoken word. Similarly, Jacka's were hunting for a response.

Should he say what he knew or would it be kinder to let him think he had no information to impart? The question needed some kind of response as a pained individual who had been separated from his family for almost three months could not bear the agony of not-knowing for any longer. Billy Bod had no time to fully assess the advantages or disadvantages of both sides and thus spoke forth the first thing that came into his head.

"*N'ora vy tra vëth!*"

It was a white lie that he knew nothing at all—though it was a necessary lie. It would indeed be better for his pard if he could live for another week without tears and inconsolable anguish over the fate of Davy. Bodinar had been told by Jacka's aunt Jane only days before leaving on this rescue voyage. It was a sad state of affairs that had fallen upon the Pengilleys. Little Davy was dead and Wella had left home.

All he had learned from Jane was that there had been some terrible accident at "Wheal an Gweal" just days after Davy had started working on the surface. His eyes began to well-up and so he quickly turned away, making himself appear busy tidying ropes on the deck. It was not fast enough though to avoid a split-second hint of sadness being conveyed to Jacka. God knows how this could happen but in that short amount of time he could see his entire emotional load being accidentally loosed.

Jacka followed Billy Bod across the deck and pulled him around by his shoulder to face him. There was no escape in such a small boat.

"*Pandr'yw cabm?*" Jacka asked with a fear of the response filling his suddenly paled face. There was no opportunity to avoid answering the question of "What is wrong?"

With that, the volcano of tears exploded like hot embers in a way that Jacka had never witnessed in his friend.

"*Davy yw marow!*"

It was then the world stopped.

Jacka could no longer hear the waves crashing onto the sides of the lugger. He stood there as though time itself had become petrified like an ancient ant in amber. Billy Bod's look of horror was frozen too. Both were stunned to silence by the shock for an indeterminably long moment. Slowly, Jacka's lips formed the words he had just heard. He repeated *"Davy yw marow"* three times as his body collapsed to the deck between the barrels of tobacco and salt.

"Marow? Marow? Marow?"

Jacka's reflexes moved his shaking arms into a cradling action as though a gurgling baby innocently lay within his gentle protection. He lovingly gazed down at the empty space which he held so tenderly and wrung out a painful smile. His friends, old and new, watched on; helpless to console, helpless to redeem, helpless to repair. Wanting to make it all right was of no use. The only person who had the power to find resolution was now hunched and destroyed on the deck of his presumed salvation.

Jacka was so sure he could feel Davy in his arms. His distraught mind told him so with the memory of neural pathways which sang and danced to the ecstasy of a newborn child staring back. Though his eyes saw nothing but his own hands before him, a vision manifested itself in his grasp. Defiant of reality and desperate for things to be different, Jacka mouthed words which willed his beloved child to sleep.

"Cùsk, cùsk, whegyn vy."

How he had wanted so see this little boy grow up into a fine young man with the strength to take forward his name and the love to bring up another generation of Pengilleys. Oh, how there was desire burning in him to stand there as a proud father at Morvah church and see him kiss a beautiful bride. What dreams he had spun in his nightly slumbers where this happy child sang the songs of old.

None of this was now going to happen. A line had been drawn in his life. There would be no resolution. Momentarily, Jacka cursed himself for breaking down in full view of a mortified audience. He looked around at them standing like the Merry Maidens: stonelike, grey and timeless. It was up to him to be strong and supportive—not a cowering wreck on the fish-stained boards of a lugger. His boldness lasted only five seconds at the most as he stared down defeat. However, reality walked a close pace behind. It soon caught up and smothered him.

The whole crew—Billy, Joshua, and Nolwenn—all remained around him holding a silent vigil. They were powerless to make the world right. They could do nothing save watch their friend sob inconsolably—repeating "*marow*" in his croaking voice. It was only another few seconds, in truth, before Nolwenn crouched down and wedged herself alongside Jacka. She threw her shawled arms around his quaking body. She squeezed him as supportively as she could.

"*Tety valy—segh dha vejeth,*" she lulled in one of the few bits of Cornish she really knew for an occasion like this. "Deary me—dry your face," was the only sentiment that anyone could impart as the sobbing continued.

Jacka wept for many hours until his energy gave out and, once more, he fell asleep. The dreams were charged with the bitter-sweet memory of his son. Bitter; for even in his dreams, he felt the pain of loss. Sweet; for during a short time in the safety of slumber, he could enjoy being with his entire family for one last time. He saw himself returning home again with Davy standing next to his elder brother Wella and his little sister Jane. They were all being cradled in the arms of Mary, standing behind them in the doorway.

His children were smiling and laughing as he approached the little row of granite cottages. Their excited voices gleefully cried, "*Wolcùm tre!*" It sounded as though they were echoing in a long tunnel as they welcomed him home.

"*Parys yw kybel dobm,*" Mary said as she gave Jacka a tender kiss on both cheeks. She had prepared a hot bath in the middle of the downstairs room. The children played outside as he stripped off his clothes and lowered his tired body into the tub.

"Aaah—*gwell yw hedna!*"

Jacka slid down into the kibble so that as much of his body was covered as possible and exhaled a contented "that's better" in Cornish. He could hear Wella, Davy and Jane singing excitedly in the lane at the front of the house. Wella's voice was just about to break but his younger two still had voices that could produce such piercing notes that the sound could travel through the solid walls of the cottage and also across vast distances.

"*Devedhys yw gàn sîra tre—sîra tre—sîra tre—devedhys yw gàn sîra tre—ha lowen on nei oll.*"

The three of them had made up the words on the spot to the tune of a hymn they had sung on Sunday morning.

"Returned is our father home—father home—father home—returned is our father home—and happy are we all."

The warm water was doing its job and relaxing him enough to start sending him to sleep. As he dozed off, he could smell the wonderful cooking produced by his wife and the sweetest sounds of his children playing. Though as he wallowed in the contentment, he remembered that this was not real, he was just dreaming. Which bit was the dream though? Did he dream that someone told him of Davy's death or was he dreaming that he was alive? Sounds washed around his head. Winds blew through his hair. Voices meandered in and out of his consciousness. Time stretched. Reality hazed. The rocking of a boat replaced the warmth of a bathtub.

He awoke.

For a couple of seconds, Jacka knew not where he was or what had really just happened. It took another minute for reality to fully reacquaint itself with him. Then he remembered painfully what he had been told. He looked over to Nolwenn who was sitting right next to him.

"Davy?"

Nolwenn nodded in sad affirmation; Davy was indeed dead.

XVI
Pengilley: The TV Star

Gary finished his presentation to the school principal to a chorus of exuberant applause from James Turner and Miss James. For once, he was in the position of power—standing in front of the white board in the class room. His sole audience were looking up at him in admiration.

"That was excellent," Turner said, eagerly congratulating the student who had formerly ignited his fury.

"I was so thrilled that you've made such a discovery in your family history," he continued while beaming between Gary and the language teacher.

"I mean—I thought that this interest in Cornish was simply a rebellious and thinly veiled bit of Cornish nationalism."

Gary and Miss James were getting an insight into the man that they had never expected. Neither of them revealed how much pleasure they were taking from a total change in his demeanour. After all, it had only been a couple of days ago when Gary was facing severe accusations that he had been the guilty party in daubing the school sign with nationalist graffiti. It was only three weeks since Turner had told Miss James that the Cornish Club was being summarily disbanded.

"So," posed the principal, "I suppose you are ready to perform that presentation again at full-school assembly next Monday?"

Gary cast a quick glance over to his teacher in search of approval—to which he received an excited triple nod.

"Well yes—of course," he laughed, standing up to shake James Turner's hand. "I mean—*heb mar—mynaf.*"

The head frowned an "I-don't-get-you" look back at Gary.

"Of course—I want to!"

The following weekend was one of intense study and preparation for this big event in front of the entire school. Quite surprisingly, Gary felt an obligation to Turner to increase his revision and study for other subjects too. Part of it was down to duty and also for the fear that if he failed in his Spanish, mathematics or even physics, then he would be letting down anyone who had suddenly awarded him a heightened level of admiration. Additionally, it was possible that poor marks from members of the Cornish Club could be used in the future as proof that this was a society which was not good for the boys' future prospects.

Though these fears lurked incessantly in the troubled dark recesses of Gary's imagination, he had heard that the exact opposite was more likely to be true. It had been in one of his brother's science journals in which he had seen an article about the psychology and benefits of learning other languages. The scientist who had written the learned piece used a complex language of his own to express the results of research. Apparently, so Gary read, there was comprehensive proof that children, like himself, could expand their mental abilities by becoming bilingual. He didn't think that Eddie had noticed that edition had been removed from his pile of magazines in the study. It had been a dangerous covert operation to liberate any of these prized publications which had languished in a towering monument to science in the dusty recesses behind the sofa.

That Saturday and Sunday, the rest of the Pengilley family barely saw their eldest son. He was certainly on a mission. It was as though he had condemned himself to jail or had taken up the life of a hermit. Meals, drinks and snacks were delivered to his bedroom door. His father would knock and leave a tray on the landing. Minutes later, a dressing-gowned bleary-brown-eyed teenager, with the appearance of a young Trappist monk, would furtively open the door and slide in the tray. The proof that there was indeed life on the far side of the door was evidenced half an hour later by the crumbs of devoured food left on a plate outside his room.

It was late on Sunday evening when Gary emerged from isolation and declared that he was ready for anything the school, or even the world, could throw at him. He had filled his brain to bursting point with facts and figures, revised for a series of upcoming examinations and had successfully rehearsed his big presentation (which was being performed the following morning). If he was experiencing any nerves, he refused to let anyone else know.

"*Parys ov rag avorow*," exclaimed Gary in his best Cornish. However, his family was not quite that advanced. So, for their benefit, opening his arms as though he were a Victorian showman on the stage of a music-hall, he declared to the awaiting parents, "I am ready for tomorrow."

Sarah leaped up from the sofa and gave Gary a massive hug and a sloppy motherly kiss on his forehead.

"Well done—I am so pleased for you."

As any teenager would do at this point, Gary wiped a hand across his brow in embarrassment to remove the unwanted excess saliva. He recoiled as though she had a contagious disease and moaned; "Oh, mum!"

Laughter returned to the home after two days of tense expectation and everyone relaxed in front of the television. Though the TV was switched on and flashing its imagery before them, not one of the Pengilleys was giving it anything more than a passing glance. Each of them had forsaken it for their tablets and mobile phones.

While the news of another terror attack broke before them showing images of horror on a Syrian street, Gary, Eddie, Sarah and Geoff were engrossed in other things. A reporter was dressed in full body-armour as he performed a piece-to-camera about a bombing. There were still dishevelled civilians rushing around in the background attempting to pull blood-stained victims out from under a pile of twisted metal and rubble. Sarah was browsing an online shop for art materials. The next item to turn up in the bulletin showed a food-bank in Birmingham and had the voice of a female reporter talking about levels of urban poverty. It was clear that Geoff was partially paying attention because he lifted his head to simply comment; "what about rural poverty?" He quickly returned to his tablet where he was continuing to read through the diary translation. Eddie was engrossed in electronic circuit diagrams while Gary was engrossed in a game on his phone.

It was during the local news when an "and-finally" item caught the whole family's attention. It caused them to lift their eyes to the screen simultaneously.

"—and finally, there is much excitement among Cornish academics as it is claimed the largest piece of eighteenth-century prose in Cornwall's ancient language has been discovered in an attic," announced the newsreader with a cheesy "just-before-the-weather" grin.

"What?" exclaimed a dumbfounded Geoff, "—that is *our* diary."

"They had no right!" added Sarah.

"Let's just listen!" interrupted Gary impatiently wanting their interjections to stop so that he could hear the details.

"—a university is refusing to comment right now after an email was forwarded anonymously to us, showing an extensive diary written in Cornish."

The camera angle altered to a picture showing the newsreader and the arts correspondent in the studio.

"—we have our own expert with us now—so what do we know about this?"

The camera angle now zoomed into the correspondent to show a close up of his grinning face and shiny bald pate.

"This is a truly remarkable find, if it is what is being suggested in the un-named source. It seems the Cornish language could be about to get a massive boost with the discovery of hundreds of new words and phrases."

The screen then showed library footage of Cornish bards walking around in a circle and still images of texts pulled from the internet.

"What is even more remarkable—if true—is that this document, found earlier this year in an old trunk, could give us many songs, poems and stories from Cornwall which have never been recorded before."

As soon as the item was over and the effervescing weather woman came onto the screen to show clouds bursting with rain, Sarah grabbed the remote control and muted the volume. She was livid.

"Surely, that is *our* diary and *no one* had the right to tell anyone about it without asking *us* first."

"Maybe it wasn't the university though?" queried Gary, letting his game declare that he had lost with a low electronic anthem to failure played over a tinny speaker.

"Who else has seen a copy of the diary though?" asked Geoff; rubbing his head.

"Er—"

Everyone looked around to Eddie as he let forth the murmur.

LIKE A BURIED CITY

"I sort of showed what we had of the document in an email to a teacher."

Somehow, either the university had leaked the revelation or a minor mistake on the part of Eddie had led to someone getting hold of part of the text.

"Eddie," Sarah exclaimed as gently as possible so as not to give the impression he was in the dog-house (even if he was).

"When you say that you showed a teacher the text—who did you show and how?"

"Well—" he began hesitantly, realizing that he had totally dropped himself into a whole load of trouble, "I showed it to my English teacher and forwarded the email to him!"

It was becoming increasingly apparent how the leak had occurred. Eddie's teacher at junior school was Mark Turner who just happened to be the brother of the principal at Gary's school.

"Oh, for pity's sake!" exclaimed Geoff, exasperated at the unfolding screw-up.

"—pity's sake, pity's sake!" he continued, "James Turner has obviously been talking about this to his brother—who in turn has been able to get hold of a copy and leak it to the media?"

"But why?" chorused Sarah and Gary.

"Don't you see?" said Geoff, shooting his hands out in front of him to gesture towards the TV set.

"The arts correspondent's name says it all—Dale Turner. Dale Turner is Mark Turner's son!"

Geoff "Inspector Clouseau" Pengilley left the room in a hushed realization that a simple mistake and a line of family linkages had led to their secret getting out.

The annoyance was left undiscussed at breakfast the following morning. The whole family had gathered around the table with Gary and Eddie in their usual seats and eating the same cereals as any other Monday morning. However, for Gary, there was a distinct need to push to the back of his mind any distractions from last night's TV news. Nothing was to get in the way of the performance of his life.

Once again, he walked through the school gates and suffered the same old chuckles and dim remarks from fellow students. He boldly ignored them as his focus was elsewhere. They could have shouted all they wanted and would not have knocked Gary Pengilley off course in his immediate mission.

As he checked into the principal's office in order to be briefed about the upcoming assembly, Mr Turner met him at his study door.

"I am really sorry about the TV news story last night."

Gary decided to remain silent and let the uncomfortably apologetic head give his best reasons for what had transpired. None were mentioned past the initial plea. What followed left Gary startled and outside of what he currently considered his comfort zone.

"Since this all hit the news, a TV crew has turned up and want to speak with you. Is that okay?

The boy was struck speechless by this latest twist. He had only just pulled his wits together enough to stand up before the entire school. Now he was being asked to go on television too.

"I have just called your mother and asked for parental permission. She says she'll give it so long as you want to go ahead."

This had all descended upon Gary very quickly. He struggled to clear his mind enough to work out whether he should go ahead with small-screen stardom or not.

"I'll leave you for a few minutes to make a decision."

With that, the principal disappeared back into his study. Gary just managed to get a short glimpse of a man with a large camera accompanied by a reporter. It was Dale Turner. There was a sudden surge of anger which welled up within him. He took a deep breath and counted to ten—in Cornish.

"*Onen, dew, try, peswar, pymp, whegh, seyth, eth, naw—deg.*"

Gary stood in the corridor outside the principal's study and carefully tried to balance up the positive and negative. For instance; if he made a howler of a mistake then he would look stupid in public. If it all went well, then he would be famous and become a cultural hero. If only he had his ten-year old brother's analytical mind! He laughed at the realization it was that same mind which had dumped him in this quandary in the first place—or was it an opportunity?

Gary decided to take advantage of the situation—but under his own conditions. He knocked on the door. Seconds later, Mr Turner poked his head around the edge of it.

"I have decided to do the telly bit," he announced bravely. At that moment, all he wanted to do was collapse in a bag of nerves.

"However, I don't want them to film me giving my presentation—I'm nervous enough about that as it is!"

Turner nodded and gave Gary a pat on the shoulder.

"That's okay—no problem at all."

Half an hour later and he was standing on the stage with legs secretly trembling and heart pumping like a runaway steam engine. He looked out to three hundred of his peers sitting in a sea of regimented rows before him. The youngest were at the front and the eldest were standing at the back in a chaotic array of uncouth slouches. Miss James gave a large "okay" sign from the side of the hall. This was it—time for the hours of dedication and rigorous practice to kick in.

Gary looked towards Mr Turner and then clicked the remote control to activate his slide show.

"I have been asked to give a short presentation for today's assembly to tell you about important research which I have been involved in which could revolutionize our understanding of Cornwall in the late eighteenth century."

As soon as he took his first big breath, a voice came from the middle of the hall.

"Is it about inbreeding?"

A teacher instantly identified the heckler and strode into the line of pupils to flush him out. Gary stopped for a moment while there was a minor stand-off. The rest of the school had turned around as three boys, David Carter and his mates, were led out the side door. As soon as he had a majority of faces looking back at him, he continued.

"Just a little more than four months ago, my grandfather died and left a large padlocked trunk in his attic. It was meant to be opened exactly two hundred years after the death of one of my forefathers—Jacka Pengilley."

The slides showed images of the wooden box. Gary paused as he clicked the slides onwards to show the lid opened and a pile of paper and a clay pot.

"We found an old diary within it along with a handmade pot. The significance of the diary was that it was written entirely in the Cornish language—a Celtic tongue which I started learning here after school."

By now, Gary was certain he had everyone's attention for a total hush had descended.

"It has been said that the Cornish language lies like a hidden city beneath our feet. We pass over it without realizing it is there."

Now came his statement to hook all the would-be classicists in the room.

"We all know how Pompeii was a bustling Roman city until it was destroyed by an eruption of Vesuvius in AD 29. When it was rediscovered and excavated, the lives of the inhabitants were caught in a snap-shot of time as they carried out their everyday lives."

He could tell that he had cast some sort a magic spell for the ranks of students before him were clearly entranced by his discovery.

"Just in the same way as we can use the petrified remains of Pompeii life to reconstruct how Romans lived their lives—we can use this buried city, which is *our* Cornish language, to link us to our past."

So, he continued for another ten minutes before reaching his conclusion. The nerves had totally dissipated by now and left him able to ask, with a confident smile;

"So, are there any questions?"

Twenty arms shot up and Gary began answering questions from the youngest pupils to the oldest. Each one showed how his quest, and the adventure behind it, had hooked his audience.

Eventually, his eyes caught the face of the final boy asking a question. It was another member of Carter's gang—the one which had been causing him grief over recent weeks. Gary drew a short breath and awaited an unpleasant jibe. No remark of such kind was proffered:

"Are there any parts of this research which have yet to come up with an answer?"

Gary felt a flutter of emotion when he realized that one of his harshest accusers must have been snared too.

"Well there is—" he started as Mr Turner cast a glance at him while tapping his watch.

"Very briefly—as I'm over time now—but Jacka Pengilley left a short message at the end of his diary. All it says is that we have to search out 'Anseth Tor'. No one can find this feature on any map of Cornwall or Devon. So, at the moment, we are completely stumped."

Miss James rushed over to Gary as soon as the assembly was concluded with the school song.

"*Gwrÿs yn tâ, Gary,*" she smiled. Gary's Cornish was strong enough to understand this meant "well done."

James Turner followed closely on her heels in giving gushing congratulations and then ushering the star out of the hall and back to his study where the television crew were patiently waiting. They had been sipping dainty cups of tea and demolishing the head master's best biscuits. It was time to control his nerves once again and be the performer he had just discovered within himself.

The cameraman hauled the heavy lump of technology onto his shoulder and switched on the lighthouse-bright lamp above the lens. Just as Gary's eyes had refocused and become acquainted with the conditions, Dane Turner prodded a large fluffy microphone below his chin and politely requested Gary's name and age. The interview had begun.

XVII
Homecoming

Jacka had held his lamenting stare into the middle distance for the last two hours. His face was pained, pale and blotchy with the dry stains of tears still etched upon his cheeks. They left marks on his skin like the meandering trails carved on a beach into sand by winding rivulets of water. No one had been able to console him for his loss and no one had succeeded in enticing him to eat or drink anything. His eyes were still fixed on whatever he could see in his mind's eye when the lugger slipped into the small fishing harbour of Porthenys. He neither shifted his body position nor made a sound of celebration at being back in Cornwall. He would probably have been singing under the influence of rum or cider if he had not had such tragic news broken to him earlier in the voyage.

Joshua grabbed his hand tenderly to usher him to stand up and alight the boat once the ropes had secured the *Gwicker Frank* alongside the quay. If he had not taken it upon himself to do this, then Jacka would likely have remained where he was through the night and caught another chill. Jacka looked up silently as he was gently helped to his feet.

"*Th'ero'nei tre lebbyn,*" Joshua whispered. If he had not been told he was home now, he would certainly have been confused about his location. The houses in Porthenys looked very much like Porzhtudi in the half-light and there was still Breton being spoken between Joshua and Nolwenn. Billy Bod aided Jacka up the steps as Joshua handed his new friend onwards.

"*Ma Porth Enys gàs welcùbma,*" announced William Bodinar with a sense of officialdom as though he was running a ferry service. Indeed, he could hardly think of anything much to say other than 'welcome to Mousehole'. Anything else would have emerged from his lips as a trite or trivial throwaway comment. Such moments made him feel awkward and he was relieved to complete this trip. As Joshua, Nolwenn and Billy Bod made their way off the pier, Jacka an Lacka led a team of locals in the hushed operation of removing the contraband from the boat as quickly as possible to leave the fish on display ready for an impromptu auction.

Billy Bod glanced behind him before leading his mournful group towards the nearest tavern in the hope of breakfast. He watched a crowd of eager buyers descend on his catch. An old lady hobbled past him at that moment. She was carrying a heavy wicker basket which was very nearly as big as she was. Despite her ungainly gait, she almost collided with him. She was certainly in a hurry to get the best specimens out of the barrels while Billy Bod's attention was barely focused on the path before him.

"*Bedhowgh war!*" she exclaimed angrily, without even stopping to rebuke him at length.

"Doll!" cried Billy Bod and Joshua in unison as they recognized the fish-jowster. Their quayside collision had been with one of the area's oldest Cornish speakers—a lady who was famed far and wide.

"*William Bodinar ha Joshua Pascoe! Fatla geno'whei?*" she mumbled with a one-toothed grin that would scare even the most nightmare-hardened child. Dolly Pentreath's face had turned from an angry grimace into a sparkling picture of joy.

"*Dâ lowr!*" they replied, giving Jacka a quick look to see if he was going to join in the welcome. Jacka forlornly made a grunt of recognition and then continued to pace slowly along the quayside on his own.

"*Dr'yw cabm ganso?*" asked the puzzled old lady. What indeed was wrong with him would not be revealed willingly at that moment. Thus, because of the obvious problem with Jacka, and also Doll's need to buy a basket-full of fish, she hurried off down the quay shouting:

"*Me a vydn gàs gweles i'n tavern haneth.*"

Dolly Pentreath wanted to see them at the inn that evening. That was the group's collective plan anyway as no one had pre-ordered lodgings for Joshua and Nolwenn for that night. Billy Bod was reckoning on the chances of meeting someone in the bar who would take pity and offer a bed. His fall-back plan involved them returning to the boat and sleeping aboard. However, they had all spent too many nights on that vessel with some of them nearly losing their lives aboard it. He could not put them up himself either as his own humble cottage was far too small to accommodate anyone apart from himself, his wife and two sons. At least he need not worry too much about Jacka as it was likely that he would be able to stay at his aunt Jane's again.

The tavern on the edge of the harbour was surrounded by what seemed to be a hundred tiny granite boxes all huddled together haphazardly for warmth. The apparent chaotic layout gave the impression of an absence of planning. That was correct by and large as the port had developed in this close-knit fashion over many centuries despite massive waves, marauding pirates and even the Spanish Armada. The inside layout was equally unplanned with tiny corner seats wedged behind thick beams or crammed around the large open fire. Billy Bod had been in here innumerable times on wild evenings. However, this was so early in the morning that there was no one around.

"Anybody serving?" called Bodinar. His expectation of a reply left a momentary gap in discourse as the foursome waited at the bar. It was a tired silence—a heavy silence. It was one which ended with a lad scurrying from a door at the back of the low-hung room.

"What are ee spectin? Food? Ale?" he sang out cheerfully. The smile, which initially stretched across his dark-skinned weather-beaten face, quickly faded when he saw the exhausted crew before him. Joshua made his first faltering attempt in years at speaking English:

"T'ez far too early for ale but we'm opin for any bread and soup."

The four huddled around a large oak table near the front window overlooking the harbour for half-an-hour before the lad brought to the table a tray laden with bowls. His mother followed bearing a large pot of steaming broth. More scurrying resulted in her son returning with a basket full of freshly-baked aromatic bread.

"Will that be all for now?" the rotund woman asked as she finally deposited a pile of spoons on the table.

"*Gromassy*," stammered Jacka, "er—thank you."

It was the first sound they had heard from their forlorn friend for hours and came as a pleasant surprise.

The breakfast was consumed with a voracity which could only be compared to the way a litter of hungry kittens would suckle their mother for the first time. It was clear Jacka's shock was easing. He began to remember out loud how Davy, more than anyone in his family, loved to listen to tales of adventure and myths of spriggian. Billy Bod welled-up inside as he heard how the ten-year-old often spoke about him and his fondness for his drolls. There was a part of the old man that felt a kinship equivalent to being a grandfather for the boy.

Billy Bod nodded with tenderness as the conversation paused. Then he cleared his throat and began to sing:

> *"Davy Pengilley, gwra mos down in cùsk,*
> *Cùsk down i'n gwely ha cùsca heb tros,*
> *Davy mab Jacka pùb tra vëdh pòr wheg,*
> *Na fors an lacka rag che dhe vos teg."[9]*

Silence fell around the table as Billy chanted the final words of the short lullaby which he had written to sing to Davy when he was just three-years-old. Davy and the children had stayed with him for a short time at the request of Jacka because of some particularly difficult times in the village. It had become very unpleasant to the extent where drunkenness had reached previously unseen levels. Jacka himself had faced deep misery when a temporary vicar at the church had refused to baptize Jane in Cornish. No wonder, he mused, why the Wesleys had found such a warm reception in the district—they could offer consolation to fend off a widespread depression.

No number of green hills and fabled standing stones could bless the population enough to grant them happiness. Jacka couldn't count the number of times he had climbed the slopes of Carn Galva and sat on the rugged rocks at the summit wondering if this would be the day that he should go to meet his Maker on his own terms. Each time he remembered his duty and his family.

The lullaby took Jacka straight back to those days. He realized once again—even more now—that his family needed him. He could

9   *"Davy Pengilley go deep to sleep,*
Sleep deep in bed and sleep soundlessly,
Davy son of Jacka everything will be fine,
Don't worry about the worst for you are so beautiful."

barely imagine what Mary was going through. He felt a sudden burning urgency in his legs as though they were willing him to return as fast as he could the next morning.

Breakfast turned into lunch and, before anyone could realize, darkness fell on Porthenys. It left a myriad of twinkling lights around the harbour and the angry crashing of waves on the barnacle-crusted, seaweed-laden rocks. Each window bore a candle burning in it to make the village visible from far out to sea. That sea was now whipping up aggressively—driven by the power of a whistling south-westerly. The pounding could be heard against the granite just like it always did in Portherras when "An Cawr Keef" started throwing boulders to fend off intruding giants wishing to tear Morvah apart.

As the storm grew in force, more of the villagers resorted to the cosy confines of the tavern. Again, and again, the heavy door swung open and clunked shut—followed by the metallic rattle of the latch. Joshua found this quite annoying and had almost had enough of this constant intrusion on his evening. He wanted to spend it as a free Cornishman once again without the oppression of French soldiers bearing down on him. His celebratory mood was helped on by a steady supply of beer and the aim of getting cosy with Nolwenn. He had just grabbed his wife and given her the almightiest drunken kiss when the tavern door flew open again; this time it was Doll.

As soon as the old lady reached the bar, conversation around her turned from laughter and conversation into a mocking hubbub of voices making fun of how she spoke.

"*Dotha wotha raggies lubba*," shouted one skinny youngster. He was followed by a huddle of older women behind them in much the same vain. Of course, it meant nothing—and that was the fun of it to them. Dolly and the remaining Cornish speakers like her in Porthenys had become a joke.

"*Taw tavas!*" she yelled furiously as she slammed her crinkled palm down on the bar. But the lad directly in front of her refused her command to be quiet. It was uncertain whether he had actually understood what she had told him. He certainly got the impression that she was displeased with his unfriendly jesting when her face met his, nose to nose, with a threatening insult: "*Che gronak hager du!*"

The insult was her favourite. Anyone who displeased her to such an extent was called "You ugly black toad". She had actually just had the pleasure earlier that very day in telling an antiquarian from up country to make himself scarce using much the same language. A Mr Daines Barrington had called on her in the hope he had discovered the last Cornish speaker. Dolly had not a clue what he was saying to her. The only inkling she had of his intentions was a rough translation of his questions by two friends from across the street.

Dolly Pentreath had no wish to waste her time with such a pompous man in a tailored suit. He had carried out his research so poorly that he thought that when she "croaked"—so would *Kernowek*. She had sent him fleeing from her front door with her insult following him down to the harbour. The poor Englishman must have felt so embarrassed to be verbally abused in a strange language and then suffer the ridicule of the neighbours as they laughed at him from their doorsteps.

The barman knew better than to enrage Dolly and pushed a cruskyn of ale across the counter towards her. She grabbed it with both hands and wandered off across the room with a slow walk that would have convinced anyone who didn't know her better that, beneath the dress of this fearsome little lady, there was a wooden leg. She did have both of her pins still but her bones were misshapen through a disease that had confounded the local doctor.

Billy Bod caught her attention by waving his cruskyn-touting arm in the air and shouting "come here" in Cornish.

"*Dewgh whei obba.*"

The seventy-six-year old's haggard face swung around, ready to grimace at anyone else prepared to mock her. Instead, she found Billy Bod's beardy grin. A light instantly switched on within her which transformed her body language from that of an aggravated hag into a charming old lady.

"*Billy Bod, cothman vy,*" she laughed as she hobbled over to welcome her old friend, "*dâ yw genam' dha weles obba arta.*"

Indeed, her whole being expressed how pleased she was to see William Bodinar in the tavern again. She seemed to lose a whole ten years of age with her final steps up to the fisherman-cum-smuggler. She added a few short little skips which any doctor would have barely thought possible considering her condition. Then as she pulled up a stool, she landed a big wet kiss on Billy's cheek.

An evening of catching up on the latest news followed. Billy, Joshua and Jacka told her about their adventures crossing the channel and almost being arrested by both the British and French navies. She proceeded to explain how she had received an important visitor that very day.

As she started to relate her tale in Cornish, the whole pub fell silent to listen to the old lady and her friends in conversation. If one listened carefully enough, it was possible to detect a few more people who could translate her Cornish for an interpretation of her words was being whispered from one person to another. Their jests had turned into a local sport of "who could work out what her mumbling meant".

"Well, Billy—I was in the middle o boilin a thick fish broth for my tea when there was a knock on my door. I ad t'coose over some quick as it sounded like whoever was there was some mazed an was avin a flink—you knaw—a spasm o bad temper."

The translation paused almost in time with Doll taking a curious look around the bar to see how large her audience was and who was acting as her interpreters this time. Then she shuffled her stool back around and continued.

"When I opened the door, I found a *pinnicking* liddle man standin there who simply pointed t'isself an stated e was Daines Barrington. I ad'n a clue what e was on about but e looked some whisht after a long day on is feet. So I brewed up some tay an gave im a biskey or two. By the way e was makin notes whenever I said anythun, I can only think e was ere t'find out about Cornish."

By now there was a second wave of translation going on as Joshua had begun explaining to Nolwenn what the old lady was saying—but this was happening by means of Breton. Billy Bod was nodding as Doll continued her story so that she was encouraged to tell more. The droll was picking up pace so that anyone attempting a word-for-word translation would be struggling.

"By chance, a friend o mine stopped by t'check on me an was able t'tell me a liddle o what this curious liddle man was after. But it was gettin on an I was gettin some teasy with Mister Barrington. E could tell I was tryin t'get rid of im so e gaddled is tay an left. It was only an hour later when I found e'd left all his notes behind. E'd filled a book with bits o Cornish an ad'n come back for it. Well—I needed some extra fuel for the fire—so there up it went in flames."

Her bar room audience burst into laughter as she sloshed another clunk-load of ale and almost fell off her stool. Jacka was not laughing though. He thought it was quite sad and ironic that this old woman had taken such a thoughtless disregard for an important book. There he was writing a diary to whoever may read it in the hope that some of his community's dying embers of Cornish might be saved—only to find that a researcher had filled a whole book with copious notes and lost it to the flames to heat up Doll's tea.

"*Yw leskys an lever yn tien?*" Jacka interrupted the laughter to ascertain as to whether the whole book had been burned.

"*Nâ—ma genam' nebes folednow rag qweth frigow.*"

Doll produced some pages from her pocket that she had torn out to use as a handkerchief. Jacka squinted to inspect them. They seemed clean enough and were full of interesting scribbles.

"*Ellam gwytha an folednow-na?*" asked Jacka with a desperate desire to rescue some of Barrington's work. Doll nodded and handed the pages to Jacka with a wave of her hand.

"*Gwra gwitha an pëth yw genam' whath.*" She was happy to let Jacka keep what was left. The bar descended back into being a noisy roomful of fishermen and traders as the audience reverted to the main entertainment of consuming large amounts of alcohol. At the same time, the *Kernowek* corner maintained its conversation. Billy Bod, Joshua and Doll were on fire with poetic stories bouncing to and fro between them as though they were actors in a long miracle play full of jests, parodies and foul language.

Midnight came and went—though, there was still plenty of talking to be done. The early hours of the morning saw every drinker leave, save for those gathered in the fire-baked corner that had become Dolly Pentreath's personal lounge. She was always in the tavern providing a talking-point for villagers and visitors alike. She had become something of a local celebrity who rejoiced in her fame—even when it amounted to teasing slants whispered in half-heard drunken conversations.

The barman cleared the table before them as a cue for them to make their ways homewards.

"I'm so sorry to be asking this of you," Billy apologized as he pulled the barman nearer, "but my friends have nowhere to stay apart from my lugger out there tonight. Be there any chance of lodgings?"

"Only if you have the pennies to pay for it!" sternly replied the host, tugging himself away to continue with clearing the tables. Pennies!—they were no issue at all after such a successful rogueing run. Billy Bod reached into a pouch and pulled out a handful of coins. Forcing them into the barman's hand as he tried to get on with his work, he pleaded for a room for three:

"Es this enough for ee?"

The barman opened his hand and poked about at the shiny shillings. They sparkled brightly in the flickering flames which still burned in the nearby hearth.

"Ess—that'll do!"

Doll wheezed while standing up to make her way across to the door. As she leant on the frame to pull the heavy piece of oak open, her tongue (which so often dealt harsh rebukes) delivered a verse of beauty for the benefit of the grieving Jacka:

> "Che den crev leb eus wàr tir,
> Hydhow gwra gèn skians fur,
> Ha'n Duw uhelha 'vedn ry
> Pëth yw gwelha oll rag why."[10]

Then she was gone and Billy Bod followed her outside. Jacka was far too inebriated to go knocking on Jane's door at this time in the morning. So, the three who remained were offered a single room to bed down above the bar. It only had the bare basics—meant for those who were either too drunk to find their way home or to house tired seamen after braving the ravages of the Cornish coast. The spartan accommodation consisted of a bleak room with two small dirty windows. One looked out over the backyards of neighbouring cottages while the other gave a magnificent view of the harbour. The bedding was made from old straw mattresses which showed their age and extreme wear—each had a number of roughly repaired holes in their fabric. There were no pillows or blankets to ease the harshness of their lodgings.

---

10 *"You strong man who is on this land,*
Today conduct with wisdom,
And the God above shall give,
What is best of all for you."

Joshua and Nolwenn were lucky to be a couple in these conditions for they were able to hug each other for warmth. Jacka was too tired and had consumed excessive amounts of beer. Thus, he was not concerned with the primitive bedding and fell instantly to sleep. Joshua's snoring went un-noticed—as did the sound of a rat scurrying across the floorboards. They slept so deeply that even the disturbance caused by a fiery argument next door went on for an hour without causing them to stir.

Noises emanating from the street below and pouring in through the window were enough to abruptly awaken them. Trade had already commenced. There were rumbling carts dragging goods to the quayside and fishermen talking loudly as they repaired their nets. It was possible to view all of this activity through the dirt and grime that had built up on the tiny panes of glass.

One could see an array of tiny boats laid out on the muddy foreshore within the harbour walls. It was also possible to spot the *Gwicker Frank* tied up further out in deeper water. The gap in the harbour was visible too. Beyond those protective granite barriers lay the island. Billy Bod only ever called it "An Enys" but he had heard talk of it being named "St Clement's Isle" by some other sailors.

Joshua had hauled himself off the uncomfortable bedding and was standing in front of the tiny aperture stretching his limbs. He remained there for a few minutes to allow his body to settle into the day and contemplate what had happened the previous night. For a start, it was good to meet Dolly Pentreath whom he had known in previous years from living in the village. That was in the time before he moved to Brittany. Then he remembered what Dolly was saying about her meeting with a man called Daines Barrington and how he had been trying to find out about his language. He chuckled to himself as he imagined what that meeting must have been like. Doll wasn't the best hostess and was prone to getting teasy with anyone who didn't understand what she was saying—and that made up, pretty well, everybody!

On turning around to view his wife and friend, he noticed that they were now, to some extent, awake. Jacka was leaning up on one elbow and rubbing his sore head. Nolwenn was standing up and neatening her dress which had to double as night-clothes. Then there was a knock on the door. It was Billy Bod.

"*O'whei parys rag an jorna teg-ma?*" greeted Bodinar—checking that they were ready for the day.

"*Res yw dha nei reckna an mona warbar' ha mos wàr gàn vor' gàn honen,*" stated Billy Bod now that he had the attention of everyone. He wanted to get on with his work and go his own way.

First of all, the four of them had to deal out what money was owed to whom after the trading trip. Even though Nolwenn, Joshua and Jacka had not taken any direct role in the rogueing operation, they had experienced their fair share of the danger. Thus, he dealt out a pile of coins for them too. He then handed another pouch to Jacka who had worked with him on his outbound trip, suffered two inspections by taxmen and had been left stranded in Brittany for almost a quarter of a year.

Billy Bod hugged each of them at the tavern door and watched them walk up the hill towards the village of Paul as they set off on the road home. He, himself, smiled at the great memories he could now treasure. Then, he turned back towards the harbour and his lugger. Despite everything that had transpired in recent weeks and months, it was a calm sea and a clear day. Maybe, just maybe, it was one in which he could even earn some honest money.

XVIII

Convergence

Gary was wallowing in his success. He had been a TV star and had helped make some historic discoveries. He was particularly proud of having confounded his enemies too. In fact, he doubted he would have much more trouble from Carter and his puerile gang since the scene they made in front of the whole school. He was under no doubt that if his presentation had "gone south", then maybe he would not find himself in such a promising situation as he was now.

It was almost a film script scenario where the hero comes from no-where and has to battle extreme odds. All he needed now was to find a girl and stroll off into the sunset. That was another challenge for another day. But, for now, he just wanted to capitalize on his victory and learn to speak Cornish as fluently as possible. There was one thing that bothered him still—what *did* happen to Davy?

Gary slid his tablet off the bedside table and lay back on his bed to continue reading the diary translation:

> *August 20th, 1768: I returned home this morning to find that the house I left was neither as full nor as happy as it used to be. Mary ran into my arms weeping as I approached the door. She had waited and watched up the lane for the last month wondering where I was and what foul luck had befallen me. She had tragic tidings to impart about Davy, my ten-year-old dear son with whom I had enjoyed so many beautiful times. He had been another victim of "Wheal an Gweal".*
>
> *Mary and Jane were the sole occupants of Boswicker now that Wella had gone off to work as an apprentice. The two of*

them wept inconsolably as I entered the cottage with Joshua and Nolwenn following me. We all sat together before the hearth as she started to tell us about how Davy had died. She explained between her sobs and dabbing her tears that he had volunteered to spend some time earning pennies on the surface operation at the mine; he was there to push wagons and empty the ore into piles where it would go to the dressing floors for breaking.

He had been working with some older boys who had decided he was an easy target for pranks. The jokes had started light-heartedly by making fun of his poor English. They then became worse. On one occasion they received a severe rebuke from the mine captain for throwing Davy into a wagon and sending it back down the tunnel. The rebuke was enough to stop this harsh treatment but it had left Davy feeling very anxious about everything he did. He was always waiting for someone to play a trick on him or mock anything he said.

Then, with an explosion of more tears than I have ever seen anyone shed before, Mary told me about what happened just a month ago. Davy's nerves had really got to him and he had become clumsy around the house. Unintentionally, he had broken some pots while attempting to move them. He had knocked over a stew and scalded his arm in the process. This was all because he had become so self-conscious.

Davy was not killed by anyone or any criminal mischief but simply because he was so wound-up and distracted by his worries one day that he failed to notice a wagon bearing down the track towards him. He was crushed by the weight of a fully-loaded skip. There was nothing that anyone could do to save him.

With that, Mary and Jane led me, Joshua and Nolwenn out of the cottage and along the lane. I did not even have to ask for I knew where I was going. We walked in mournful silence as though we were recreating the funeral procession towards the church. Once we had arrived in the graveyard, I could see clearly the fresh burial with a cleanly hewn headstone surrounded by summer-meadow flowers.

The vicar had spotted us approaching and rushed out to meet us. I had not been able to attend the burial of my own dear son and he had realized that this would be the best time to, as near as he was able, to repeat the prayers. It was sadly unfortunate that this young lad who had so happily rejoiced in the songs, drolls and ways of his Cornish heritage was not able to be blessed for the life-after in the language he spoke. The priest was well-meaning in wishing to share with me the words he had used to send him on his way to be with Jesus. I stopped him from praying though by placing a finger on my lips and a hand on his shoulder.

Then I prayed those prayers myself in Cornish. I prayed for Davy to find peace in Heaven and surrounded by the angels. I prayed for him to enjoy, for all of eternity, the sweet smells of springtime heather which he had so loved in his mortal life. I then held Jane's tiny hand on one side of me and had my arm around Mary on the other side as I recited the Lord's Prayer in Kernowek. My tears were streaming as wildly as Mary's by now. They flooded so fast from my eyes that they dampened my shirt and made it barely possible to see.

Jane took leave of holding my hand and ran off towards the hedge at the back of the graveyard from where she picked a painful sprig of gorse-flowers. She made herself bleed in this action—though it mattered not to her at all. For she ran back towards me with a consoling smile upon her face and gently bent down to place it on top of her brother's grave.'

Gary himself was now sobbing as he read these tragic words which explained how this ten-year-old boy had taken it upon himself to try and help out with the family's welfare in desperate times. He also realized that Davy had paid a huge price for other people being inconsiderate towards him and carrying out a heartless campaign of bullying. Gary had been suffering the oppression of bullies too; a victim of those who wanted to "beat the Cornish out of him".

He dumped the tablet onto the bed covers and stood up before his bedroom mirror. He could feel the anger and passion burning within him. This was the fury of lost generations and lost opportunities. This was the vengeance of the souls which had never had the chance to hold beauty on the surface of their tongues—as he had learned to do. The emotion released itself: "*Gary Pengilley ov vy—ha me a vydn pêsya in olow treys ow theylu.*" That is to say he made a pledge, then and there, in a sudden burst of Cornish (which surprised even himself) that he was Gary Pengilley. He vowed solemnly to continue in the footsteps of his family.

It was as though Gary had suddenly become united across time with the spirit of Davy Pengilley. He stood there looking at himself in the mirror as though he was viewing himself through Davy's eyes. What would Davy Pengilley make of this moment? What would Davy Pengilley do now?

That evening, the Pengilley's sat around the circular dining table which formed the centre-piece of family life. Geoff was serving the tea while Sarah was busy laying knives and forks. Eddie was scanning some more reference books about the history of Boulton and Watt. Since reading the translation of Jacka's diary, he had almost turned out to be the spiritual re-incarnation of Wella.

When everyone had sat down, Gary looked around the table. Eddie had put his book aside and was twirling some spaghetti around his fork and then sucking it up with a noisy slurp. Geoff was gingerly cutting his into small pieces. Sarah's eyes met Gary's.

"What's the matter?" she asked. She could read what her son was thinking; "it's about Davy, isn't it?"

Gary nodded with the weight of grief bearing heavily down upon him. The rest of the family had already read this passage—Gary was the last to discover the tragic news. Eating abruptly halted. Gary's eyes moistened; "what does it take to change your name?"

"What do you mean?" Sarah was confused by the question. She suspected, however, that it was linked to Davy.

"I mean—can I change my name?"

Geoff and Sarah looked at each other in puzzlement.

"I want to officially change my name to Gary Davy Pengilley."

A string of spaghetti halted in Eddie's mouth in mid suck. It hung there dangling precariously while spreading drips of bolognaise over his T-shirt. A stunned silence fell across the dining-room table.

"Well, why do you want to do that, dear?" Sarah asked tenderly.

"Because—I want to honour the spirit of Davy and to achieve all the things our family dreamed about two centuries ago!"

Sarah and Geoff both frowned at each other as though their son had just informed them that he had joined an extreme religious sect.

"Don't you think that is going a bit too far?" asked Sarah as she grabbed his hand as though she was about to lose him off the edge of a precarious precipice. Her grip was met by him placing his other hand on top of hers and giving a reassuring squeeze.

"What is so wrong about wanting to add a relative's name as my middle name? After all, I've never had a middle name."

Sarah shook his hand and smiled the way that mothers do when they know something is wrong—and they had no control over it. She then gently drew it away to continue her meal. Geoff took over the conversation to see if he would have any better luck in making sense of this.

"Yes—it is possible. However, you need to think about it a little longer. If, after lots of thought, you still wish to go ahead, then we will investigate deed poll.

It was not a matter of "if" for Gary so much as "how soon?" He saw a clear line through history emerging before him. It was as though Jacka had placed a spell on the diary to create a victor who could achieve what he and his generation never could.

Conversation eventually mutated into some of the more mundane subjects. As the final morsels of apple-turnover were mopped up, Geoff began specifying how he would take the car in for its MOT and service in the morning. Sarah added an item to the action list by announcing that she had to make a trip into town to collect some more clay for her latest masterpiece. Eddie had nothing to contribute apart from; "can I get down from the table please?"

Tea was finished and the dish-washer had been stacked. Gary returned to his room to continue his homework. But, before settling down, he closed his bedroom door and stood before his mirror once more—just as he had done earlier.

Gary fixed eye contact with himself for a few moments, maybe even a full two minutes, then he made a pronouncement to his own innermost being:

"*Davy Pengilley ov vy—dewhelys ov!*"

"I am Davy Pengilley—I have returned!"

XIX
Good Fortune

Wella Pengilley was up early to see the sun spread its first rays onto the tiny houses huddled together around the harbour at St Ives. As the morning made its first appearance from across the bay, it sent sparkles and glints of silver dancing across the waves. Far out from the cliffs, there was a single fishing boat making its way out to sea chased by an eager mob of ravenous seagulls. They darted and swooped over the little lugger as it bobbed slowly over the swell. It reminded him of his visits to Billy Bod with Davy and his *sîra*. They were a soothing memory whose recall brought an instant sense of relaxation. This had become a necessity ever since the twists and turns of fate had transformed his life into a busy swirl of people, places, deals, delights and the occasional disaster too.

He had been employed as an apprentice for John Smeaton for almost a month now and he was just as anxious to get working on this clear morning as he had been on every other. His life had experienced a complete transformation ever since he had moved from the rural cottage, in which he had been raised, to the bustling town clinging to the edge of Cornwall. This place was full of so much action and opportunity. There were people trading and conversing, running and shouting, laughing and drinking nearly everywhere he went. It was in stark contrast to Morvah. Life was slower there and revolved around the church and mines. Here was something different to consider and muse on every single day.

Below his lodgings' window, Wella could watch John Smeaton's pier taking shape at a pace which he hadn't thought possible. It was being built out of Cornish granite hewn from the moors. Each block was cut accurately and squarely to within fractions of an inch. The clean straight lines were pleasing to his eye—unlike the ragged edges of the boulders which he was accustomed to seeing strewn across the slopes of hills near his home.

It was his enjoyment of accuracy which had amazed him and everyone who became acquainted with him. His task was to check that every block fitted exactly into the gap assigned to it. John Smeaton would wander past from time-to-time at the start of his apprenticeship in order to double-check Wella's measurements. However, as things progressed, Smeaton was able to rely on his young apprentice's accuracy.

The pay had even increased to a level where the young man could afford a fine view over the harbour and see the new quay taking shape from an elevated position. He was proud of what was unfolding before him and took great pleasure in having a place of his own for the very first time. There was even plenty of money left at the end of each working week to send some back to his mother and sister.

His views through the window looking across the lazy waters towards Godrevy were important to him, not only because he could survey his first ever proper engineering project, but also because he needed somewhere from where he could contemplate. Each morning, before doing anything else, he would stare out across the harbour towards the little island in the far distance and watch the waves crash over it. He would then say a short prayer for his *sîra*, followed by one for his poor late brother.

"Dear Lord—I pray to Thee for my family to be held in Your Divine care. Look favourably upon them. Let my dear departed brother, Davy, find a place of joy in Thy house and that he will be the finest droll teller ever in Heaven."

Then as a thoughtful nod of respect to his *sîra* and brother, he added a final, "*Indella re bo*—Amen."

With that, he slung his holdall over his shoulder containing some essentials for the day including a pasty wrapped in cloth. It had been baked by the landlady for him that very morning. He could still feel its warmth permeating through the material. It reminded him momentarily of the cottage under Carn Galva—those times when he would set out through the front door of the little cottage. There he would be with Jane and Davy as his mother waved them off for more educational instruction at the vicarage. Mary would prepare a small pack for each of them containing their croust.

The difference between then and now covered many aspects. Firstly, his appearance was as smart as any gentleman from up-country. John Smeaton wanted his apprentices to look the part of a professional engineer and so purchased the finest clothes Wella had ever seen. His jacket had tails and his hat was tall. He never wore anything like this when he was back home. His standard wear had been a pair of badly worn flannels and an exceedingly itchy white shirt with permanently rolled-up sleeves. The final difference was probably the most startling to Wella. He had barely spoken any Cornish for the whole month. Everyone in St Ives, or so it seemed to him, was speaking English.

Wella bounded down four stairs at a time as he raced towards the front door and out into the street. He moved so quickly that as soon as he was in the open, he had to hold onto his gentrified hat so that it would not be carried off in the breeze which whipped down the tiny opes and alleys. He hardly stopped for breath as he rounded a corner and flew along the back of the sands bordering the seafront.

He was early enough on the building site to see John Smeaton arriving with a couple of visitors. They were dressed just as impressively as he himself but had the extra adornments of pocket-watches and eyepieces. Wella noted that they were fast heading his way and knew beyond all certainty that his employer would expect him to give the best impression possible. So, he pulled his jacket into place and adjusted his prized hat with seconds to spare. Smeaton and the party of two other men stopped in front of him.

"I do like to make sure that I give local boys the best opportunities I can—and here is one such example," Smeaton proudly announced as though it was a royal presentation being held for the King. "We have here a great lad from a tiny mining village which lies a short distance to the west of where we are now."

"Sir," Wella said as he bowed formally.

"And who might you be?" requested the younger of the two gentlemen, looking him up and down as a sergeant might do during an inspection of new recruits.

"I am Wella Pengilley—at your service."

The visitors laughed heartily for a few seconds and then started to move on to examine the fine finger of Cornish granite projecting out into the Celtic Sea. However, they were stopped in their tracks with only a couple of paces taken.

"Pardon me sir," Wella asked in the highest-class English he could manage, "—but may I ask of thee who thou art—and what your expertise might be?"

The younger of the guests turned around and stepped back towards the cheeky youngster. In some places of work, such forwardness would have been punished as impertinence. If he had said anything of such a nature at the mine, the captain would have sent him away without any pay for a week or more. Wella felt that he now had opportunities to ask questions which he would never have dared to ask before. This was a time of learning and self-improvement in the company of engineers which he certainly did not wish to waste. The men with whom he was in the company of now excited him with their passion for designing a new world with wonderful machines and solutions to make lives better, people richer and give every man, woman and child the chance to live happier lives. Such optimism had not occurred to him until now. The world was surely opening up before him.

The visitor placed his hand on Wella's shoulder and shook it enthusiastically.

"I love a lad who is enthusiastic like you."

He stood there looking deeper into Wella's face as though he was attempting to fathom his abilities by simply measuring jaw-bone angles and facial dimensions. Surveying a man's fortitude and morality was no different to him than calculating levels and angles in a mortar and stone construction.

"My son," he continued, "I am Mr James Watt —and I am exceedingly impressed with how you were so bold as to ask me such a testing question at your age."

Watt spun around to Smeaton and engaged the astute gears of business which could power up as readily in his brain as the ones he reserved for designing engines.

"I know that I told you I was coming here out of curiosity to see your great works—but I am also in Cornwall to investigate these Newcomen steam engines."

Smeaton nodded submissively with the anticipation of business being started early.

"I know that Mr Watt—and it is no trouble at—"

"—But there is something else that I'm after," James Watt interrupted with a glint of determination in his wiley eyes.

"I am searching out fine youngsters such as your Mr Pengilley who can be in my employ—and I am prepared to pay you handsomely for his transfer."

Lives can change without anyone realizing a fresh wind is blowing. People can turn corners without seeing there is something new just out of sight. Wella Pengilley's day had started just as days had begun for the past three weeks. He had been expecting to dutifully spend another fourteen hours measuring, checking and marking figures on a plan. However, an hour after first meeting James Watt, he was sitting in Smeaton's office with this surprise arrival. He was filling out paperwork consisting of legal letters which now needed Wella to leave his mark. He carefully wrote his name as he had been taught. He could even hear Mrs Prendergast shouting out a warning that anyone whose writing was not neat enough would receive a fearsome punishment.

Wella was starting to realize that life outside of Morvah moved at a startling pace. The ink on the letter, officially contracting him to James Watt, was barely dry and now he was in a carriage making haste along the main road back eastwards. Though the route was rutted and made the journey extremely bumpy, Watt handed him some paper, a board to lean on and a quill.

"It is best you write a letter to your family now and explain that you may be away for a number of years."

The violent motion of the carriage made such a mess of Wella's handwriting that he was sure it would be completely indecipherable:

Mabm wheg—

Mester Smeaton o dean pur thaa ka ev a ros thebm mear a skeeans war byldya cay. Lebben, therama moas mes dhurt Kernow gen dean kries James Watt. Gynner ew. Na ellam doas trea arta lias blethan bus me vedn screfa jo chons.

—Tha vabe, Wella.[11]

---

11   Mabm wheg— Mêster Smeaton o den pòr dhâ ha ev a ros dhybm meur a skians wàr byldya cay. Lebbyn th'eroma mos mes dhort

The letter was handed over to another coachman as the carriage took a short stop at the London Inn in Redruth. From there it raced along lanes and trackways with hedges brimming with gorse and white-thorn. It was nothing like the slow laboured journeys which wound across the barren uplands of Penwith and down to Billy Bod's boat. Those excursions went at a pace where each field could be examined from fast-changing angles and every point of interest was debated. This rapid progress through unfamiliar countryside revealed a Cornwall which he had never experienced before. Wella knew none of the drolls or the names of local buccas. He had never heard of most of these villages before—even though their Cornish elements informed him about what to expect from their history.

There were huddles of houses which pulled on his inquisitive nature such as Marazanvose and Parkandillick. The first led him to ask what day the "Market of the Wall" was held. The latter made him laugh and wonder why it was so important for locals to remark on a certain field being full of horse-dung. A multitude of alien territories spun past his eyes before the carriage pulled in to a tavern in the middle of nowhere.

This hamlet was surrounded by wild moorland with an array of haphazard boulders and green slopes dotted with the occasional sheep or cow. Wella could make out granite walls and stone-capped carns similar to the ones which ran along the north coast of his home territory. But there was no one here that knew him or his father. He could not simply take fright and run to the comforting bosom of his mother. He was now out on his own.

That evening he slept in a strange bed in a room above the coaching inn boasting furnishings fit for a gentleman. It appeared that he had been given the finest lodgings he had ever seen. Then again, he had not seen that many in his life. He had shared a room at home with his siblings. He cast his mind back to the times he had spent at Aunt Jane's in Porthenys and the recent experience of having his

---

Kernow gèn den cries James Watt. Jynor yw. Na ellam' dos tre arta lies bledhen bùs me a vedn screfa p'o chauns. —Dha vab, Wella.

Dear Mother— Mr Smeaton was a very good man and he gave me much knowledge on building piers. Now, I am going away from Cornwall with a man called James Watt. He is an engineer. I cannot come home again for many years but I will write when there is a chance. —Your son, Wella.

own accommodation in St Ives. This was the first time though that he had enjoyed multiple layers of sheets and a finely sewn quilted-top. The chamber pot was also a new addition to his life. Mr Watt had obviously thought very highly of him to spend his money like this.

Once back on the road, the journey took a whole week of travelling from one county to the next and staying in coaching inns along the way. After adventures in Bristol and Manchester, the party of engineers finally arrived in Glasgow. Wella soon became deeply involved in a world of nobles and learned elders discussing ingenious solutions to make mining more profitable. They spoke of inspirational ideas and contraptions which he had never considered possible.

His days were filled with oil, grease and workshops. The evenings were taken up with accompanying James Watt and his entourage to fine receptions in hotels and grand houses. His knowledge of mining was highly prized, even though most of it had been learned from his father and other men around the parishes of North Penwith. These occasions were hosted on shiny-tiled floors and lit with crystal chandeliers. The conversations were a convoluted mix of broad Glaswegian and haughty English. Dining had been a completely foreign experience. It meant having to learn the complex etiquette of which knife, fork or spoon to use for which course.

A whole year passed at James Watt's side. Though Wella had started out as an apprentice, he had become such an indispensable assistant that he was now on a considerable wage. It amused him to consider how it would put him on a par with a mine captain back home. It was at another societal reception where Glasgow's elite were gathered when he found himself in a deep discussion about pottery and porcelain. He was sipping wine which had just come off a ship from Italy and ended up explaining how his family had recently been making some rather fine examples of Cornishware.

"Master Pengilley," began the trader, while running his nose over the scent pouring off the surface of the glass, "I have never heard of any such wares arriving from Cornwall."

Wella felt embarrassed to be entering a discourse which was totally out of his depth. Thus, he allowed this bespectacled man in his mid-thirties to lead the conversation. He took another sip of the vintage, which he had only just imported that week, and smiled condescendingly.

"However, as a trader and a gentleman, I am prepared to always try new things and experience new places in the hope of making myself a profit."

Charles Gainsford's statement was issued formally and decisively as though the gaunt-faced trader was thinking out his business plan aloud.

"Master Pengilley," he continued, while placing his glass on the top of a nearby fireplace, "I have heard much about you as being a clever and inquisitive young man who is always keen to learn new things."

Wella had heard this kind of announcement before. It was exactly this feeling he had when Smeaton sold his services to Watt.

"How would you like to accompany me on my trading travels around Britain and Europe for a year or two?"

Wella politely thanked Gainsford for his interest but declined as he was already learning such a lot from his current employer. The encounter had been forgotten for a good two months when James Watt called him into his office.

"Master Pengilley—you have been a stunning apprentice and an equally amazing assistant over the last four months."

Wella fidgeted in his seat on the other side of a vast oak desk which was chaotically littered with leather-bound ledgers, half-built valves and a rack of pipes. James Watt selected one of them and pressed a wodge of tobacco down into the end.

"However, I am not a selfish man in any way and feel that I have benefitted long enough from the fine work you offer."

Watt leaned across his desk to ignite the tobacco from a large candle. As the flame took hold, he pushed himself back into his seat and took a couple of long drawn breaths on the pipe. Almost instantly, the room was filled with a highly perfumed aroma. Wella choked slightly.

"I have signed an agreement with a Mister Charles Gainsford. I believe you know of him."

Wella nodded as he realized that whatever he had said out of loyalty to Gainsford had been totally ignored.

"Charles told me how you had been a decent enough person to vow to give your continued services to me—and I appreciate that immensely. However, I also realize that this is a wonderful opportunity for you."

So, once again, Wella found himself travelling. This time he ended up on a graceful tall ship with vast sails, creaking and fluttering in the wind. The salt in the air had a familiar taste as the vessel sped out to sea from the Clyde. It moved as swiftly as a seagull catching a rising thermal and then swooping down wind. The billowing canvas sent timbers ploughing up steep waves and plummeting down into cavernous troughs for three days. Their passage headed down the Irish Sea and around the wild waters of Land's End.

It was the closest Wella had been to home in far too long. He had sent letters back every week to explain what he was up to, whom he had met, and describe some of the ideas he was developing. He had also received letters from home nearly as often. His mother and father had explained about grieving for Davy while trying to carry on for Jane. Jacka had given expansive details about how Joshua and Nolwenn had helped them set up a fine pottery in St Ives. Business was going very well and they had received high praise from far and wide.

Wella had these letters in mind as the ship came into sight of land. He could see the cliffs at Pedn an Wlas where monstrous waves smashed against the towering monolithic cliffs. It was then that the winds blew the spirits of home across the foamy sea towards him. Wella began to quietly sing to himself:

> *"Ple ero'whei ow mos, mos, fettow teg,*
> *Gèn agas bejeth gwydn ha'gas blew melen?*
> *Mos dha'n venten, syra wheg,*
> *Rag dêlyow sevy a wra mowysy teg."*[12]

It was the first time in eighteen months that a word of Cornish had danced upon his tongue. He had quite forgotten about the songs he used to sing and the conversations he would have with Davy. Even Jacka, in his desperation to make a living, had found himself

---

12 *"Where are you going, my pretty maid,*
"With your white face and your fair hair?
Going to the well, dear sir,
For strawberry leaves make girls pretty."

speaking English more often. His father's letters to him rarely displayed any language but that of the Saxons.

Wella mused to himself that all those years of torment had been for his own good. Having Cornish beaten out of him now meant he was a respectable member of society to a degree where he was now in the employment of one of Britain's top traders in everything from fine wines to porcelain and steam-boilers to gold. His family had adopted English and now were proud owners of their own business making beautiful pottery.

Still, those words in Cornish hung in his mouth with as much bitter-sweet flavour as he had ever experienced from the cuisine and grapes of the wealthiest banquets. He stopped singing and rested himself on the side of the ship to watch the cliffs retreat into the misty distance. There he left one single word drifting: "*hireth*—longing".

XX

Dartmoor

There were two issues worrying Gary about his continuing quest. One was the location of Anseth Tor and its relevance to the life and legacy of Jacka Pengilley while the other was more to do with his personal mission. It was one thing to research a family tree and find out about some interesting artefacts. It was a completely different affair when that history and those items change your whole perspective.

Maybe, it might have been far easier if that box had been opened in the solicitor's office to reveal some gold bars or a diamond necklace. For, if that was all that had been left, Gary, Geoff, Sarah and Eddie could have cashed in the wealth and disappeared off on a relaxing holiday or two. The riches, once handed out to every eligible member of the family, might have even enabled the purchase of a new car. That was not the case though as each and every one of the family had read the entire translation of Jacka's diaries and they all knew that he was trying to tell them something across the centuries.

It was clear to them all how Jacka was aware he was living at the end of time. This was not the ultimate finality concerning the destruction of the world by the hand of God, but this was about the extinction of his way of life. He knew he was among the last of his kind singing songs passed down from father and mother to son and daughter. He felt the deep burning pain of losing that connection. The only way he knew to alleviate the agony was to record those final days. Maybe then he could inspire someone else to take up the fight.

Those beyond-the-grave dreams had fallen upon the twenty-first century shoulders of the Pengilleys. Geoff had realized that he had two sons who bore the talents displayed all those centuries ago by Wella and Davy. Though he found it difficult to say out loud; he was proud of Eddie the scientist and engineer and free-thinker Gary. Strangely enough, his own wife, though not related to Mary Pengilley by blood, was displaying an extraordinary link to the past through clay.

Gary, by this experience, had been the most fundamentally affected of all of them. He had read the diaries, researched the background and was now becoming increasingly dedicated to the Cornish language. With his mock exams out of the way and the summer bringing a flourish of colour to the landscape, he had taken more time to continue his passions. He had a stretch of a couple of months before he went back to school and study hard for his GCSEs. Thus, every opportunity to continue his research was cherished. Every clue was stowed carefully like treasure in his mind as he peeled back the layers of history as an archaeologist would do with the careful scrape of a trowel.

The devotion filled his weeks: Monday nights entailed Sarah driving him to a pub near Helston for a gathering of Cornish speakers. While many were sampling beers and talking in *Kernowek*, Gary sat drinking a coke and ice, listening intently. As he watched lips move and sounds fill the bar, there was the inclination to believe he was sitting there enjoying to the same sounds as spoken and sung by Billy Bod, Dolly, Joshua, Mary, Wella, Davy, Jane and Jacka.

Geoff took over taxi duties on Tuesday nights and drove Gary, clutching his violin like a new-born baby, over to Perranporth. There, he began to play alongside other musicians. They filled a waterside bar with sweet, energetic and earthy melodies. Wednesday nights were Eddie's turn: he was inspired by the history of steam which had emerged from the diaries. Jacka had told tales about the great Newcomen engines pumping water from the mines. Now Eddie had begun helping out with a local society which looked after some of that machinery with a semi-religious fervour. The rest of the week, despite being spent at home, had become full of activity and endeavour.

Geoff and Sarah even caught the bug—the former earnestly asking around his friends about the location of Anseth Tor, while the latter becoming the protective keeper of the pot found in Jacka's trunk. She found a deep beauty in the deep reddish-brown earthenware. The glaze enhanced its rusticity with patterns laced across its fractured glaze which mimicked the clefts in cliff-faces.

The only distraction from this onward march of cultural conquest was an event which all his year-group was encouraged to partake in before they entered their GCSE ordeal; the "Ten Tors". Gary had spent many a night lying awake in a vain attempt at conceiving plausible excuses to get out of it. How could he give a believable reason that would exempt him? He was too cultured to get lagged in mud and wet through to the skin in a stank across the wild wastes of Dartmoor. Where was the pleasure in catching cold when he could be in a warm house with his music and books?

No excuses had been devised which were good enough to persuade Mr Turner to let him off. So, it was not long before Gary found himself up to his knees in a swampy mire on the west flank of the moors. The rain heaved down and bit through his clothes with an intensity which made each drop like a needle piercing his skin. Gary dragged his sodden hair out of the way of his eyes as he huddled together with Josh Johns and David Uren. They were trying to examine the detail of the map. However, the protective case was leaking and the paper had started to get wet.

"We're bloody lost!" exclaimed Josh as he attempted unsuccessfully to tighten the fasteners on his coat. Every time the wind gusted with gale-force, it blew down the hood leaving him exasperated.

"We should have taken the track down from High Willhays heading west. Now we are stuck here and can't see anything," he continued to protest.

David Uren wrestled the map away from Gary and held it as close to his face as he could.

"May is meant to be sunshine and blue skies—*not* bleeding driving rain."

Gary simply laughed at both of them.

"Come on you two—see the funny side."

"There is no *funny* side of it," admonished Josh.

"Okay, okay," admitted Gary stomping off, "I am going to climb up that tor over there and wait for a clearing in the rain to see if we can spot the best route out of here."

With that, he felt a wave of heroism sweep over him as he laboured through the boggy terrain. If only his audience to witness this consisted of creatures more intelligent than sheep!

"*Me a yll bos hardh ha crev,*" he told himself in an attempt to become the brave adventurer the competition aspired to make him. However much he told himself that he could be bold, strong and clever enough to discern the correct way, he knew he was battling against the clock. Firstly; there were hundreds of other teenagers who were probably ahead of them and, secondly; the weather was getting worse—definitely *not* better.

Gary reached the tor and hauled himself up between a gap in the rocks. For a moment there was some relief as the overhang protected him from the pummelling wind and the piercing rain. He found another finger-hold in the granite and heaved on the next layer of rocks which sat upon each other like a pile of bacon in a butcher's window. A few more pushes and he would be up on top with a view of the surrounding hills—so long as they were granted a break in the torrential conditions.

"*Onen, dew, try—*" Gary counted ahead of another exertion where he pitted his cunning and strength against the ageless eroded peaks of a long-forgotten mountain range.

He slipped.

His boot failed to find the tiny ledge which would have acted as a step and his hands were too numb and wet to be able to maintain their grip. He felt them slowly lose their grasp, finger by finger, as the moisture-laden air blew in a swirl of liquid and noise around him. Then he felt that he was flying. For a moment he could look down and see the green landscape stretching out before him. He had become a bird—maybe a seagull with a carefree wish to remain airborne until its safe ledge could be spotted on the precipitous cliffs of Bosigran.

The clouds had cleared. There he spotted far below a row of cottages and a man returning home to his wife and daughter. They were all crying. They hugged and wailed as he swooped by them. His attention was fully absorbed in the moment of that image. He could make out the little girl's messy brown hair and her mother's apron being used to dry her face. Gary thought he knew these people. He felt he loved this family. But why were they crying.

There was not enough time to discern the cause of their distress or what was happening next for the clouds closed in again and the wind and rain blew hard on his face as time regained its hold on his body.

He thought he felt his body come into savage contact with the ground below him. But he could not be sure.

There were moments which followed where he saw bright lights. In one of those moments, he caught sight of a face looking down on him and inspecting right up close. Time lost its meaning once more and he was in a boat out at sea with five older men and one boy just a little older than him. They were fishing and laughing. They were all talking Cornish.

"How—*fatla genowgh why*?" called Gary as he greeted the crew. He did not quite hear their replies before he was asleep once more and drifting. He could hear a mechanical whirring and throbbing noise which was deafening and made him want to flinch against it and cover his ears—but he couldn't. The noise became louder and louder and was starting to frighten him. It was then he realized that the bright light had turned into the flash given off by an explosion. The thundering noise around him had turned into the sound of rocks falling. This was followed by darkness and fear.

Next, he felt hands lift him. Was he being removed from these fallen rocks? Where had this happened? Bright lights again. They were racing above him as though he was lying on his back on a trolley and hurtling along a corridor. He was.

The cacophony of noises blurred along with the lights and faces. He understood nothing and recognized no one.

Davy had no knowledge of how long he had been unconscious. All he could remember were some vague visions and sounds: He was now in a strange place where the people looking at him wore masks. One of them said something. It was unintelligible. Davy attempted to answer back.

"*Pleth esof vy*?" he asked to ascertain his location. No answer that he could work out was returned.

"*Pandra wrug wharvos*?" he asked again as he attempted to discern what was happening. There was still no response that would help him. The masked people around him tried to speak to him. It sounded foreign. Davy passed out again.

Later—much later—but how much later? There was more noise. He could hear someone asking him something again. He had no idea what was being said and so went back to basics.

"*Davy Pengilley ov vy*," he announced as though he was new to the world which blurred around him.

He heard something that sounded like: "*yarr ow ke Gary.*"

Whatever that meant was a conundrum.

Things started to clear a little more and he began to understand that he was in hospital.

"*Clâvjy?*" he murmured. It was decidedly difficult to talk, though, as he seemed to have been fitted with a sprawling web of tubes in his mouth supplemented by wires laced all around him. He felt trapped and started to try and tug out the wires. He recognized a lady dressed in white telling him "No, Gary!"

Regardless, the meaning was apparent. But why was she calling him "Gary". As far as he could remember, his name was Davy—Davy Pengilley.

Time drifted and Davy-Gary understood little. He had learned to hear Gary when he meant Davy. He had begun to make out some of the sounds. The fog which filled his mind was still clouding his reasoning and hindered him as he attempted to work out what put him into hospital in the first place. Was it something to do with flying? He seemed to remember that feeling of weightlessness for a moment. There was wind and moisture around him. Once more he could see that parting in the clouds and the upset family at the door of the cottage. Why was this of importance?

A nurse helped him sit up in bed a little better and checked his monitors. That's right—those were monitors beside him making a beeping sound. He hadn't been ensnared by a web or strings and ropes either. Instead, he was hooked into a monitor.

"*Yma sëhes dhybm,*" Gary-Davy informed her as she checked a drip which was feeding a liquid into his arm.

She smiled and said something that sounded like: "*Nâ chet.*"

He was not aware of a verb in his language which sounded like that, even though he could tell she was speaking in the negative. The questions now involved trying to understand whether the hospital staff understood him. The whole process of thinking was tiring enough and, just as he had seemed to do hundreds of times within the last few days, Gary-Davy fell back to sleep.

The next time he awoke, as far as he was aware, he was in a different room and did not have all the tubes and wires feeding into him. His head felt a little clearer too. Gary-Davy looked around and spotted five other bays in the ward which were occupied by older men. He could just about glance to his left where there was still a heart monitor beeping away. There was also a table full of cards.

"Hope you get well Gary—from Josh."

"Get well soon Gaz—from David."

"Praying for you Gary—Love Mum & Dad."

"Hang in there bro—Eddie."

"*Omwelha yn scon*—Jenefer James."

Clarity suddenly hit him.

At that point Eddie rushed into the ward shouting, "he's awake!"

Sarah rebuked Eddie for creating a disturbance but understood how he felt. After all, it had been touch-and-go as to whether Gary-Davy would live or not.

"Mum—Dad—Eddie!" Gary-Davy grinned as they gathered both sides of his bed.

"I am so glad you are speaking English again Gary," Sarah replied in sheer relief that he had actually said something comprehensible.

"How long have I been here and what happened?" he demanded for fear that the haziness would return before he received any answers.

"You, my dear boy, gave us a bleedin fright!" Geoff smiled in a half-joking rebuke.

"Well, tell me then—what happened?"

Mum and Dad spent the next twenty minutes at his bedside recounting how he had slipped and fallen from a tor during the Ten Tors' Race, and how he hadn't been the only student who was rescued that day—but he had certainly been *the* news story.

Gary-Davy had been on television once again as an air ambulance had been despatched after a panicked phone call from Josh Johns. Doctors in Plymouth had given him a twenty-five percent chance of making it through as he had severe concussion.

Gary-Davy had been recovering in hospital and falling in and out of a coma for a month. He had only just started to become conscious within the last few days. However, during that time, there was a fear he had become brain-damaged. At one point, all he was speaking was a handful of words in Cornish and showed no understanding of anything in English.

"You had also been adamant that your proper name was Davy Pengilley!" laughed Eddie as he tried to lean over the bed and give his brother a hug.

He looked back at his visitors in astonishment.

"—and isn't it?"

XXI
The Return

Wella knocked three times on the pottery door in St Ives. When it eventually swung open, he was not presented with the smiling face of his mother or father.

"Ess—can I elp ee?" asked the bald-headed bearded man standing before him, giving Wella's attire a disapproving glance. He clearly thought he had fallen out of a royal coach.

"I am Wella Pengilley, sir. Who might you be?"

"Ah—*Wella yonk*! Young Wella! I am Joshua Trengove—I work with your *mabm* and *sîra*."

With that Mary Pengilley stepped into the doorway and stood there in shock for what seemed to be an eternity. Then she screamed excitedly, "my boy's back—my dear dear boy's back!" There was a smash of a pot being dropped from sheer surprise followed by Jacka appearing at the door, his face beaming as though he had been blessed by Heaven and every angel within it.

"*Wella, Wella—mab ker vy!*"

They hugged and kissed their returned son before beckoning him into the pottery. This all happened with hardly any notice being taken of Charles Gainsford who had also been standing at the door. He followed in anyway while enjoying the melodrama of a family reunion unfolding before him.

"Sorry, *Mabm, Sîra*," apologized Wella, suddenly remembering that he had his employer with him. "This is Mr Gainsford under whom I serve."

Joshua, Nolwenn, Mary, Jacka, Charles and Jacka pulled two benches together in the middle of the pottery to carry out a mixture of catching up on life and introducing his boss to the workshop. It was the first time that Wella had seen his father since he had gone away to Brittany with Billy Bod. He hadn't even had the opportunity of sharing in the family's grief over the loss of his brother.

It was inevitable that this would be a bitter-sweet moment. They cried again and, even though time had moved on, their grief had failed to do so. It hung around their heads like a dark chain of musty black flowers. They had waited a year-and-a-half before deciding to move out of the Morvah area. It did not seem right to leave the house where Davy lived at a time when, for all they knew, his spirit still lingered. What would it have been like if the poor boy had come to visit and they had not been there?

Eventually, decisions had to be made as their business was growing and the best opportunity for trading was in St Ives—especially now that Smeaton's pier was looking so fine and attracting many a splendid ship to tie-up. Thus, they had managed to buy the pottery and living space above it with proceeds from the cottage and by selling good quantities of earthenware to visiting traders.

"Well, that is the other reason I am here," smiled Wella warmly. He had barely been able to keep the secret for so long as to why Mr Gainsford was in attendance.

"My employer and I have been travelling around Europe for the last year or so and have come across a number of wealthy individuals who are interested in buying fine wares."

Nolwenn grabbed her handkerchief to her mouth in anticipation of an exciting business proposal. She was not to be disappointed.

"I have exhibited a couple of items of yours already which you sent me a little while ago. Mister Gainsford—would you like to continue?"

His employer removed his spectacles to reveal his gaunt face and deep eye sockets behind them. He glanced to-and-fro a couple of times to assess the nature of the people he was intent on carrying out business with. Finally, he cleared his throat and made a straight forward proposition.

"I desire to purchase your pottery from you for the price of four hundred and fifty pounds."

"Four hundred and fifty?" whispered Jacka.

"*Pajer cans ha hanter!*" he stammered, barely believing the figure being offered.

"What is more," continued Charles, "you will be retained in my service to operate the business on a very healthy wage too."

Negotiations continued throughout the day. Gainsford was also privileged to be given a master class in firing pots as Jacka and Joshua were in the process of loading up the kiln. It was during these discussions that his new boss handed over a key to a bank account set up in London containing the money to buy the business. Jacka smiled and put it in his pocket for a moment until he had a chance to inspect it further in privacy. It felt wrong to pour too much admiration over monetary success. It did not feel right to him as he was simply happy that he could offer his family and friends security. He only took a proper look at the piece of metal once he was alone with his pipe.

It was three inches long and made of a flat piece of polished steel. There was also a number engraved on one side of the head. Turning it over displayed the bank name: Royal Kensington & Mayfair. Jacka put it back in his pocket as Joshua and Charles returned to the room with a view to joining him smoking. Gainsford caught him secreting the item into his jacket.

"You need not be ashamed of money my man—enjoy it—after all you have earned it."

That evening, the group of friends, family and new business colleagues gathered in a waterfront tavern and drank as much as they could to seal the deal. It was only when enough ale had been heartily consumed to cause considerable issues with standing up straight that Wella called the party of revellers to attention.

"There is a second reason that I have returned home," he slurred at the same time as attempting to hold onto the thick oak table in front of him. The tavern fell quiet while Wella gathered enough strength to elaborate on his call for hush.

"I wish to take you—*mabm ha sira—dha Loundres genam*—er—to London with me—to meet *gen* Penny. *Me a vedn demedhy Penny.*"

On announcing that he was to take his parents to London to meet a maid called Penny and that he was wishing to take her hand in marriage, the tavern's clientele, including parents, Joshua and Charles, erupted in ecstatic applause. The drinking continued long into the early hours with the subsidized aid of Mister Gainsford. The only ones who were not privy to the news was Wella's sister Jane, who was fast asleep above the pottery and Nolwenn who was looking after her.

The following morning, Nolwenn, Joshua and Jane waved farewell to Wella, Charles, Jacka and Mary as they piled their trunk onto the top of the stage coach to London. A small crowd had turned out to watch the departure. Some even helped the Pengilleys load up. Last time Wella had made this trip, he wasn't seen off by anyone and was in the company of James Watt.

But now, the Pengilleys were heading for London, England. "What a turnaround in life has visited upon us!" rejoiced Jacka.

"It's hard to believe," Mary added, "being just three years ago we were facing destitution."

The couple were now flying along the coaching road from inn to inn up country in order to meet their future daughter-in-law: a Miss Penny Spiers from Berkshire.

"When will the wedding be then?" asked Jacka as the coach rocked and tilted. The ruts and bumps along the road across the wild expanses of Devon tossed the rickety carriage side-to-side and bounced it high in the air as though the very frame was celebrating the joyous news.

Up until this point, there had been little conversation about plans. The last two days had seen discussions over the shape of the business and remembering times past too. But that struck a chord of sadness within Wella.

"Father, you can speak to me in Cornish if you so wish?" Wella begged as he clung on to the window frame of the violently rocking coach.

"Oh, no don't worry son," replied Mary as she leant forward to pat Wella on his knee, "your father and I are doing well now with English—as you can hear. It's necessary for trade you know!"

"You never told me you spoke Cornish," interjected Gainsford inquisitively.

"Well—I never had cause to," answered Wella before facing his father again, "you know Davy would want it—*heb mar dâ via gèn Davy.*"

Jacka nodded slowly and smiled at his son.

"*Me a or*! I know! I know!"

He paused for a moment as he remembered those halcyon days of excursions, fishing and playing with his three beloved children. He thought of Jane (who was now with her de-facto nanny, Nolwenn) and Wella (who had done so well in business through means of his engineering and trading acumen).

Then his memories caused him to drip a lamenting tear down his cheek as he remembered Davy on his knee listening attentively to stories about "An Cawr Keef" and Cormoran. Wella could see his father's lips move as he silently recounted a tale to an imaginary son still seated on his lap.

"However much we loved those days with Cornish on our tongues—those days have gone and we have entered a new era."

Wella was visibly shocked by Jacka's reaction. All those years of standing up and being counted as one of the last families in the area upholding the old ways—and now that tradition was being completely dismissed. His mother was sensitive enough to her son's confusion to lean forward once more and grab his hand. She then leant over to Jacka and softly muttered in his ear.

"Ah yes—" continued Jacka, "*mabmyk ha me*—er—your mother and I were discussing things last night and it's about my diary and a pot we've just fired." Jacka glanced sideways to his wife for support as his emotions were bubbling under the surface. He did not want to appear to be a helpless blubbing wreck in front of the new owner of his business.

"We have made up a special trunk to be handed down through the family and you will receive it as part of your wedding gift."

Mary hugged tightly to Jacka's right arm as he continued to make his announcement.

"As you know, I *have* been concerned about the loss of our way of life and language. So, over the last three years, I have written a diary in Cornish cataloguing those years—along with some stories and songs. For safe keeping, I have also hidden some notes that were nearly lost, made by a man called Daines Barrington. I got hold of them from Doll as she was using them for fire kindling and a handkerchief too. They are safely in the lining of the box."

Wella was startled to discover that his father had been making such early plans for the future.

"But why are you doing this now—*Rag fra lebmyn, a sira*?" asked Wella confused at such haste to pack up the past.

"Because—" he paused to wipe away another tear, "because we have to say goodbye to what is gone now—and look forward to a bright future for the Pengilleys—however—at the same time, I do want our family to have a chance at some point to know what our lives were like."

"And also—" prompted Mary.

"—and also, we have just hidden something else in there—now that we are living comfortably. After all, who knows—my great great grandson might need some help in the future—or his great great grandson."

"But what is it and where is it hidden?" demanded Wella caught in the intrigue.

Jacka did nothing but tap his nose and smile.

"Whosoever reads my diary and has enough knowledge of Cornish will understand where to look."

It was clearly apparent that the bequest in the oak trunk (currently being used as a settle in the kitchen) was going to stay locked with all its secrets intact. Jacka was content now that he had placed his past in a strong box, closed it, and was planning on moving forward with life.

Wella leaned back and took in the passing countryside for, as his parents had both fallen asleep in their seats, he had the chance to ponder what his father had just told him. He could hardly believe that Jacka had so easily sealed the lid on those years.

"If it was I," he began to contemplate as the scenery passing his window became a blur, "then I would not be so hasty to bury my past."

It had already come up in discussion previously. Jacka vehemently claimed the family was waving goodbye to a whole era, a whole tradition and Davy with it. Those tears which welled into little salty pools in the corner of his eyes told him that he was still wrought with grief. Wella knew his father's heartbreak was manifesting itself in stubbornness and a determination to be progressive. He couldn't have thought this was possible a few years ago. However, those times were different and sometimes it was necessary to recognize defeat.

If Wella had been overly sensitive to these emotional situations, he would have likely taken a minor level of offence at such devotion to one of his three children. Despite this, he knew that Jacka loved them all equally. It was just that Davy had formed a very special bond by sharing in so many of the things which his father had hoped to preserve. He knew he saw Davy as the boy who would take forward his drolls and continue to sing his precious songs. Wella would dearly have loved to step in to his brother's shoes. Dearly loving to was not the same as being able to.

Dare he take a look inside that trunk and read those diaries once it was handed over to him as a wedding gift? Dare he try and dig out those secrets which had been left hidden for the future family?

The remainder of the journey was filled with idle chat about St Ives' townsfolk and some of the traders who regularly visited the port. A few days of buttock-bruising travel passed before they reached their penultimate stop on the road to London. The coach had pulled in at a low-slung tavern with creaking low ceilings in the middle of the tiny village of Bray. The chaotically built inn was freshly thatched and was surrounded by bustling customers, traders and boys whose job it was to tend to the tired horses. It was here that they would stop the night and dine with Penny Spiers and her family before making the last haul into the capital.

As soon as the carriage came to a rest, Wella spotted Penny outside the oak-beamed entrance. He leapt out of the coach door even before the wheels had come to a complete halt. He bounded excitedly across the cobbled yard towards her. His forward momentum was carried through into whisking Penny off her feet in one effortlessly balletic move. They hugged, laughed and kissed.

Mary had only just completed her careful descent of the coach steps, ably balanced by Jacka's hand, when Wella and Penny came skipping back towards them like naughty children; grins stretched ear to ear.

"Penny, my dear," Jacka put on his highest-class English for the introduction, "it is an absolute pleasure to do your meeting."

She laughed with a tinge of embarrassment at her future father-in-law's slightly clumsy English. She quickly recovered herself and held her hand out to Jacka and then Mary.

The meeting was enough to mask all that emotion which was so difficult to lock away in a trunk. Another evening of barroom celebration was staged with a new addition to the family and a crowd of at least twenty flam-new names and faces to learn. There was James Spiers and his son (who was also James Spiers). There was a clutch of new nieces and nephews too. This made Jacka glow with pride.

Suddenly, he became aware that Wella had sidled up beside him and was enjoying the two families getting along so well.

"*Obba an termyn vedn dos,*" Jacka smiled while continuing to gaze ruefully across the room. Finally, he turned to his son and touched his glass to Wella's.

"Here's the future, son."

XXII
Two Worlds

"You took quite a tumble there." Gary fully awoke as soon as he realized that a doctor was standing at the side of his bed.

"We nearly lost you twice," he continued while making notes. He was scribbling down readings from the monitor above his patient's head. Next, he placed the clipboard back on the end of the bed and checked Gary's temperature.

"You should be ready to go home in about a week, I hope."

A week sounded as though it was a long time. Add that onto the month-and-a-bit that he had already been in hospital after the Ten Tors accident at the start of May. This meant it was almost half way through June. He was a little concerned that he might not have enough time to complete everything that he wanted to do this summer.

"But I would not go overdoing it young man," replied the doctor to Gary's unspoken desire to get out of bed and back to his life.

"When you say that you almost lost me," asked Gary with a worried frown scrunching up his forehead, "what do you mean by that?"

The doctor prodded his finger towards the heart monitor.

"You were in surgery at one point and your heart stopped. We had to resuscitate you on the table. Medically, you were dead for a whole ten minutes."

Gary was visibly shocked.

"The second time was in the ward. All the alarms went off at night and we had to get in a 'crash team'. That time you were gone for almost fifteen minutes."

The doctor was obviously pleased at his own skills in pulling another customer through.

"Son, you are indeed a miracle. Then of course we were worried about you being brain damaged—what with all that garble you were talking. Now, it seems you are right as rain again."

Gary was quick to fire back a retort with a little more than a hint of anger in his voice.

"Garble?"

The doctor had disappeared down the ward to check on another patient and conveniently chose to ignore the fact that he had caused a patient to become agitated. In his mind, it proved a point which showed Gary was well enough to take up a fight—all be it verbal.

He was still grumbling to himself when the ward sister came over to the bed to inform him that he had a visitor. She turned around to go and fetch the person in question after getting a nod from Gary. There was no need to usher the guest in though as she was right on her heels—it was Miss James.

"*Otta jy, Gary,*" she greeted him in a voice which was just a little too warm to be that of a class tutor. It was more like the tone adopted by a long-lost aunt meeting her wayward nephew after years apart.

"*Dâ yw genama dha weles mar vewek ha lowen,*" she continued as she sat down in the chair next to the bed. She was indeed glad to see him so lively and happy.

"*Dâ yw genama dha weles jy inwedh,*" replied Gary, returning the compliment.

"One thing," he asked, returning to English for want of saving his brain power, "did I say anything *unusual* when you last came to visit?"

Miss James fidgeted and shuffled uncomfortably in her seat. For a moment she wondered how he knew that she had been there, before surmising that he would have assumed so much from seeing her card on his bedside table.

"Well, yes—as a matter of fact," she began tentatively. She hesitated momentarily to create space for choosing her words carefully.

"You said nothing unusual in a manner of speaking—but the staff and your family were a little worried that you had lost your marbles—if I can put it in such a way."

Gary's frown, which had previously locked onto the doctor, was back in use for another outing.

"How do you mean?"

"You didn't seem to understand much English up until a week ago and you were insistent that your name was Davy Pengilley."

The doctors had been right. For a whole week, all he had been able to understand or speak was Cornish.

"Do you realize, Miss James—" Gary paused for a moment to check that he was understanding everything correctly, "—that for a whole week—I was a monoglot speaker of Cornish—perhaps the first such person in more than two hundred years?"

His teacher was momentarily struck speechless by such an amazing consideration. The more Gary thought about it, while recovering from the coma, he realized that he had seemingly existed within the lives of his distant relatives. To all intents and purposes, he thought he was Davy Pengilley living in the late eighteenth century.

"Even before I had this accident, I was considering changing my name to Davy. That hasn't changed. So, I don't really consider that bit to be weird at all."

He paused for a moment to see if she showed any signs of being uncomfortable by what could be considered a character change or a mental impairment. There were no obvious clues being given off by her body language.

"I do still want to do that," he insisted, "and I will put that into effect as soon as I am able to—legally."

Another wordless moment gave Miss James cause to nervously shift in her seat as though she could anticipate the build-up of some strange notion in her pupil's mind.

"The truth of the matter is that I remember seeing some things and hearing some things when I was unconscious—maybe even dead."

Now Miss James was visibly uncomfortable and Gary rejected her attempt to hush him. He did not need any rest now—what he needed was to explain his visions.

He went on to describe how he thought he had flown weightlessly in the wind when he fell from, what he continued to think of as, Tor Anseth. He described how he had watched from the air as he flew like a bird over a tiny cottage. He had seen a man return home to a distraught mother and daughter. He had recognized that cottage as Boswicker. He then relived the moment with the language teacher how he had been in a boat with a group of fishermen speaking Cornish too.

It had all made some sense to him when the doctors explained that he had died twice before being resuscitated. Did those moments and visions coincide? How real were they? Was he fabricating these moments from what he had read in Jacka's diaries or did he have an out-of-body experience where he actually crossed the expanse of time to see these moments?

"There is no way we can ever know for certain what goes on inside our minds," Miss James pondered, "—but I suggest you get some rest now."

"Do you believe in re-incarnation Miss James?" Gary added.

She didn't answer but began to leave. Her exit faltered a moment as she looked back at Gary.

"You just said something though that has given me a theory on part of Jacka's diaries."

"*Pandr'yw hedna*?" Gary asked to find out what she meant.

"Anseth Tor—you said you fell from Tor Anseth. That would be the Cornish word order. As we know, we haven't actually found this Anseth Tor or Tor Anseth."

Gary was puzzled.

"Give me a day or so and I will be back to you with my theory."

Gary was left lying in his hospital bed staring at the ceiling above him trying to work out what Miss James had discovered. Had he really provided the answer unwittingly? Maybe it wasn't him at all who had provided the vital clue. Maybe it had been the real Davy hiding within him who was trying to escape.

"Perhaps I am going mad!" Gary mumbled to himself.

"*Fol yn tien!*"—completely mad.

XXIII
The Wedding

Weddings were traditionally a simple affair in the tiny village of Morvah. If one were to be held in the months of summer, then fresh flowers would be cut from any field or hedgerow that had not been attacked by the voracious mouths of sheep or cattle. Everyone with a space in their oven would bake something for the celebrations and there would be niceys for all the children. This was different though as, for the first time in many years, a Morvah boy was marrying someone from outside of the parish. It was even more extreme and worthy of gossip as this was not even being celebrated within the blessed land of Cornwall.

The marriage of Wella Pengilley and Penelope Spiers had been planned in the parish church of the bride's hometown of Bray for this very day in June 1772. It was where this particular branch of the Spiers family called home and where generations had lived, been baptized, married and buried. The church sat close to the sleepy waters of the Thames surrounded by trees of more species than anyone in Cornwall had ever seen. The fields and hills back home were virtually barren of leafy boughs because of the relentless onslaught of savage winds from the Celtic Sea. But this parish was sheltered and cool—even when the sun beat down as it did on this very day. The aisle and porch had been adorned with wild flowers of every size and colour. Also, a garland had been stretched across the top of the rood-screen. It sent branches of ivy cascading down towards the flag-stone floor.

Wella waited patiently beneath the benign watch of the vicar as he heard the sound of his bride and father entering at the church door. It was far too early for him to take a look over his shoulder even though the anticipation within him cajoled the reaction. Eventually he took a fast look back and saw Penny wearing white silk which hung from her body like boughs of white blossom. Her face was obscured enough by the veil to delay the final look of his betrothed.

The father and daughter smiled at as many of the weeping relatives on both sides of the church as they were able. Their feet appeared to dance lightly on a cushion of ecstasy as they walked towards the altar. At one side were three fiddlers playing a traditional Cornish "furry" while the procession was followed closely by two bridesmaids. They wore miniature recreations of Penny's dress; one was a Spiers niece while the other was Wella's young sister, Jane.

Penny had been brought to Wella's side exactly as the echoes of the last notes faded. Her father helped her lift the veil back over her head to reveal the smiling beauty whom he had met on his first trip into the centre of the City of London. Gainsford took him there to encounter other traders exporting pottery to every corner of the world. Penny had happened to be accompanying her father on business at the same time. On that occasion, she was wearing a hooded heavy coat that kept out the freezing cold of winter and the heavy rains which danced like piskies on the cobbled streets.

Jane laid the bridal train flat down the aisle while half tripping over her own delicate dress. She had never worn anything so fine in all her life. Her best clothes had always been her Sunday-wear. Now that the family lived in St Ives, even her finest clothes usually had random clay stains on them. This was a day when she felt like a queen herself. For the first time in her life, she had been wearing clothes which had not been stitched back together or passed on from some other child in the village.

"We come together in the sight of God—" began the vicar as silence descended within the ancient flint walls. The only noises that could be heard were the echoes of a couple of fidgety children and the minister's words bouncing off the pillars and high ceiling. There was also a faint sound that seemed to be an echo. Wella realized after a minute that this was Mary translating the occasional phrase for her aged mother who had arrived by stage-coach only that morning.

As Wella looked at Penny, the vicar's words, along with the world around them, seemed to stop and blur. It was apparent that time had come to a halt for her too as she had her deep green eyes locked into a soft gaze. The service continued in the background of their thoughts as though they were in a living dream where reality and myth collided.

"Wilt thou have this woman to thy wife, to live together after God's ordinance in the Holy estate of matrimony? Wilt thou love her, comfort her, honour and keep her, in sickness and in health? And forsaking all other, keep thee only to her so long as you both shall live?"

The vicar rattled the all-important line off as though it was for the third time without answering—and it was. The couple had been standing there oblivious to events around them and the minister had asked for the legally necessary words to be replied to twice already.

"So—wilt thou?" smiled the vicar, realizing that the man and woman standing before them were hypnotically engaged with each other.

"*Manaf*—I will!" replied Wella with a broad smile flashing across his face.

"And wilt thou have this man to thy wedded husband—to live together after God's ordinance—"

Once again, the vicar's words appeared to mush into a background echo. The dream-state which surrounded them was like Wella had heard his father talk about in the land of the spriggian. They didn't live quite in this world or the next but occupied a half-way existence. Perhaps that was really where they were now? If he listened hard enough, maybe he could hear his brother Davy laughing at his attempts to speak English. Maybe if he looked hard enough out the corner of his eyes, he could even *see* Davy there too. Perhaps he did, but it was too short a time to tell as the wedding service had moved on.

It was Wella's turn.

"I, Wella Pengilley, take thee, Penelope Spiers, to my wedded wife, to have and to hold from this day forward, for better, for worse, for richer, for poorer, in sickness and in health, to love and to cherish, till death us depart."

Before either Penny or Wella knew, they were outside the church in the bright blessed sunlight that found every conceivable path through the leaves of a giant oak and that of a nearby yew. The rays of sun half blinded them as they stepped out of the church porch.

The family stood around cheering, laughing and throwing blossom petals over their heads.

The whole party walked down the lane and up to the banks of the Thames where wine and cider was ready for the family and friends. As they stood there chatting, hugging and kissing, there came a shout from the distance. The whole party turned around and looked down the flowing waters of the Thames to see from where it had come.

It was hard to make out with the bright sunlight causing all manner of reflections and sparkles to shine off the surface of the water. The ripples made the sun dance and sparkle leaving the only clues as to who was making such a hubbadullia from the Thames in the sounds of the voices. They were indeed familiar—very familiar. It could not be so—but it was. A Cornish lugger sailed up to the bank of the Thames and a rope was thrown and ably caught by Jacka. It was Billy Bod and his son, Billy Bod Bian, in the *Gwicker Frank*.

"*Re'n Jowl!*" laughed Wella as he recognized his father's old friend—his surrogate uncle.

His mother, Mary, slapped him gently on the shoulder with her maternal discipline on display for possibly the last time.

"Wella Pengilley—you shouldn't be using such bad language in the sight of the Lord—whether it be in Cornish or English!"

Wella smiled at her and kissed his mother on the cheek.

"Isn't it just great to have Billy and son here too?"

The wedding party sat on the banks of the Thames as the light faded. Billy Bod went back on board and got out some oil lamps and placed them on the grassy slopes down to the water. The drink flowed and the two families from completely different backgrounds, different locations and entirely different cultures got on as though they were one and the same—and always had been.

Eventually, as the evening threw up a chilled breeze, the wedding party repaired to the Hind's Head Inn, where they stayed until the bar man pleaded for them to find their rooms. This was not before Wella and Penny had managed to step outside once more to grab another kiss beneath the stars.

"Who would have thought it?" remarked Wella as he stared towards the heavens.

"What do you mean?" asked Penny—though she plainly did know what he meant.

"Well—us two. You English, me Cornish, you from a good background, me from a childhood where the only riches we had were in our hearts."

"That is what love is about though," she mused, "and we are the proof of it."

Wella paused as he took in the moment. He breathed the air deeply into his lungs. The air even tasted different without the strong saltiness he was used to at home.

"Even the air is different. Though nothing matters now apart from us and the future we make together."

Penny was not used to Wella coming out with any poetry in his language. He was more likely to find beauty in the balance of a caber beam on a steam engine or in the chemical reactions that produced the glaze on a pot.

"When did you suddenly become a bard like Shakespeare?" Penny gently laughed as she caressed his cheek with the back of her fingers.

"Maybe it's not me—maybe it is my brother's spirit talking."

Penny leaned back and looked Wella full on in the face which was now illuminated by the rising moon.

"No—this is you speaking to me—and I love it."

From this moment on, Penny and Wella's union brought them joy and peace—but also; prosperity. It wasn't long before Wella was presenting exquisite wares to royals and famous foreign officials. The couple worked hard and saved hard. After a couple of happy years, they bought a three-floored townhouse on the outskirts of London. This meant that the docks were only a horse-ride away. Wella could meet traders as they stepped off their ships and entertain them with the finest wines brought in from the heat-hazed vineyards of Southern France.

Wella knew how difficult life could be and thus was not tempted by overspending. Yes—he bought Penny the finest clothes befitting such a beautiful wife. Yes—he also lavished love and attention on his children, James and Clarice. However, he believed in the future too. He believed in his father's dreams which he had once spoken of—the time when the language and culture of their childhoods could return.

In many ways, Penny was more interested in the dreams that Wella had harboured than he was himself. Though they often spoke about Cornwall and finding a way of making a future out of what Jacka believed in, nothing happened. Penny would spend long cold nights cuddled up to Wella asking him about his childhood and the legends from that little place next to the vast waves of the Celtic Sea—but she had never been there.

Then on James' fourth birthday and a few months before Clarice's second, his son was sitting on his knee and was desperate to be entertained by his father.

"Daddy, tell me a story of monsters and giants!" he demanded with his big green eyes begging for a magical trip into the world which every child longs for. Wella nodded slowly as his son waited expectantly. His memory took him on a journey of his own back to that long granite-lined track across the moors of Penwith. There he was riding bareback on the family pony with Davy behind him. Jacka pulled on the reins and led the tired beast of burden back home after a couple of days in Porthenys. As the wheels of the cart creaked with the load of goods to use in the home and some to sell to neighbours, Jacka began to tell the droll about Cormoran. In exactly the same tone, the words came flooding out of Wella's mouth in English.

"This is a story about some giants from West Cornwall. Cormoran lived in a big wood next to the sea and within sight of St Michael's Mount. He and his wife decided to build a castle on the island. They wanted to see all the land around and about. With this, they could secretly watch people as they went about their everyday lives. Cormoran called to his wife for help in carrying the big white rocks to build the castle. Unfortunately, she was busy making pasties. His wife, Cormellian complained that she had other things that she needed to do. However, she gave in and helped out. The work was so tiring that Cormoran decided to take a nap. His wife found him asleep and was very cross. So, she decided to stop moving the rocks too. She left them exactly where she stood as her husband snored. Those rocks are still there to this very day. You can walk past them at low tide between Marazion and the Old Grey Rock in the Wood—or St Michael's Mount."

Wella was about to continue telling James more of the story but heard his soft snore. His son had already drifted off to that dream world which he used to inhabit. It rang to the persistant sound of knockers and was filled with the magic of spriggian, buccas and piskies. It was then that Penny looked from her chair over to Wella to speak the desires of her inquisitive mind.

"I would love to spend more time in this land that you tell your son about. I wish I could walk that long track past Lanyon Quoit and see that castle on the island in the distance."

"Well—maybe we could," mused Wella as he gently laid James down in another chair and placed a blanket over his sleeping body. "We have established a healthy business here in London—one which does not really need me anymore. Maybe, just maybe, it is time to return home. Would you like to move to Cornwall?"

If it had not been for their money and their security, the Pengilleys would not have had the wherewithal to be able to make such a decision on the spur of the moment. But now they were among the class of people who had made a living for themselves based on hard work and honest trade. They were able to make such a choice.

It was only a matter of a week since the Pengilleys' decision to return across the Tamar—now the stage coach was being loaded up with cases, trunks, two children, and the dreams of a family ending its self-imposed exile.

It was 1776 and Wella's memory of the last time he made this journey was not very clear. He could not remember any of the taverns or towns. He had forgotten the places where the road was safe and could not place exactly the sections of rutted track way where highwaymen were meant to lay in wait for their next victims. A week of travelling left the family tired and the children crying from not having their own beds for a week.

Eventually, they arrived in St Ives to see that great bay and beach stretching out to the Island. There on the far end of rows of tiny huddled-together houses and shops was the pier which Smeaton built. It was the pier where his family's story began.

"This is where we're going to live Penny: you, I, James and Clarice."

Penny hugged Wella and gave him a long kiss on the lips. James saw fit to comment in the way that a five-year old can be expected to: "Yeeeuchh!"

The romantic moment was spoiled—but humour was welcome. Wella bent down and picked up his son. He then raised him high in the air. James screamed with laughter until Wella placed him back upon terra-firma. Clarice had clung around her mother's leg mimicking her older brother's noises of delight.

"So, what do we do now that we've moved here?" asked Penny as the family took in the view. Jacka, Mary, and Jane were hurrying towards them—having spotted them arrive just a minute earlier.

"It's about us," smiled Wella, "It's about *Mabm* and *Sîra*. It's about James and Clarice. It's about all those Pengilleys yet to come."

"What do you mean? I don't understand." Penny frowned at him as though he had suddenly lost his mind.

"It's about Jacka's legacy—the legacy of my father. He dreamed of taking this feeling for place forward into the future. Davy was going to be the one that conveyed Cornish to the next generation while I was away, playing around with engines and piers."

Jacka held Penny by the shoulders and looked her straight in the eyes.

"But Davy isn't here anymore so I have to make sure that James and Clarice convey that culture across the generations."

Jacka, Mary and Jane were panting after their sprint along the seafront to where the coach had halted. Arms were thrown around each member of family with the laughter and tears echoing up the tiny alleyways between the houses. Exactly who greeted whom with what phrase or in which language did not matter as it was a joyous reunion. The chatter continued as they walked back towards the pottery with the accommodation above it.

"We'm opin t'find a pretty cottage with a view over the arbour dreckly. For now, we've made space for ee," advised Mary.

"*Gromassy, Mabm*," thanked Wella, giving her another hug.

Jacka took his grandchildren to heart over the coming years, treating them with tenderness and attention, just as he had doted on Davy, Wella and Jane. James and Clarice were still young enough to effortlessly absorb knowledge, incisive or spurious, thrown their way. Before long they knew how to proudly count to a hundred in Cornish and recite parts of epic poems too.

The family was not the same as it used to be all those years ago—back in that tiny cottage under the long leering shadow of Watch Croft. For one thing, they could afford to do things which they had never dared to dream possible. Jacka now had his own boat tied up along Smeaton's Quay. It was big enough to take the whole family for trips around the coast to watch the seals near the Knavocks or the proud soaring choughs as they swooped high and low.

Their favourite excursion was across the bay to Godrevy where they would land on a gently sloping beach and then tuck into a large basket of food in the evening sun. Wella would sit and think of his brother on such trips as he listened to Jacka teaching James and Clarice the droll of Matthew Trewhella and the Mermaid of Zennor or as he explained the noises the knockers made down the mines.

The first year spun by so quickly. Wella made three journeys back to London in that time in order that he could keep a check on business. There were causes for celebration as Joshua and Nolwenn had a daughter. There were also causes for grief as Jacka took his family to the tiny parish of Paul to witness the funeral of Dolly Pentreath. On this occasion, rather than stanking across moorland on foot and mule, the family made the trip by boat around the wild seas off Penwith.

Jacka had named the vessel *Cov Davy*—the memory of Davy. He was very proud of her with her gleaming brass fittings and newly varnished woodwork. He guided the boat into the harbour at Porthenys and threw a rope across to Billy Bod so that she could be tied up next to the *Gwicker Frank*.

It was probably one of the last times, if not the last, that Wella ever saw William Bodinar. It would have been easy to have had hindsight as they sat in the tavern on the harbour-front and chatted for many hours before they had to walk up the steep hill to Paul Church. Wella would have asked more questions about the past at that point. All he could remember was much reminiscing about Dolly. Inevitably, with her in mind, conversation returned to that of the language. Billy Bod admitted that he rarely had much opportunity to speak Cornish anymore—much the same situation as Jacka and Mary avowed to.

William Bodinar did note there was one instance though which was of much importance to him.

"*Dr'yw hedna dhana, sos*?" asked Jacka wanting the details. Billy went on to remind him of the day they last saw Dolly and she had been talking about the visit of a man called Daines Barrington. He had turned up in the hope of finding the last Cornish speaker ever. Doll had packed him off running and used some of his notes to stoke her oven.

"*Ha my wrug sawya nebes a'n volednow*," added Jacka to remind Billy that he had rescued some of the pages from out of her hands in the very tavern where they were sitting now.

"*An keth sam den-na a screfas lether i'n paper nowodhow hag gofen pyw eus ow clappya an tavas whath*," Billy continued to explain that Daines had written a letter and asked if there was anyone who knew anything of the ancient tongue. Naturally Billy Bod had written back:

Blŵth vee Eue try Egence a pemps. Theara vee dean Bodjack an puscas. Me rig desky Cornoack termen me vee mawe. Me vee demore gen seara vee a pemp dean moy en cock. Me rig scantlower clowes Eden ger Sowsnack cowes en cock rag sythen ware Bar. Na rig a vee Biscath gwellas lever Cornoack. Me deskey Cornoack moas da more gen tees Coath. Na ges moye vel pager pe pemps en dreau nye Ell Clappia Cornoack leben—poble Coath pager Egance Blouth. Cornoack ewe all neceaves gen poble younk. —William Bodinar.[13]

---

13 Bloodh vy yw try ugans ha pymp. Th'ero'vy den bohojek a'n pùscas. Me 'wrug desky Kernowek termyn me a veu maw. Me veu da mor gen sîra vy ha pymp den moy in côk. Me 'wrug scantlowr clôwes udn ger Sowsnek côw[s]ys i'n côk rag seythen warbar'. Na wrug avy bysketh gweles lever Kernowek. Me [wrug] desky Kernowek 'mos da mor gen tus coth. Nag eus moy 'vell pajer pò pymp i'n drev ny 'yll clappya Kernowek lebbyn—pobel coth pajer ugans bloodh. Kernowek yw oll nakevys gen pobel yonk. —William Bodinar

My age is three score and five. I am a poor fisherman. I learnt Cornish when I was a boy. I was at sea with my father and five men in a boat. I scarcely heard one word of English spoken in the boat for a whole week. I have never seen a book in Cornish. I learned Cornish by going to sea with the old folk. There are not more than four or five of us in our town who can speak Cornish now—old people of four score years. Cornish is all forgotten by the young people. —William Bodinar.

Since then, there had been the occasional passing phrase whispered in the street or shouted angrily in the harbour. He would still sit on the quayside and listen to some of the fishermen counting their catch in Cornish.

"*Wonen, dew, try, pajer, pymp, whe—*"

Apart from that, Porthenys was more or less converted to the speaking of English with a fair few Cornish words wedged into the conversation. Even if Dolly was not the last speaker, her passing seemed to highlight the severity of the situation. There were so few people left speaking *Kernowek* that every time someone like this old lady passed away, they took with them another sacred piece of the puzzle which had previously fitted together to form the fabric of society.

The family slowly marched up towards Brewinney (or as some called it "Paul") with friends and other grievers in a long line of solemnity; those who had laughed at her, those who had taunted her, those who had longed to see her die along with her language, those who were her friends, those who drank with her, and those who mourned as much for her as for the passing of an era. The parish church of Pluw Bowl in the middle of the village was filling up with them all. Billy Bod spotted Anne Wallis with her family. The pew in front of him contained John Tremethick. Sitting immediately behind him were the Quicks and the Berrymans. Across the central aisle were two entire rows filled with the Davy family who had arrived en masse from Zennor and Boswednack that very morning.

Billy Bod and Jacka had never heard so much *Kernowek* spoken for a very long time. For once in their lives, it seemed that the language had returned in force. Jacka thought for a moment that this boded well and his fears about living through the last days of Cornish were unfounded. Yet, looking closer at the situation, he could tell that all of those people who were chattering away in Dolly's tongue were ageing and their grandchildren were all using English.

He looked to his own children: Wella and Jane. Yes, they were engaging with these relics of a dying civilization. Despite Wella's insistence on upholding the language, Jacka looked at Clarice and James as they laughed in the pew next to him. They were happily living their early lives in this foreign tongue. They couldn't be blamed. They would go on to do well and achieve much. Their mother, Penny, couldn't be blamed either for she was honestly passing on her own culture to them—as was her duty. No one was doing any purposeful harm that he could tell. Yet, why did he suddenly feel so depressed about the future?

As the service proceeded in the solemnity of the dark building, lit by stray beams of sunlight slipping through the narrow windows, Jacka's thoughts drifted away from the words being spoken by the vicar and towards the loss of his own son. This funeral was a surrogate for the service conducted for Davy back in Morvah when he was stranded abroad.

Jacka and Mary softly sobbed in the pews. It mattered not to the rest of the congregation who these tears were for. Many had their own to shed. Who was to say which had whose name swimming in the glistening pearls of sadness which rolled from eyes?

Jacka's thoughts eventually gravitated towards his legacy. He scanned his eyes across the congregation again to look at all the women in their gowks and the men in their smartest jackets. He looked back along his own pew to see his family and friends intently listening to the word of God. If, perchance, his grandchildren did not end up fluent in Cornish, then it did not matter—for Jacka had continued his diary. He believed with every fibre of his being that his account would make sure that something was saved.

Wella was sitting right next to his father and could see from out of the corner of his eyes that he was distracted. He could tell that Jacka's mind was wandering elsewhere and that it was likely to be focused on Davy rather than Dolly. He too was aware of the future— after all, he had left home at an early age while his father was abroad in order that he could build a future for the next generation.

"Isn't this what it is all about Penny?" mused Wella one evening, days later, as they sat on Porthminster beach.

"Legacy is not only about the children. It's also about what they believe in—and the memories that they hold."

"But what about Dolly?" pondered Penny, "she had no children— so what was her legacy?"

Wella sat there and thought a few moments more as a mild breeze rustled Penny's hair and the Cornish Heavenly choir (the seagulls) swooped and cried above them.

"*Kemeneth Dolly yw kemeneth nei!*" he replied with a far-off stare searching the horizon for answers.

"I don't understand much Cornish," Penny was irritated that she was being left out of the meaning with no translation provided. Wella never did give her the translation as he hoped one day, this English lady whom he had married would understand in her own way.

He offered his hand to her and pulled her up to stand with him on the white sands.

"It doesn't really matter what the translation is," Wella continued, pointing to her heart, "what matters is what is in there."

XXIV
Riches

Gary awoke with a start. "*Duw! Pleth esof*—God! Where am I?" Calm returned almost immediately as he realized that he was no longer in hospital. As the feeling of disorientation died away, like a faint echo at the end of a long tunnel, he felt his injured leg still encased in a restrictive cast. Following his hand higher up his sore body, he located a similar cast on his left arm. Usually, he would experience panic in situations where immobility thwarted him— such as being pinned down by bullies. However, this time, he could render a relieved smile—for he was home.

His condition meant that he was not able to rush out and enjoy the summer weather with a carefree jaunt to the beach on just a momentary whim. It also meant that picking up his violin was firmly out of the question. Despite these negative aspects of his predicament, he did have plenty of time for whimsical thought.

"After all, everyone needs a purpose," he muttered to himself, "don't they?"

"Some people have a purpose hinging on paying the bills while others spend their years on this planet planning for the afterlife. Some individuals wander aimlessly through their existence without ever working out what that cause of being is," he continued with growing confidence.

"And, others spend their lives believing assuredly that they knew there was something more."

This is when it occurred to Gary that, in many ways, *he* was Jacka Pengilley's afterlife. This was not just about genes and procreation. *This* was about legacy.

This train of thought was going as deep as Dolcoath now, forcing a desire within the burgeoning thinker to grab a pen and paper. Holding any writing implement was a struggle with his left arm firmly encased in plaster. He transferred the pen to his right hand and made an effort to write again. Still no success.

Gary opened up a document on his tablet and began typing painfully slowly with one finger on his right hand:

My life, all be it young, has taken many complex turns in recent days, weeks and months and I have been led to making some startling conclusions about who I am. I was indeed born Gary Pengilley and have been raised by my wonderful family in a homogenized society surrounded by mass-media and mind-numbing reality-television with its hangers-on and tired plastic celebrities.

My family has dug beneath this surface and uncovered a civilization of great beauty. This buried city lay beneath us without any previous realization of its being there. However, now its streets and treasures have been unearthed, we cannot ignore it anymore.

For this city which lay smothered in dirt and noise of modern life contains the streets, houses and shops where the Pengilleys lived. They were there at a time when their entertainment was not poured out of a television set or from the screen of a mobile phone but from the mouths of parents and grandparents. The stories they told were not about who had been sleeping with whom. The stories were not about the fickle lives fed to us by faceless corporations solely aiming to make some money.

The stories of my heritage were told about myths and legends which grew out of a beautiful landscape. These were called drolls and had been passed down through the generations until the world around filled minds with technological progress and insincerity.

I was born Gary Pengilley—but, whether by breeding, circumstance or by some supernatural force, I have become Davy Pengilley. It does not matter to me whether anyone finds this strange or not. It changes nothing whether anyone

*wants to try and extract if this is down to genetic memory or
by being brainwashed by a society—or by re-incarnation.
From now on, I am Davy Pengilley.*

Davy emailed this declaration from his tablet to his entire list of
contacts. He posted it on his social media too. If he was going to get
to grips with his life being part of a greater legacy, then there was no
point in hiding it any longer.

There was a desperately nervous sense of hush at the dinner table
that evening. Eddie cast a few glances towards Davy, almost to say,
"Weirdo!" Geoff and Sarah mumbled a few things to keep the pretence of normality going:

"Eat up then!"

"Is that nice?"

"Oh, look at the weather outside!"

Davy started to push his food around with just a fork on the plate
as he attempted to ascertain whether his family was with him or not.

"Oh, for goodness sake! Say what you're all thinking!" Davy burst
out, infuriated by everything that was not being said. His mother
was the first to reconnect.

"We know you have been through a lot and if you are sure that
this is what you want to do—then we will go through the legal
paperwork to make the name change."

Davy looked at his father.

Geoff simply muttered a "fine by me" without even looking up.
Davy could tell by his tone that it was fine. It was as though the
Pengilleys suddenly created a bridge linking the generations and
they could all hear the whisper of Jacka across two centuries saying:
"Davy, you never died. You never left us."

So, he finally looked towards his brother who was hiding away in
another blog. The expectant silence from around the table was
enough to alert him to everyone looking at him. Eddie looked up
and smiled that brotherly grin which transcends play, bickering and
fighting.

"Davy—you weirdo!"

There was barely an opportunity for the laughing to fade naturally
when the doorbell rang. Sarah dropped her knife and fork in irritation and headed out of the dining room to the front door. Everyone
else went quiet to try and hear who it was.

"Gar—er—Davy—it is Miss James for you!"

Davy was unable to move fast enough to find out why he had such an unexpected visit because he was hindered by the cast on his leg. Instead, Sarah brought Miss James into the dining room.

"Oh—I'm sorry to disturb you," she apologized as she noticed they had hardly started eating.

"No worries at all," replied Geoff getting up from the table to fetch a chair, "can I get you a cup of tea or something?"

"No need—but thanks anyway."

"So, what is this about then?" asked Davy.

"Well—first of all—congratulations on your name change, Davy. I just received your email."

She looked around the room to see a family waiting for some revelation which would change everything. After all, it is not a usual event for a teacher to suddenly happen upon your doorstep. They were not to be disappointed.

"I have worked out what Jacka Pengilley was talking about when he said you have to think of Anseth Tor."

An expectant hush descended.

"It occurred to me that the translation you were given did not match the original Cornish. The vital change was Dr Casement writing 'Anseth Tor' when a Cornish place name would have had the 'Tor' first."

Everyone was still listening while trying to decode what Miss James was saying.

"I was at first thinking that it could be Brea Anseth—or even Brea Anserth. Then I looked at Carn Anseth and Carn Anserth. None of these names existed anywhere."

Miss James looked around her audience who were hanging on her every word in the same way that an inspector might reveal the guilty party in a murder-mystery whodunnit tale.

"So, I then looked at the original manuscript which did indeed say 'Tor Anseth'. But—I have to tell you—it is not a place name at all!"

Stunned silence followed. It took Eddie to speak up for a change.

"So, what is the meaning?"

Miss James looked at Davy as though he could suddenly generate the correct answer himself. Nothing emerged from his lips for half a minute. All that anyone could tell was that he was playing with the words in his head. His lips moved as the thought process escalated. Finally, his eyes lit up and looked back to his Cornish teacher in amazement that he had solved the problem.

"*Torr an seth*—it is not a place name at all but a command. Jacka is telling us to break the pot!"

"What pot?" asked Geoff.

"And now I understand what Aunt Elaine was saying at the solicitor's office," Davy continued as though he had not heard his father's question. Geoff moved his lips to attempt asking the question once more but his son persisted: "She was talking about the supposed 'gobbledygook' that Granfer Jack used to come out with."

Davy fell silent and looked around the room to see that he had everyone's attention.

"She said something like '*taranzeith na geweith*'," whispered Davy above the hush that had descended on the dining room.

"*Taranzeith!*" exclaimed Miss James. "Can it be true?"

"*Taranzeith!*" repeated Davy, "'*Torr an seth*'—break the pot!"

"Pardon me for sounding a little impatient here—" grumbled Geoff, peering over his hands clenched in front of his puzzled face. He leaned forward on the dining table: "—but can someone tell me which pot we are going on about here?"

"There is only one pot that Jacka can mean," Sarah replied as she headed out to her art studio. A minute later she returned with the article which had been discovered in the trunk along with the diary. She held it in her hands and turned it around several times to see if there was anything noticeable about it without destroying such a beautiful antique.

The only writing on the bottom of it was the word "*gavr*"—the Breton for "goat". It held no significance to anyone in the room.

Sarah then held it up to the light and looked inside. She could see that the bottom of the pot was not as uniform as the external appearance. It seemed to be a little cracked and lumpy as though there was something which had caused it to not fire properly in the kiln.

"I think I've found something," she cried with latent excitement bursting out of her eyes. She disappeared back into the workshop. There was some noise of toolboxes being sifted through and then the rush of feet as she reappeared in the dining room bearing a hammer in one hand and a tray in the other.

"Davy—you do the honours!"

Sarah handed the hammer and tray to her son and then placed the pot in the middle.

"You're sure you want me to do this?"

The tension in the room produced the answer without anyone needing to utter a single word.

Davy picked up the hammer and held the pot against the cast on his left arm. With one hefty whack the antique, which had remained in a dusty trunk for two centuries, lay in bits spread out across the tray. The intake of breath was audible as the family viewed the dust and debris which lay strewn before them. For, there, gleaming among the terracotta shards was a small piece of shining metal.

Davy picked it up and held it aloft to the light in order that he might be able to examine it closer. The light glinted along the metallic shaft as he rubbed some remaining clay from it and read the letters upon it:

"R. K. & M."

"R. K. & M.?" asked Eddie.

"R. K. & M.!" repeated his mum.

"So, what is that?" pondered Davy.

"Those initials—my lad," replied Geoff, "stand for the Royal Kensington and Mayfair Bank."

"It's a very old one which is now used by the rich, famous and royalty," added Sarah.

"So—we're rich?" asked Eddie.

Geoff smiled back at the family.

"Let's find out."

Excerpts from Jacka Pengilley's Diary

Miz Ebral an pajurra jorna 1768
Thew calish creolgy bos bownar morhagar,
bar Dew. Hethou, then ve pur ogoaze lether
en droglam en bal. Thera ve cones oladn an
oloar perig cotha radn an carn awarra
warnam. Edn olean an para ve a ve lether
en truan. Cowetha erol a theath scon thom
savia en towla mez bern broar a vein. Pur
looan en ve oloar olhe'n gwelz arta ha gwelaz
a wreag ha' flehaz ena. Ethick ew peolery
fatel veea ractans na viama whath bew.[14]

---

14 Mis Ebrel an pejwora jorna 1768

Th'yw calys crejy bos bôwnans mar hager, abarth Duw. Hedhyw, yth en vy pòr ogas ledhys in droglam i'n bal. Th'eren vy ow conys 'dadn an dor pàn wrug codha radn a'n carn awartha warnam'. Udn den a'n parra ny a veu ledhys yn truan. Cowetha erel a dheuth scon dha'm sawya in tôwla mes bern brâs a veyn. Pòr lowen ev vy dos dhe'n gwels arta ha gweles ow gwreg ha flehes ena. Uthyk yw pedery fatla via ragthans na vien ma whath byw.

Fourth of April 1768

It is difficult to believe that life can be so unpleasant, by God. Today I was nearly killed in an accident in the mine. I was working underground when part of the upper rock fell on me. One man of our team was unfortunately killed. Other comrades came quickly to save me by casting aside a huge pile of stones. I was very happy to see the grass again and to see my wife and children again. It is awful to think what would have become of them were I no longer alive.

Miz Ebral an pempaz jorna 1768
Mary ha me a bassiaz mear a dermen
hethou en pedery an peth tho weel gen agon
bounaz. Scant nag eze wheal orall en pow
buz peth an bal. Na venjama boaz lethez en
tewlolez oladn an oloar, na whath. Thera nei
suppoga olraljama gwainia nebbaz mona gen
Billy Bod. Metessen Mary alja gweel
neppeth gen prei ha gwerra sethaw.[15]

---

15   Mis Ebrel an pympes jorna 1768
     Mary ha me a bassyas meur a dermyn hedhyw in pedery an pëth dha
     wil gen agan bôwnans. Scant nag eus whel eral i'n pow bùs pëth an bal.
     Na venjama bos ledhys in tewlder 'dadn an dor na whath. Th'eron ny
     sopojya der aljama gwaina nebes mona gen Billy Bod. Metessen Mary
     alja gwil neppëth gen pry ha gwertha sethow.
     Fifth of April 1768
     Mary and I spent a long time today considering what to do with our
     life. There is hardly any other work in the area other than mine work.
     Still I would not like to be killed in the darkness underground. We
     reckon that I could earn some money with Billy Bod. Perhaps Mary
     could make something with clay and sell pots.

Miz Ebral an wheffas jorna 1768
Mary o whath pùr drewethack hethou rag
an flehaz ve keskez en scol arta, drefen na
orans mear a Sowznack. Moy vel hedna,
thera gon contrevegion a keel geaz ahana nei
drefen nag eu Sowznack cowzez lies en chei.
Na wela ve destny teag rag gon tavaz nei en
termen a vedn doaz rag bohez eu an bobel
eze ort e clappya whath.[16]

16   Mis Ebrel an wheffes jorna 1768
      Mary o whath pòr drewedhek hedhyw rag an flehes a veu keskys i'n
      scol arta, drefen na orans meur a Sowsnek. Moy 'vell hedna, th'era gàn
      kentrevogyon a kil ges ahanan ny drefen nag yw Sowsnek cowsys lies
      i'n chy. Na welaf vy destny teg rag gàn tavas ny i'n termyn a vydn dos
      rag bohes yw an bobel eus ort y clappya whath.
      Sixth of April 1768
      Mary was very unhappy today because the children were scolded in
      school again, because they don't know much English. More than that
      our neighbours were mocking us because not much English is spoken
      in the house. I cannot see a great future for our language in the future
      for the people who still speak it are few in number.

Glossary

abm kiss.

bal-maiden a woman who works above-ground at a mine.

balyer barrel.

bowgie (Cornish *boujy*) shed for sheep or cattle.

bucca a Cornish spirit.

cloam earthenware, pots.

coose to hunt or chase game out of woodland.

croust pasty time.

cruskyn tankard.

crowjy shed.

come us come on, hurry up.

cùrun a spern hangover (*lit.* 'crown of thorns').

dâ lowr okay.

Duw God.

droll a traditional Cornish tale.

fearie Cornu-English dialect for *fairy*.

furry A festival observed at Helston, Cornwall, on the eighth of May; also, a peculiar dance used on that occasion..

geek to peek.

gowk A large bonnet similar to a Quarker's bonnet, with a "curtain" behind; worn by mine, clay-work, and country girls or women.

Guldize harvest festival (*Gool dheys*).

hubbadullia (Cornish *hùb-badùllya*) a lot of noise.

kan-ha-diskan a type of Breton song sung by two alternating voices

keels skittles.

kibble tub, bucket.

kiddleywink, wink an illegal drinking house

mabm mother.

mizzick sea mist.

niceys sweets.

ope a passage between houses.

osket containers for putting pilchards in.

pair a team of miners.

pard mate.

pasty traditional meal encased in pastry with a crimped crust.

pinnicking weak, puny.

piskie one of the "little people" of Cornwall.

Poria Porth Ia; St Ives.

pronter vicar.

ronk snore

sîra father

spence larder, pantry

spriggian ['sprɪdʒən] *pl.* Cornish spirits. (In the nineteenth century this loanword was re-analysed in English as a singular *spriggan* ['sprɪgən], plural *spriggans*.)

stagged stuck.

stank tread, long walk, stamp.

stem shift in a mine.

tacker a small child

tas father.

tattie potato

teasy annoyed, angry.

tus wocky stupid people.

whisht melancholy, dismal, sad.

Lightning Source UK Ltd.
Milton Keynes UK
UKHW040635191121
394250UK00001B/131

9 781782 012962